"And v

"Will you have trouble sleeping tonight?" She knew she was baiting . . . teasing . . . tempting, but she didn't care.

"I don't know. I suppose that will depend on you, my love." His mouth met hers again, hungrily exploring the sweetness.

My love. The words echoed enticingly in her ears. Greg had never used such an endearment before. Was he suggesting that she stay with him tonight? Chelsey wanted so much more from him—a commitment—but was he ready to give one?

"Let's go to the house," Greg urged.

Chelsey wanted time to think, but her mind refused to function. His heady kisses made her powerless to make a sound judgment.

"Greg, I don't think we should."

Amid her whispers of indecision, Greg slid Chelsey out of the car and lifted her in his arms. Their mouths met again and again. Hungry, sweet, mindless kisses that blocked out reason and the last shred of sanity.

ABOUT THE AUTHOR

Lori Copeland fell in love with romance novels six years ago. Now the author of twenty-five titles of her own, Lori believes that a good love story makes anyone's day. She hopes that through her writing she makes yours.

Lori lives in Springfield, Missouri, with her husband, Lance, three sons, two daughters-in-law and two absolutely perfect grandsons.

The Trouble with Thorny

Lori Copeland

Harlequin Books

TORONTO • NEW YORK • LONDON
AMSTERDAM • PARIS • SYDNEY • HAMBURG
STOCKHOLM • ATHENS • TOKYO • MILAN

To Lance, the best decision I ever made

Published September 1988

First printing July 1988

ISBN 0-373-16261-8

Printed in U.S.A.

Chapter One

"Greg, I think it's time we did something about Father."

"Come on, Camille. Pop is doing fine."

"You might happen to think he's doing fine, but I don't," the voice on the phone continued. "I want you to promise you'll see about placing him in Rosehaven. It's close enough you can keep an eye on him, but he'll be properly supervised and cared for in your absence."

Greg swiveled in his chair and stared down at the busy boulevard below. Since Thorny, their father, had come to live with him, his sister was getting to be a royal pain in the—

"Are you still there, Gregory?"

"Yeah, Camille. You were saying?"

"I know you don't agree, but we don't have any other choice at this point. With your demands at work and my living so far away now, Father needs proper supervision. Since you travel several times a month and can't keep decent help, what other option do we have?"

"Pop seems happy," Greg argued.

"And why wouldn't he? With you gone, he has the run of the house. His diet flies out the window; he totally ignores his medication, and he's implied that he even goes so far as to entertain women on occasions. . . ." Camille's voice trailed off helplessly.

"Women? Oh, surely not. Why, the man has lost his mind," Greg returned dryly. Ordinarily he would try to lighten his sister's mood, but today he didn't bother. He didn't want to put Thorny in a retirement home. The two of them were doing fine, if Camille would only leave them alone.

"It's precisely that cavalier attitude that assures me Father must be placed in a retirement home as soon as it can be arranged."

"Camille—"

"Would you like for me to fly down there and personally take care of this matter, Gregory?"

Lord no, he didn't want her flying down. That was the last thing he wanted. "Okay, Camille. I'll check it out."

"You've promised me that before. I want action this time."

"Just give me a few days."

"One week, Gregory."

"Come on, Camille. One week is not enough—"

"One week."

"Give me a break!"

The line clicked, and the dial tone buzzed loudly in his ear.

Snapping the receiver back into its cradle, Greg sighed. "Okay. One week."

GRACE MARTIN'S VOICE drifted pleasantly over the office intercom the following afternoon. "Ms. Stevens, your four o'clock appointment is here."

Chelsey glanced at her watch. She wasn't aware she had a four o'clock appointment, but a hurried check of her appointment pad reminded her she was scheduled to meet with Gregory Bradford concerning his father, Thorton.

"Thank you, Grace. You may show Mr. Bradford in."

Chelsey rose from her chair and stretched, then absently massaged the small of her back. The beautiful early-fall afternoon beckoned to her, and she sighed as she recalled how she'd hoped to slip away early today. She could only hope Mr. Bradford wasn't long-winded.

She strolled to the window, and a tiny smile played at the corners of her mouth as she viewed the small group of elderly men and women sitting together on the large veranda.

If the conversation were the usual, the men were talking about the weather, while the ladies talked about the men, their fingers flying through colorful yarn as they knitted and crocheted exquisite handmade items for Rosehaven's annual Christmas bazaar.

Ida Munsington caught sight of Chelsey and waved. Chelsey smiled and lifted her hand to return the greeting. Ida was a dear old soul who needed a lot of affection, and Chelsey was always glad to give it. People like Ida were only one of the reasons Chelsey loved her job.

The door to her office opened and Chelsey turned.

"Ms. Stevens?" asked a pleasant baritone voice.

"Yes?"

"Your secretary said it was all right for me to come in...."

"Oh, yes." Chelsey moved quickly away from the window. "Please do, Mr. Bradford."

She wasn't sure what she'd expected in Gregory Bradford, but she knew it wasn't remotely close to the striking man walking through the doorway. She judged him to be about her age, and he was slim, with an imposing six-foot frame and magnetic brown eyes. He was tanned, relaxed, and if clothes were any indication of a man's success, Mr. Bradford had done well.

She stepped behind her desk and extended her hand. "Please make yourself comfortable, Mr. Bradford. I'm Chelsey Stevens, chief administrator of Rosehaven."

"Good afternoon, Ms. Stevens." Chelsey smiled pleasantly as his hand engulfed her smaller one, clasping it warmly for a moment.

His direct gaze met hers. "Nice to meet you." He returned her smile easily. "I'm afraid I'm a little early."

"No, it's perfectly all right." She motioned for him to sit in the wing chair opposite her desk.

"Thanks." He seated himself and proceeded to study the serious-looking woman before him, immediately pegging her as a typical businesswoman—all work and no play. She was moderately attractive, with a nice shape she concealed inside a depressingly drab, blue business suit. Her hair, a shade of honey blond, was pulled into a severe knot that tempted him to pull the pins and let the soft mass have a little breathing space. Her nose wasn't bad, if you liked tilted noses—which Greg could take or leave—and her complexion was all peaches and cream. The serious look in her emerald eyes staring at him through oversized glasses could intimidate the average man, Greg quickly decided, but not him.

In fact, Ms. Stevens's puritanical manner brought the playful side of his personality to life, and he found himself wondering just how he could shake her up a bit.

Chelsey opened a manila folder containing the Bradford application and tried to ignore the invigorating fragrance of after-shave teasing the air. She found it oddly disturbing.

"I understand you're here concerning your father," she began.

"Yes. Thorton Bradford—that's Pop."

Chelsey raised her eyes. "Pop?" The sobriquet never failed to annoy her. A pop was a soft drink, not a parent.

"Yeah, Pop." Greg thought he detected her disapproval and wondered about it.

"May I ask why you're considering placing your father in Rosehaven?" Chelsey asked, though she didn't need to. She had seen Greg Bradford's type before. A playboy who no longer had time for his aging parent and wanted to get rid of him. She would bet on it.

Having been raised in a succession of foster homes, Chelsey had always considered parents a luxury—not a burden; therefore, without realizing it, she made her first snap judgment about Greg Bradford.

Greg unconsciously edged forward in his chair, sensing her disapproval, but not disturbed by it. "Well, you see, Ms. Stevens...." He paused, as he looked her straight in the eye. It had been a long time since he had taken pleasure in teasing a woman, and he found the sudden challenge stimulating. "I live on the estate adjoining Rosehaven," he confided, making sure he dominated her gaze. "And my sister—and I," he added, and Chelsey noticed a slight hesitancy in his voice. "Well, you see, Camille thinks it's time to place Pop somewhere because I have to travel frequently and she lives out of state. I want to find Pop a home where he'll be happy and he won't think... he's actually moved."

You mean a place where he won't think he's been dumped, Chelsey amended silently, giving him a cool smile. "I see."

"If he moved into Rosehaven, he'd have similar surroundings, and I'd be close by if he needed me," Greg reasoned. "When I travel, I don't like to leave Pop alone. Not to say he can't take care of himself. He doesn't need a nursing home, but he does need someone to supervise his medication, do his laundry and provide three square meals a day. Know what I mean?"

She did, all too well.

"Yes, of course." Chelsey let her gaze slide to her hands as she folded them primly on top of the folder. "Where are you employed, Mr. Bradford?"

"I'm president of Bradford Electronics. It's a family-owned business. I took over when Pop retired ten years ago."

"Are you familiar with our services here at Rosehaven?"

"I've heard nothing but good things about your establishment," he said smoothly, trying to capture her gaze again.

He noticed her smile was genuine this time. "We're proud of our reputation."

"You should be."

"Then you know we strive for a congenial, homelike atmosphere and a happy, productive life-style for our residents in their twilight years."

"It certainly seems like a nice old folks' home," Greg agreed, then winced inwardly as a shadow of irritation skimmed over her flushed features.

"Old folks' home?" Chelsey edged forward in her chair. "Mr. Bradford, Rosehaven Retirement Center is not an old folks' home. We encourage our residents to remain resourceful and productive if their health permits, and the term old folks' home has a negative connotation, don't you agree?"

Greg cleared his throat patiently. This had started out to be a bad day, and it looked like it was going to end up as one. Chelsey Stevens was going to be one tough cookie, or at least she was doing her best to make him think so.

If his situation weren't desperate, he'd just get up and walk out. He didn't need this kind of hassle. But his fourth housekeeper had quit this morning, and he had exactly one week to find someone to look after Pop before Camille took charge.

Thorny was basically healthy, but the heart attack he'd suffered ten years ago limited his activities somewhat. He had to contend with the usual ailments of many men his age—high blood pressure and occasional gout. It was important that Thorny's medication and meals were on schedule, and it was up to Greg to see that they were.

He loved his dad, and since Camille insisted Thorny be placed in Rosehaven, Greg would go along with it. But he hadn't planned on having to deal with Ms. Stevens.

Greg reminded himself that he usually enjoyed a challenge, so he decided he wouldn't let her condescending attitude bother him. He'd always called a spade a spade, but if it offended Ms. Stevens to call Rosehaven an old folks' home, then he would appease her. "Of course, Ms. Stevens. How thoughtless of me. It's a fine, as you say, retirement center."

"It's essential that we bolster the morale of our residents," Chelsey reminded him. "Therefore, you can understand our concern about your choice of words. Rosehaven is not a nursing home. It is a minimum-care facility for the aged. Of course, we do have provisions for those who need closer medical supervision, but in general our residents are still more than capable of caring for themselves."

Greg leaned forward and covered her hand with his, and a devilish delight raced through him as he saw her stiffen. "Oh, I agree. It's a wonderful minimum-care facility for the aged."

She shot him an annoyed look as she quickly removed his hand from hers. "You mentioned your sister, Mr. Bradford?"

"Yes, Camille. She recently married and moved to Montana."

"Are there other brothers and sisters?"

"No, just Camille and me."

"And your application indicates your father is mobile."

"Oh . . . very mobile." He grinned lamely. "Pop had a heart attack several years ago, but he's fine now. Camille just thinks he needs closer supervision than I can give him."

"I understand."

"Pop came back to live with me three years ago when Mom passed away. At first the arrangement worked out fine, but lately Camille thinks Thorny—that's what Pop likes to be called—is left alone too often. I'm gone more than I care to be, and I can't seem to keep a housekeeper. The fourth one this month quit this morning." His voice trailed off thoughtfully. Drucella Medley had been one to overreact when it came to having her fanny pinched. Greg had warned Thorny to refrain from such behavior, but...

"Anyway, since our property adjoins Rosehaven, Camille figured Pop might be happier living here than at some other retirement place. It wouldn't mean that much of a change in his life...."

Chelsey found her attention wavering as she tried to concentrate. His trousers fit like a glove. A nice soft leather glove that clung to all the interesting places—and he did have a variety of interesting places.... His thighs were well shaped and muscular, and she caught herself staring. Self-consciously she urged her concentration back to the conversation.

"Rosehaven comes highly recommended. I think Pop would probably enjoy being with people his own age. I understand you have various activities...."

Greg's voice droned on as Chelsey's gaze drifted involuntarily to his hands. They were large, masculine hands, tanned, with nails well manicured. He was wearing a college ring on the left hand; his right hand was bare.

She was surprised to realize she'd been looking for a wedding ring, and even more surprised when she wondered why. Well, no matter she decided, he was the typical playboy, and, if the truth were known, he wanted "Pop" out of the way for his own selfish reasons.

But it didn't matter what Mr. Bradford's current status was. Chelsey never mixed business with pleasure, and certainly not with a man like Greg Bradford.

"...so Camille thought I should come and take a look around," Greg finished. He leveled his gaze at Chelsey pointedly. She'd been staring at him for the past five minutes, and he couldn't figure out why.

Chelsey suddenly realized he'd noticed her preoccupation with his physique, and she averted her gaze quickly. Clearing her throat, she tried to join the conversation again. "You mentioned you live on the estate adjoining Rosehaven?"

"Yes."

"And you think your father would be happier living in a retirement center? Rosehaven is not a nursing home," she clarified again.

Greg sighed. "No, Thorny wouldn't be happier, but Camille thinks moving him here will contribute to his welfare. To be honest, Ms. Stevens, I don't know what Pop wants. I've brought up the subject of placing him in Rosehaven a few times, but he's been noncommittal."

Chelsey rose and walked to the window, and Greg's eyes discreetly followed her trim form. She had good legs, long and slim. And her fanny was nice. Pop would definitely deem it pinchable. He quickly made a mental note to warn Thorny that Ms. Stevens's fanny was strictly off limits.

"How old is your father?" Chelsey inquired.

"He'll be seventy-three this January."

"Hobbies?"

"Pop is interested in everything. He likes golf, swimming, music, pool—he loves to shoot pool and..."

Once more Chelsey found her attention fading. Instead of listening to what Greg was saying, she was listening to the mesmerizing cadence of his voice.

"...so Camille—and I—think he'd be better off living here. Actually, that's not quite true. Camille frets over Pop more than I do," he confessed. "I think Pop and I manage just fine, but since the day he turned seventy, my sister thinks our father needs someone to blow his nose for him."

"Well, I think the first order of business would be for you to tour our facility," Chelsey concluded, finally turning from the window. "Your father sounds independent enough."

"No problem there. Thorny's independent all right."

Chelsey's right brow lifted a fraction. Somehow, the way he said independent sounded different from the way she said it.

"Independent?"

"Oh, not overly so," he corrected.

Actually, he thought, that wasn't true, either. Thorny could be a problem at times. He was too independent for his own good, but Ms. Stevens looked as if she could handle a nuclear meltdown and not bat an eye.

And it was imperative Greg find someone to care for Thorny. He summoned his most persuasive smile and leaned forward, capturing her reluctant gaze once more. "You'll like Pop," he promised.

He loved the way her eyes spoke volumes, none of which was very flattering to him.

"I'm sure I will." Chelsey stood and removed her glasses. "If you'll follow me, Mr. Bradford, I'll show you our facilities."

"I'd be most happy to, Ms. Stevens."

Definitely *not* his type, he thought as he fell into step behind her.

Chelsey was determined to ignore Greg Bradford. She had seen his kind before. She'd seen *all* kinds since she'd accepted the position of chief administrator of Rosehaven two years before. But she prided herself on being able to take on anything that came her way with cool professionalism.

Greg Bradford was someone she could handle. Obviously, he'd been born with a silver spoon in his mouth, and he didn't seem to have the faintest idea what life was about.

But Chelsey was good at her job—as good as any man—and she didn't permit her personal feelings to interfere with her duties. She'd worked long and hard to achieve an important role in administration, and she would prove to the regional director that he'd made a wise choice in selecting her over Walter Bishop, a coworker at Rosehaven.

If people like Greg Bradford and his sister wanted to abandon their parents, then she would see to it that Rosehaven provided a loving home for their outcasts.

Chelsey had ranked Greg Bradford pretty low by the time she led him out of her office and paused to speak with her secretary.

"Grace, I'm going to show Mr. Bradford our facilities. If Walter Bishop comes looking for me, tell him I shouldn't be gone long."

"Yes, Ms. Stevens." The thin, older woman glanced up from her typing and smiled.

"We'll start with the grounds first," Chelsey announced briskly, and Greg nodded agreeably as he followed her down the hall.

"Your parents still alive, Ms. Stevens?" Deciding he'd teased her enough, Greg wanted to make casual conversation. Her persistent coolness was wearing thin.

Chelsey kept her gaze averted from his. "No, Mr. Bradford. They died when I was very young."

"That's too bad." There was sincerity in his voice that Chelsey was surprised to hear.

The tour took a little over half an hour. Rosehaven was indeed as comfortable and attractive as it was touted.

The main buildings were nestled snugly in a grove of tall sequoias on five acres outside of Carmel-by-the-Sea, California. The grounds were appealingly landscaped with flowers, and purplish ivy trailing down the sides of the red-brick structures added to the feeling of serenity.

While birds chirped overhead and the smell of freshly mowed grass permeated the air, Chelsey and Greg walked briskly along the flagstone path. "As you can see, Rosehaven maintains high standards, and our residents are well supervised and cared for," Chelsey pointed out. "The east wing houses our residents who need closer supervision. Should your father decide to join us, Mr. Bradford, his new quarters will be in the west wing. His needs will be cared for, and medication administered regularly, but he will have the freedom to move about as he pleases—within the grounds," she added. "Should he wish to journey outside Rosehaven, I will need either verbal or written permission from you."

They had passed several small groups of elderly men and women along the way, and as far as Greg could tell, everyone appeared cheerful and content.

"We offer a variety of crafts and activities designed to alleviate boredom. We have bingo games, bowling, woodworking, basket weaving, and a potluck supper on Saturday evenings."

"Sounds nice," Greg had to agree. He had been favorably impressed with all he had seen and had no doubt Ms. Stevens was more than capable of keeping the troops in order.

Chelsey always felt a sense of pride whenever she toured Rosehaven. She loved her job and the residents. The home ran like a well-oiled machine—with only a few minor exceptions.

Their footsteps slowed as Chelsey noticed a couple of the minor exceptions sitting at a picnic table playing cards.

"Hello, Lars, Otto."

Lars Metcalf was a small man in his early seventies, with thick glasses and a winning smile. He raised his balding head and grinned. "Hello, Ms. Stevens."

"Who's winning?"

"Ian," Otto Cameron relayed in a friendly voice, his gold front tooth sparkling brightly in the late afternoon sun.

"Ian?" Chelsey glanced around. Ian Landers, Otto Cameron and Lars Metcalf were usually inseparable, but at the moment Ian was nowhere to be seen.

"Yeah," Otto glanced at Lars. "Uh . . . Ian had to leave for a minute, but he'll be right back."

"Leave?" Chelsey felt a chill slither up her spine. While Ian, Lars and Otto were pleasant men, the trio tended to be her Waterloo. The three men were unpredictable, and what Ian couldn't think of to eradicate boredom, Otto could. Lars was a squeamish follower.

Lars cleared his throat. "Yeah . . . but . . . Ian . . . he'll be right back, Ms. Stevens," he promised.

If it had been anyone but Ian, Chelsey would have let the subject drop. But she knew Ian became bored the easiest.

"Where did Ian go?" Chelsey persisted.

Otto hurriedly got to his feet and extended a hand to Greg. "Hi there! I'm Otto Cameron and this is Lars Metcalf."

"Oh . . . yes." Chelsey belatedly recalled her manners. "Gentlemen, this is Greg Bradford." To Greg she said, "Otto and Lars have been with us for over a year now."

Greg reached out and shook each man's hand firmly. "Nice to meet you, gentlemen."

"Yeah, same to you," they chorused.

"You visiting?" Lars inquired.

"I'm considering bringing my father to Rosehaven."

"Oh, he'll like it," Otto assured, and Lars nodded his head in automatic agreement.

"Where did you say Ian went?" Chelsey prompted again.

"Oh . . . I think he was gonna wash his hands," Otto said thoughtfully.

"Oh." Chelsey glanced around uneasily again, then decided she was being unnecessarily concerned. Ian had behaved quite admirably for the past few weeks. "Well, don't let us keep you from your game."

"Thanks, Ms. Stevens." Both Lars and Otto smiled and waited until Chelsey and Greg had continued down the path.

When they were out of hearing range, Lars poked Otto in the ribs with his elbow. "Why did you have to go and lie to her again!"

"Ouch! I didn't lie to her!" Otto said.

"You did, too! You told her Ian was washing his hands."

"Did you want me to tell her the truth?" Otto challenged. "Did you want me to tell her Ian's down at Taco City buying our dinner? Why, she'd have a hissy!" he predicted.

"Well, no, but you didn't have to say Ian was washing his hands," Lars objected. "I can't abide lying. Never could—never will. You should've just said we didn't know where Ian had gone," he complained. "Didn't have to lie about it."

The two men returned to the table and picked up their cards. They sat in silence for a moment, then Otto said, "Well, Ian probably will wash his hands if that's what's worrying you."

"Yeah, maybe." Otto could see the thought made Lars feel a little better, but only a little.

"I just don't want to get in trouble again," Lars grumbled. "I like Ms. Stevens, and I promised I wouldn't sneak off the grounds again—and I haven't. It was Ian who didn't want creamed chicken for dinner. He wanted that blasted burrito instead. . . ." Lars's eyes narrowed with defense. "Well, I'll tell you something, Otto, it's going to be Ian who gets in trouble if he gets caught, not me!"

"I know, Lars. Don't go getting all flustered," Otto soothed.

Lars suddenly felt better that his friend could see his point. Otto usually didn't. "Well, just so Ms. Stevens knows the burritos aren't my idea," Lars said. "Now all I have to do is eat the burrito and hope it don't keep me awake all night with indigestion."

"Well, I read in *TV Guide* there's a good late movie on if it does," Otto consoled him.

"Oh? Well, I guess if I have to eat the burrito and be up all night, then at least I'll have something to do."

"Yeah, guess so."

When Chelsey and Greg arrived back at her office, Greg admitted he was impressed. "I'd like to bring Pop by tomorrow and let him tour Rosehaven."

She made a point of avoiding his eyes this time and glanced at her appointment pad. "I'll be able to meet with you around nine in the morning, if that's convenient."

"Nine will be fine." Greg reached out to shake her hand. "I like your operation, Ms. Stevens."

"Thank you, Mr. Bradford. I'll look forward to meeting your father." Chelsey noticed he held her hand for an uncommonly long time, and it annoyed her.

She started to see him out when she felt his hand casually settle on the small of her back, guiding her to the doorway. It was an innocent gesture, but she stiffened.

Exactly *what* was he trying to prove?

Greg glanced down at her and smiled. "Until tomorrow, Ms. Stevens?"

For a moment she couldn't find her voice. The man was insufferable. He might be an exceptionally attractive man who could turn the eye of most women, but she wasn't most women. Greg Bradford merely irritated, not stimulated, her.

"Cat got your tongue?" Greg inquired lightly. Her eyes widened as his gaze moved lackadaisically over the outline of her lips. The smell of his after-shave closed in on her again, and she hurriedly stepped back.

Greg had no idea why he was tormenting this woman. Perhaps it was his ego. He wasn't above admitting he had plenty of that. But it bothered him to watch how she could turn him off at will. It suddenly became a challenge to see if he could get a response from Chelsey Stevens.

Surprisingly Greg discovered her lips looked warm and inviting, but he'd bet it had been a long time since any man had dared to invade such formidable territory.

His underlying tone of arrogance snapped Chelsey out of her momentary daze.

"The cat hasn't got my tongue, Mr. Bradford." She opened the door. "But if there were one present, it wouldn't have any trouble locating his dinner." She couldn't come out and call him what she was thinking, but she hoped he would get the drift.

He did, and amusement flickered in his dark eyes as they met hers. "Until tomorrow, Ms. Stevens?" he said again.

"Until tomorrow, Mr. Bradford," she returned pleasantly.

After he stepped into the outer office, Grace Martin nearly jumped out of her chair as the door was slammed shut behind him.

Grace lifted an inquiring brow. Greg winked at her and confided in a solemn whisper, "I think Ms. Stevens might be having a bad day."

Chapter Two

"I think you'll like the place, Pop." Greg and Thorny walked into the kitchen together the following morning.

"Maybe."

"Oh, you will. With the exception of Ms. Chelsey Stevens, Rosehaven has a cordial atmosphere."

Thorny was surprised to hear Greg stress Ms. so distinctly. "Who's Chelsey Stevens?"

"Chelsey Stevens? A wet blanket if I ever met one." Greg opened the refrigerator door and peered inside. "What do you want for breakfast?"

"I'll have ham, three eggs over easy and biscuits and gravy." Thorny sat down and shook the newspaper open, adjusted his thin, wire-rimmed glasses and began reading the headlines.

"Come on, Pop. You know you can't eat like that. How about some scrambled egg substitutes and whole wheat toast with a little honey?"

Thorny lowered the front page and peered over the rim. "The only honey I'd be interested in is Phoenix Sommerville."

"Who's Phoenix Sommerville?" Greg removed the carton of low-cholesterol egg alternative and closed the door.

"A sassy little fox I met at the car wash yesterday." Thorny glanced at the skillet Greg was preparing to pour the liquid eggs into and frowned. "If I have to eat that, just fix me a little."

Thorny couldn't understand it. Greg never let him eat what he wanted. He wasn't allowed to have real eggs anymore. He had to eat turkey instead of beef—turkey meat loaf! Who'd ever heard of turkey meat loaf? And fats had suddenly become a four-letter word. If he ate one more piece of broiled fish, he was going to sprout gills.

What he'd like to have is a nice big thick steak and a mound of greasy French fries swimming in catsup, he thought wistfully.

"Do you want bacon with your eggs?"

"Is it real?"

"What do you mean, is it real?"

"Did it come from a hog or did some mad scientist invent it to taunt people over fifty?"

Greg shook his head tolerantly. "It's low cholesterol, Pop, and it's good for you. I eat it."

Thorny dropped his gaze back to the paper, grumbling under his breath. The boy was getting to be downright annoying.

"I don't know why we have this argument every morning. You know you have to watch your diet," Greg reasoned as he popped two slices of bread into the toaster. "You want a cup of coffee?"

"Is it decaffeinated?" Thorny knew it was.

"Yes, caffeine—"

"Isn't good for me," Thorny finished.

"Right." Greg dished up the eggs and low-cholesterol "sizzlers" and turned off the burner. "After we eat we're going to tour Rosehaven."

"I can hardly wait."

"Now, come on, Pop. You know we've discussed the subject before. I'd like nothing better than to have you live here, but Camille thinks you aren't getting the proper care."

"Camille, samille. Your sister's more like your mother every day. Always worrying, always worrying."

"I know, but Camille does have a point. You are left to your own devices too much."

"So what? I managed to make it on my own for thirty-three years before either one of you were born." Greg blocked Thorny's knife as he started to dip generously into the tub of butter.

Thorny's face clouded with disappointment. "No butter?"

"No butter. Here," Greg absently shoved a smaller container toward him. "Try this instead."

"Oh, brother." Thorny obediently smeared his whole wheat toast with the low-fat spread. As soon as Greg left for work, Thorny planned to eat the whole tub of butter on a loaf of white bread.

"Rosehaven seems to be just what we're looking for," Greg continued, trying to ignore the resentful scowls coming his way. "I think after you take the tour this morning, you'll agree. You'll still be able to live your own life and have proper supervision in my absence. When I'm home I'll come and get you, and we'll do the things we've always done."

"I thought you said the woman who runs Rosehaven is an old biddy." Thorny could see this Chelsey Stevens now—sixty, sexless and senile. Just the kind of woman he wanted to be stuck with for the rest of his life.

"Chelsey Stevens?" Greg recalled how he had purposely antagonized the prim Ms. Stevens the day before, and wondered why he had delighted in her discomfort. "I didn't say she was an old biddy, Pop. She's just uptight. I think she's one of those feminists." Greg took a bite of his toast and chewed thoughtfully. "She'll remind you a whole lot of Mom."

"Of Elizabeth?" Thorny stifled an audible groan. He had loved his deceased wife but, Lordy, that woman had tried his patience at times. She was always on her soapbox about something.

"Well, you won't have to worry about Ms. Stevens," Greg promised. "I doubt she'll be around that much." He got up to retrieve the coffeepot before he went back to the subject at hand. "I think Rosehaven offers a man your age a lot of possibilities."

Multitudes, Thorny thought. There'd be basket weaving, ceramics and bingo, none of which Thorny found the least bit interesting.

"Ms. Stevens assures me you won't be bored," Greg promised.

"I'm not bored here."

Well, maybe that wasn't exactly true. He did get bored once in a while. And Greg was gone a lot.

Greg's face softened. "I know, Pop, but—"

"It's what Camille wants," Thorny finished. If he'd heard it once, he'd heard it a hundred times. Camille worried about him. Well, maybe moving to Rosehaven wouldn't be all that bad, although he was having trouble working up any enthusiasm for the idea.

But he guessed there'd be people his own age over there—and that might be a nice change. This big old house could feel awfully empty at times. He had seen a couple of women over at Rosehaven he might like to check out. Maybe he could even find someone to play cards with him; he'd like that. He guessed if Greg wanted him to go over and take a look around this morning, he could oblige. Lord knew he didn't have much else to do with the rest of his life.

"What time did you say we have to be there?"

"Nine o'clock." Greg, sipping the remains of his coffee, was engrossed in the sports page.

"I thought you were flying to Canada on business today."

"I postponed the trip. I need to get you settled before I take off again."

Thorny ate his last bite of egg substitute and washed it down with the decaffeinated coffee.

Well, maybe Rosehaven wouldn't be all that bad. It might even have butter.

CHELSEY WAS GOING OVER the morning mail when Grace Martin tapped on her door.

"Yes?"

"Sorry to disturb you, Ms. Stevens, but I wanted to be sure you had the meeting with Ferris Winslow this Friday at two on your calendar." Grace stepped into the office carrying her memo pad.

Chelsey was not in the habit of forgetting meetings with her regional director, but she was grateful for Grace's efficiency.

"Thank you, Grace. I do have it on my calendar."

"And the meeting with the head dietician this afternoon?"

"Yes. One-fifteen?"

"Correct, and Frank Williams in marketing would like to meet with you sometime before the week is over."

"Call Frank and see if we can postpone the meeting until the first of next week. Oh, and Grace, I need to speak with Mary Beasley concerning the Halloween party at her earliest convenience."

Each year the Rosehaven auxiliary hosted a Halloween party for children of preschool age. The residents dressed in costumes and, allowing the children to trick or treat each room, handed out candy and various gifts they had made. It was an enjoyable evening for the residents, and every year they looked forward to Halloween as much as the youngsters.

"Certainly. I'll set up the appointment this morning. You have Friday at three open."

"If it meets with Mary's schedule, the time will be fine with me."

"Oh, yes. Dr. Matlock has called twice. He wants to have dinner with you Thursday night and discuss placing one of his patients here."

Both Chelsey and Grace knew the well-known heart surgeon and notorious womanizer, Dr. Neil Matlock, didn't need to have dinner with Chelsey in order to place one of his heart patients in Rosehaven, but neither one mentioned it. Grace suspected Chelsey enjoyed Dr. Matlock's company, and it worried her.

"Thank you, Grace. I'll personally return Dr. Matlock's call." Chelsey stood up and reached for her coffee cup. "Is that all?"

"Greg Bradford and his father are here for their nine o'clock appointment," Grace reminded her.

"Oh, yes, Mr. Bradford." She smiled. "I'll let you know when to send Mr. Bradford and his father in."

Chelsey slipped out of her office by a connecting door to the hallway and went in search of a fresh cup of coffee. Let Greg Bradford cool his heels for a while, she thought smugly. She was still smarting from her encounter with him the day before.

It was close to nine-twenty before Chelsey finally gave Grace permission to show the Bradfords in. There was an indefinable sense of satisfaction in keeping the man waiting, but Chelsey was powerless to explain why.

By the stormy look on Greg's face when Grace showed the two men in, he knew exactly what she had done.

Chelsey smiled at him pleasantly from behind her desk. "Forgive the delay, Mr. Bradford. It's been frantic around here this morning."

Greg didn't believe her flimsy excuse, and he certainly didn't appreciate being kept waiting for twenty minutes. She looked cool as a cucumber, sitting there idly sipping her coffee, and it annoyed the hell out of him. It annoyed him even more when she took three phone calls and excused herself twice before she settled down to business.

"So sorry, gentlemen," she apologized again as she sat back down at her desk. "There are just some things that can't wait." She extended her hand to Thorton. "You must be Thorton Bradford."

"Yes, I am." Thorton got politely to his feet, doffed his hat and held it over his chest. "Nice to meet you, ma'am."

"Very nice to meet you, Thorton. I hope you'll find Rosehaven everything you're hoping for."

Thorny glanced at Greg with a puzzled expression on his face. He had expected Ms. Stevens to be close to his own age, with Oxford shoes and support hose, not this lovely young creature. "Oh, I'm sure I will, ma'am."

Greg noticed Chelsey was dressed as conservatively as the day before. Still, he had no trouble detecting her ripe curves beneath the dark green fabric of her business suit.

"Well, Mr. Bradford. Your son has told me all about you," Chelsey began.

"He has?" Thorny squirmed uneasily. He certainly hoped not.

Chelsey studied Greg's father, searching for a family resemblance and finding none. Thorton Bradford was small in stature, not much taller than Chelsey's five foot three. The elder Bradford was nearly bald. He had a thick, bushy, red mustache and wore thin, wire-rimmed glasses. But he looked gentle in nature and extremely tidy.

"I've been telling Pop how impressed I am with Rosehaven," Greg said, for the moment swallowing his injured pride at having been kept waiting. "And its lovely administrator," he added graciously.

Since Chelsey hadn't appreciated his behavior the day before, she'd made up her mind to simply ignore him this morning. She was determined he wasn't going to get under her skin today.

Rising from her chair, she met Thorny's eyes directly. "Then I'm sure you're anxious to see what we have to offer, Mr. Bradford. Would you follow me?"

"Of course, Ms. Stevens." Greg and Thorton both sprang obediently to their feet.

Chelsey was tempted to tell the younger Mr. Bradford to sit back down, but she knew she couldn't do so without appearing blatantly rude to his father. She leveled her gaze pointedly on Thorny again, hoping his son would take the hint that she would prefer to show Thorton around alone. "Thorton. Would you follow me, please? I'm sure since your son has already seen the facilities he would rather stay here in the office and have a second cup of coffee while I show you around."

"Oh, no, Ms. Stevens. If you don't mind, I'll just go along with you and Pop." Greg wasn't about to appease her after the way she had treated him this morning. "You don't mind, do you?"

Yes, Chelsey did mind, but what was she to do?

"Of course I don't mind," she said.

Stepping hurriedly to the door, Greg opened it for her. As she walked stiffly by him, she heard him remark in a low tone, "I love that perfume. It's that new Elizabeth Taylor one, isn't it?"

The man certainly knew his fragrances, she thought. Her face responded as he knew it would: it turned glacial.

"Grace, I'll be showing the Bradfords around," Chelsey announced curtly as she left the office.

Grace offered Greg a timid smile. It was evident she thought he was the best-looking man she'd seen in years. "Yes, Ms. Stevens."

The low heels of Chelsey's black pumps clicked rhythmically down the corridor as Greg and Thorny trailed behind her. Before they realized it, she was a good fifty feet ahead of them.

"She seems a little testy, don't you think?" Thorny was having to hurry to keep up with Greg's long strides.

"Didn't I tell you?" Greg asked out of the corner of his mouth. "Ms. Iceberg herself."

"To the left is the recreation lounge, and the Rose dining room is on the right." The dining-room decor was a charming blue and mauve, complete with matching tablecloths and fresh flowers on each table. A large piano stood in the corner. Grouped around a massive fireplace were various rose-colored wing chairs, sofas and love seats. Several residents sat watching Bob Barker on the popular television show "The Price Is Right," encouraging his audience to "come on down!"

"We have two additional dining rooms, allowing you the freedom to circulate." Chelsey was far ahead of the two men by now and she slowed her pace. "We have bingo in the rec room on Friday nights, and a family potluck dinner in the dining hall every Saturday evening. Weather permitting, we cook outside during the summer months, and have watermelon feeds."

Thorny and Greg hurried to catch up. "That sounds good." Watermelon gave Thorny heartburn. He wrinkled his brow and glanced at Greg imploringly.

"Residents are permitted to roam as they please, but we ask they return to their rooms by nine every night for medicine and bed check."

"She hasn't got a bad tush," Thorny noted under his breath, dismissing all thoughts of watermelon.

"Her tush is to be left alone," Greg warned.

Thorny frowned. "Did I say I was going to bother her tush?"

"I can read you like a book, Pop."

"Fine, then you make sure you leave it alone, too."

"You can be assured I plan to."

Chelsey slowed and waited for the men to catch up. "The visiting area is to the left. You'll notice we have a lovely solarium, which we encourage our residents to use as often as possible."

"Do I have to give up my car if I move over here?" Thorny fretted.

"Yes. Since you've had three speeding tickets in the past two months, don't you think it's about time?"

They emerged into a spacious area housing a large, circular desk. The efficient-looking staff members were bustling about their work.

A man in a wheelchair spotted Chelsey and he rolled over to her hurriedly. "Hi, Ms. Stevens. Did you see about my phone?"

"Hi, Charlie. Haven't you got that phone yet?"

"Oh, they brought it, but they haven't plugged it in for me."

"I'll be down sometime this afternoon to take care of it, Charlie."

"Thanks, Ms. Stevens. I appreciate it. I want to call my daughter."

The small party continued on. "Down the next few corridors are the various wings. The Chalet, the Amsterdam, and the Matista. As you'll notice, a new wing is currently under construction. It will be for people with Alzheimer's. We hope to have it in operation by the first of the year."

Thorny could see the rooms were airy and comfortable.

"We also have small apartments available, should you choose to have more privacy."

Chelsey reached the double French doors leading to the veranda and paused. "Am I going too fast?"

Greg and Thorny caught up with her again, and Thorny slipped through the door ahead of them.

"No, not at all, Ms. Stevens." Greg held the door for Chelsey and she unwillingly met his dancing eyes. "I like fast women." He winked at her suggestively.

Taking a deep breath, Chelsey continued in a carefully controlled tone, "There is also a happy hour twice a week."

"A happy hour?" Greg found that hard to believe. For the moment they had forgotten all about Thorny.

"We serve alcoholic beverages, and fruit punch for those who abstain. Wine and hors d'oeuvres are served between four and seven in the recreation room."

"How interesting." His eyes insisted on flirting with hers.

"I'm glad you find it so."

"Did anyone ever tell you your eyes turn two shades greener in a certain light?" he whispered.

"There are two church services on Sunday morning. Catholic and Protestant."

Greg was still intrigued with the news of a happy hour. "Can anyone attend the happy hour?"

"The families are encouraged to visit as often as possible." She stared back at him coolly. "I don't suppose that will be a problem for you, Mr. Bradford?"

Greg smiled indulgently. "Not at all, Ms. Stevens. Have you ever thought of wearing your hair down?"

His outrageous remarks were not going to annoy her. "I prefer to wear it this way," she stated calmly.

Greg shook his head pensively. "What a pity."

Thorny had taken in their strange exchanges with growing amusement. It was unlike his son to heckle anyone. Was it possible Greg was finally getting over his wife's death and finally taking a real interest in a woman?

Thorny recalled the bleak days and months after Mary Beth's death. Greg had seemed to retreat from life. He no longer went to the office. He would go for days without eating, bathing or shaving. Instead he would sit in his room for hours and never speak to another soul. After a few months, he finally came out of his self-imposed hell, only to bury himself in work, sometimes working fifteen hours a day, to avoid coming home to an empty house.

As the years passed, Thorny watched for signs to indicate that his son's pain was abating, but the signs had been slow in coming. Thorny thought Greg was too young to give up on the opposite sex. He needed to find a good woman who would heal his wounds and give him children. If just once in the past five years Greg had become seriously involved with another woman, Thorny would have felt encouraged. But Greg had kept a cool distance from any serious involvement. He dated, but Thorny knew Greg had never found anyone to replace Mary Beth. Still, Thorny found it strange he was deliberately annoying Ms. Stevens.

"Greg, I want to see the grounds," Thorny requested, interrupting the tense conversation as he saw Chelsey's eyes glisten with suppressed anger.

"Good idea, Pop." Greg politely motioned for Chelsey to precede him.

"You're an ass, Mr. Bradford. Are you aware of that?" Chelsey challenged quietly out of the corner of her mouth as she passed.

Ordinarily she would never have dreamed of speaking to anyone in such an offensive manner, but the man had pushed her to her limit.

"I'm sorry, Ms. Stevens. Did you say something?" Greg paused as Thorny came within hearing distance and waited for her to answer. He grinned at her obvious reluctance to repeat her defamatory statement.

She smiled. "No, Mr. Bradford. I didn't say a thing."

"Oh? I could have sworn you did."

"After we view the grounds, we'll look in on the basket-weaving class." She made up her mind to go back to her original solution: completely ignore him.

Greg smiled. "Sounds exciting."

Chelsey conducted the remainder of the tour with swift expediency. While she found Thorton pleasant, she couldn't help but hope he wouldn't agree to the move. If she had to contend with Greg Bradford, she wasn't sure she could remain civil.

When they were once again seated in her office, she faced Thorny, holding her breath, praying he had found something about Rosehaven he didn't care for.

"Well, what do you think, Pop?" Greg anxiously watched his father for signs of disapproval, hoping he would refuse outright to make the move. It would mean Greg would have to start all over again, but he'd decided a steady diet of Chelsey Stevens was going to be hard to swallow.

"I like it, son. It's real nice."

Greg's shoulders sagged as Chelsey bit her lower lip painfully. "You do?" They looked at each other warily, then brought their gazes hurriedly back to Thorny.

"Where do I sign?"

"Wait a minute, Pop. Don't you think we should look around a little? Maybe Camille will want to fly down and look the place over before we do anything permanent."

"Nope, it looks real nice to me," Thorny repeated. "Where do I sign?" If Camille and Greg were going to insist he make this move, Thorny was determined to be pleasant about it. Although he had no idea why, the move suddenly seemed to be a good idea.

"Are you sure, Mr. Bradford?" Chelsey found it hard to conceal the disappointment in her voice. "I recommend you take a few days to think about it."

"No, my mind is made up. I think I'm going to like it real well around here," Thorny announced confidently. "I'll move first thing tomorrow morning."

"First thing tomorrow morning..." Chelsey smiled lamely. "Wonderful."

Chapter Three

Thorny's move to Rosehaven was made quickly and efficiently. To Chelsey's relief, Thorton Bradford fit right in with the other residents; to her dismay, he gravitated to Ian, Otto and Lars. Together they formed a tight foursome.

She could only view the disturbing combination with apprehension. If the elder Bradford was anything like the younger one, she would have to deal with the equivalent of gas and a lighted match.

Thorny had been at Rosehaven a little over two weeks when Chelsey happened to bump into Greg Bradford at the local drugstore. She was reasonably sure he hadn't been to visit Thorny lately, but had overheard Thorny telling Violet Appleton that his son was in Canada on business.

Standing at the cosmetic counter examining the newest shade of lipstick, Chelsey tensed as she heard a familiar baritone voice comment, "Buy it. The color would be perfect for you."

Chelsey frowned when she noticed Greg standing at the magazine rack. Dressed casually but elegantly in slacks and sport coat, he was even better looking than she remembered.

"It isn't my shade." She quickly replaced the cap on the tube and stuck it back in the display case.

Greg smiled, made his selection, then followed Chelsey to the toothpaste display.

"I understand the red-and-white one makes the mouth more kissable," he commented, glancing interestedly over the assorted pumps and tubes.

"And I'm sure if anyone would know, you would." Chelsey selected a green tube and placed it in her basket.

He made a reproving clucking sound. "My, my, Ms. Stevens. Did we get up on the wrong side of the bed this morning?" Greg trailed behind her as she moved down the aisle to the shampoos.

"Buy the green one. The fragrance drives a man wild," he confided a few minutes later as she paused to decide if she should try the new brand.

"Don't you have to be running along, Mr. Bradford?"

"I'm playing hooky this afternoon."

Greg watched her deliberately select an amber bottle and place it in her basket. Chelsey walked off and left him standing alone amidst the conditioners and hair-coloring kits.

"How're things going at the home?" he asked conversationally as he stood behind her at the checkout a few moments later.

"Things are fine at the home."

Greg knew by her chilly response that he'd used the wrong term again. "Good. That's good to hear."

She knew she shouldn't encourage the conversation, but she had the uneasy feeling he was one of those men who thought that because she was a woman she was incapable of running a smooth operation.

It took a minute, but she finally swallowed her resentment and asked in a more collected tone, "Why do you ask?"

At first Greg didn't answer. He knew she'd been trying to avoid him. Now she was looking at him as if awaiting some sort of response. He cocked his brows and said, "Beg your pardon?"

"I said *why* do you ask?"

"About the ho—Rosehaven?" He caught himself before he raised her ire again.

"Yes."

"Oh, I was just wondering how you thought Pop was adjusting to the move."

Without appearing obvious, Chelsey tried to see what magazines he was buying. Frivolous trash, no doubt.

"Thorton is adjusting fine." Chelsey placed her purchases on the counter. "You should stop by and visit him occasionally."

"Now, now, Ms. Stevens." Greg leaned closer and smiled at her patiently. "Aren't we unnecessarily testy this afternoon?"

She turned away, determined to ignore him since he was obviously trying to provoke her.

Greg had to admit she looked good today, not nearly as forbidding as she had the last time he'd seen her. She was wearing a pastel shade of green that made her eyes look as if they had been specifically ordered with the dress. Her hair was still in a knot, but today it didn't make her features seem so severe. Actually, he decided, she was damned attractive. Still not his type, but he was willing to admit she wasn't all that bad.

"Didn't Pop tell you? I've been out of the country for the past couple of weeks." Greg went on with the conversation as if she were a willing participant.

"Thorton didn't mention it to me." And Thorny *hadn't* mentioned it to her, but to Violet.

"Well, I was. That's why I haven't been around lately."

Chelsey doubted he would be around any more frequently now that he had returned, but she refrained from saying so.

The clerk handed Chelsey her purchases, and she headed for the exit. She knew she should at least be courteous enough to say goodbye, but she declined. The man annoyed her; it was as simple as that.

Still, her conscience nagged her as she started out the door. As much as she hated to admit it, there was something about Greg Bradford she found titillating.

Outside the drugstore, she noticed the skies had turned threatening and a peppery rain was beginning to fall.

Realizing her umbrella was in the back seat of her car, she held the paper sack containing her purchases over her head and started for the car in a run.

The rain fell harder as her feet flew along, trying to avoid the puddles gathering on the sidewalks.

"I just love to walk in the rain, don't you?"

She tensed as she heard his voice. He was running along beside her.

Suddenly the skies opened up and a deluge assailed them. Greg reached out and pulled her protectively under the shelter of an overhanging awning. The unexpected gesture caught her by surprise as the rain continued to come down in heavy sheets and pedestrians scattered for cover like buckshot.

Regaining her composure, Chelsey quickly moved out of his embrace. They stood without speaking, watching the downpour for a few minutes until Greg finally spoke. "Looks like it's set in for a while." He shouted over the noise of rain pelting down on the canvas awning. "Where are you parked?"

"Another block down!" Chelsey tried to rearrange her hair, which was slowly coming loose from its pins. She finally gave up as the thick blond mass tumbled down around her shoulders in wet ringlets.

When Greg turned his glance to her, his gaze lingered. With her hair down, she looked different. For the first time since he'd met her, she wasn't wearing her glasses. The rain had washed part of her makeup away, and she suddenly looked young and vulnerable. Her nose had a cute tilt to it, and across its bridge he discovered an enchanting sprinkle of freckles he was sure hadn't been there previously.

He was staring at her again, and Chelsey lifted her left brow defensively. "Is there something wrong?" She knew she looked a mess, and if he was determined to hassle her again, she was through being polite about it.

"Wrong?" Greg shrugged. "Nothing's wrong, Ms. Stevens. I was just thinking that maybe we could share a pizza while we wait out the storm."

Greg decided he might enjoy sharing a meal with her, whether it was raining or not.

Though he was trying to be pleasant, Chelsey was hesitant about accepting his offer. What was he trying to prove this time? she wondered.

"How about it, Ms. Stevens?" He said her name differently this time, in a voice that bordered on sincere cordiality.

"Thanks, but I have to be getting back."

"Are you sure?" He wouldn't let her off the hook so easily. She was beginning to intrigue him. "It's obviously going to rain for a while, and you haven't eaten yet, have you?"

"No, but..." Her tone softened when she realized he was actually serious about wanting to share a pizza. For some reason, she had no idea what, especially after the way he'd annoyed her, she found herself declining the invitation this time with a little more civility. "Look, I'm expecting a friend to drop by. Maybe another time."

"You have a date?" he asked casually.

Now what sort of man would interest Chelsey Stevens? Greg found himself wondering. Certainly not the president of an electronics corporation. She'd made that crystal clear.

Not that *he* was interested, but her continuing obstinacy made him curious.

"An old sorority friend is coming by, and I really must be going."

Greg shrugged and surveyed the darkened sky. "You're going to get wet."

"I won't dissolve."

He didn't argue. She wasn't made of sugar, he could attest to that.

"Well, see you around," he said.

"Sure. See you."

Chelsey found herself oddly regretting the fact she already had plans for the evening. A pizza with Greg Bradford would, at the least, be stimulating. Holding the soggy paper sack over her head, Chelsey said goodbye and dashed down the sidewalk.

Greg stuck his hands into his pockets and leaned idly against the building, watching as she ran lithely down the sidewalk.

A pity. Pizza had sounded good.

WHEN THORNY MADE his declaration, he was sitting with Otto, Lars and Ian on the veranda, drinking in the warm afternoon sunshine. "I'm not going to basket-weaving class," he said.

"Why not? We don't have anything else to do," Lars countered. "I can't understand you, Thorny. When someone tells me to go to basket-weaving class, then I go—especially if Ms. Stevens tells me to go. I specifically heard Ms. Stevens ask you to attend the class this afternoon."

"We'll find something else to do," Thorny replied. "It's too darn nice to be sitting in that stuffy room on a day like this. Besides, wicker makes me sneeze."

Thorny had been at Rosehaven almost three weeks, and his new home was all right, except he got tired of doing the same thing every day. The longer he was there, the more he realized how much he missed the freedom he'd had living with Greg. But at least Camille had piped down, so he guessed he'd done the right thing.

He'd tried his best to adjust to his new surroundings. He'd joined in every activity Rosehaven offered, but he found he was easily bored. Thorny bet he'd already woven more baskets and painted more duck decoys than Otto, Lars and Ian put together. Today he was ready for a change.

"They're having a sing-along in the recreation room at two," Otto reminded him.

"I don't want to go to a sing-along," Thorny grunted. He'd gone to one the week before and hadn't cared for it. Ella Mae Wilcox had a voice that could shatter plate-glass windows. The whole experience had given Thorny a headache.

"We could just wait here until the meeting about the Rock and Roll Marathon begins," Ian suggested.

"What time does that thriller take place?"

"Three."

A notice had been posted on the bulletin board urging all Rosehaven residents to participate in the annual fund-raiser. Some in wheelchairs would roll while others rocked in rocking chairs. Various other fund-raising activities were planned to capture the public's attention—and donations.

"Afternoon, Ms. Stevens." All four men rose and tipped their hats as Chelsey walked by.

"Good afternoon, gentlemen. Going to basket weaving, Thorny?"

"Thinking about it," he lied.

"Better hurry. The class starts in five minutes," she reminded them. The four men watched Chelsey get into her car and drive away.

"Where's she going?" Otto asked. Thorny had quickly discovered Otto was downright nosy. No one entered or left Rosehaven without his knowing why.

Thorny settled back in his lawn chair and pulled his hat over his face to shade himself from the sun. "Don't have any idea."

"She's a cute little thing," Otto lamented. "Wish I was forty years younger."

"Don't we all," responded the other three simultaneously.

They sat for a moment in silence, listening to the birds and squirrels chirping overhead.

"Your son date anyone seriously?" Otto asked.

"Nah, not seriously."

"That's strange. He's a nice-looking young man. You'd think women would be after him all the time."

"Yeah, he'd make someone a good catch."

Otto thought for a moment. "You say he dates some?"

"Yeah, some."

"Then he'll probably marry and settle down one of these days. You seen the way he looks at Ms. Stevens?"

"I've seen, but Greg's definitely not interested in her."

"How do you know?"

"Because I asked him."

"Well, why not? She's a handsome woman," Otto protested.

"Beautiful, Otto, not handsome," Lars corrected.

"Handsome, beautiful—call her whatever you want. Looks to me like your boy would notice that. She's got real class."

"Greg doesn't seem to notice," Thorny admitted. "His wife, Mary Beth, died in a car accident several years ago, and he hasn't gotten over her yet. In my opinion, I don't think he's looking for anyone to take her place."

"That's a shame," Otto said. The other men nodded in mute sympathy.

"She must've been young," Lars speculated.

"She was. One day she ran up to the local convenience store for a carton of milk and never made it back." Thorny shook his head sadly as he recalled the tragedy. "Greg's never been the same."

"Well, I say it's a shame," Ian declared. "If you ask me—which no one has—Ms. Stevens and your son would make a real nice pair. He's handsome and successful, and she's as pretty as a picture."

They sat in silence again for a few moments, then Thorny asked, "You really think so?"

"What?" Otto sounded as if he'd forgotten the subject already.

"That Greg and Ms. Stevens would make a nice pair."

"Well, sure. Why not?"

"Well—" Thorny sat up and pushed his hat back on his forehead thoughtfully "—something just occurred to me."

"What's that?"

"You know, if Greg got married again, and his wife stayed home during the day, then I could probably live with my son again."

"Oh, I don't think your daughter would let you," Ian warned.

"The devil she wouldn't. If Greg had a wife, then she could look after me," Thorny reasoned. "Camille wouldn't have a thing to say about it. The only reason I'm here is because she thinks I'm not capable of taking care of myself. Why, if Greg were to remarry, Camille would have to quit mollycoddling me." Thorny was beginning to warm to the subject.

"Oh, I don't know, Thorny. Sounds dangerous to me. You're getting ready to stir up a hornet's nest," Lars predicted. "You better leave well enough alone."

"Now, why do you say that, Lars?"

"Well, just because you are. Don't you like it here at Rosehaven?"

"It's okay, but I liked it at Greg's better."

Lars shook his head worriedly. "I don't know..."

"Look, we all agree Greg needs a woman, and it appears Ms. Stevens could use a man to loosen her up a little, so why couldn't the four of us sort of ease the two of them together? If the plan works, then I can move back to Greg's house."

"Well, how would that help Otto, Lars and me?" Ian objected. "We'd still be stuck here at Rosehaven."

"True, but I could slip a little real butter over the fence once in while, or maybe a little brandy...."

Ian chuckled. "Your son wouldn't like what you're planning."

"I know. That's why we'll have to be careful. He'd be real upset all right."

"You don't think he'll suspect what we're trying to do? He appears to be a right bright boy to me," Ian reminded.

"He should be," Thorny boasted. "He's my son, isn't he? And he's been to the finest schools money can buy." Thorny recalled how his own education had been aborted in the eighth grade, when his father had died unexpectedly. Thorny had been left as the sole support of his mother and three sisters. But he had pulled himself up by the seat of the pants, and by the time he was thirty he owned his own electronics company. He'd made sure his children had what he'd always wanted—a high-school diploma and a list of college degrees anyone would be proud to possess. "He won't suspect a thing. I've always let him live his own life. We'll catch him completely off guard," Thorny promised.

Otto moved closer to Thorny, clearly caught up in the thrill of anticipation. "Have you thought about what we could do to get the ball rolling?"

"Listen, men," Lars protested. "I don't think we'd better do this. You know I don't like messing around in other people's lives! It makes me nervous. Your plan will backfire, and we'll all be in a peck of trouble!"

Otto dismissed his remark irritably. "No, we won't. What can it hurt?"

"It'll make Ms. Stevens mad at us," Lars predicted.

"She won't know what we're doing, Lars!" Ian pointed out. He turned back to Thorny. "Where do you think we ought to begin?"

"Well, let's see. There's this big swimming pool over at Greg's house. Now, what would happen if we just moseyed over there this afternoon and had ourselves a refreshing swim?"

"We would get in a peck of trouble; that's what would happen!" Lars protested. "You know we aren't supposed to leave the grounds without letting someone know."

"Good grief, Lars!" Otto snapped. "Aren't you listening? If we asked someone's permission, we wouldn't be doing anything wrong!"

"You're missing the point, Lars," Thorny said patiently.

"Which is?"

"The object is to bring Greg and Chelsey together. Right?"

"Yes..."

"And I'm afraid the only way to accomplish that is for us to force the matter."

"How are we going to do that?"

"Well, for starters, we'll start disobeying rules."

"Count me out," Lars objected. He shook his head stubbornly. "Uh-uh. No way."

"And when we do, who do you think will come looking for us every time she finds out we're missing?" Thorny continued, ignoring Lars for the moment.

There was a shared moment of silence, then Otto and Ian answered at one time. "Ms. Stevens?"

Thorny nodded smugly. "And whose house are we always gonna be at?"

"Greg's?"

"Right. And who's going to be as mad as a wet hen and *demand* that Greg prevent us from going over there?" Thorny knew he couldn't miss on this one. Chelsey would be fit to be tied if Thorny, Ian, Otto and Lars kept running off.

"But I thought we'd try to bring them together," Ian fretted. "This sounds like we're only going to upset Ms. Stevens and make Greg mad at you."

The possibility had occurred to Thorny, but the way he saw it, if he didn't want to be knee-deep in wicker for the rest of his life, he had little choice but to approach the problem from this unorthodox angle.

"It'll work, I tell you. Now look. If anyone wants out, now's the time to speak up," he warned. With an iffy plan like this, there was no room for dissension in the ranks. He'd better make that clear right off.

"Count me in," Otto stated flatly.

"I'll go along," Ian agreed.

"You're putting me in a terrible spot," Lars said sourly.

"How do you figure that?" Thorny countered.

"I don't want to be left out, but I don't want to be branded a deserter, either. You'd think after a man reached his seventies, life would start to get a little easier!"

"Lars?" Thorny patiently awaited his answer. "Are you in or not?"

"We're gonna get in a peck of trouble," Lars warned.

Thorny nodded agreeably. "That's just what we're planning to do. You in?"

Lars glanced at Otto and Ian, then back to Thorny. Thorny could tell Lars wished he'd gone to the basket-weaving class. "I'm in," he said finally, sighing.

Thorny smacked his hands together gleefully. "Let's go swimming."

Chapter Four

That afternoon Chelsey was conducting the meeting concerning the Rock and Roll Marathon. Ordinarily Mary Beasley, head of Rosehaven's volunteer program, took care of such matters, but Mary had called earlier and asked Chelsey if she could fill in for her.

"And Margaret Winslow has graciously offered her services as program chairman for this year's fall fund-raising event," Chelsey concluded now. "Now, are there any further questions concerning the Rock and Roll Marathon?"

Kenneth Laibrook's hand immediately shot up.

"Kenneth?"

"What happens if we give out before our time is up?"

"The schedule has been designed so that each participant will be replaced every fifteen minutes. Should anyone feel their allotted time is too taxing, then by all means, have the next person take over earlier."

Kenneth turned and gave Vivian Mendel a relieved grin. "Just wondering. Never know how the ole lumbago will be acting that day."

"Any further questions?" Chelsey waited as a low stir broke out among the group. When she saw Mary Beasley enter the room, she smiled. "Then, if there's nothing further, I'd like to ask Thorton Bradford if he would please stay for a moment after the meeting."

Chelsey had decided Thorny would be the perfect person to put in charge of rotating the shifts for the marathon. She glanced around the room trying to locate the familiar face. "Thorton?"

An uneasy silence fell.

"Is Thorton Bradford present?" Chelsey prompted.

"Uh...he may have gone to the bathroom, Ms. Stevens." The vague reply came from someone in the back of the room.

"Oh?"

"Yeah, that's it. He went to the bathroom," a second male voice confirmed from across the room.

"Oh." A frown played across Chelsey's features. "Well, it's getting late so if there's no further business, we'll dismiss for the day." She closed the folder and smiled at the residents warmly. "I believe you're scheduled to meet again next Wednesday at four. I want to thank all of you for your attendance."

Chairs shuffled, their metal legs clanging, as the meeting broke up.

Mary Beasley hurried over to speak with Chelsey. "Thanks for filling in. I'm running hopelessly behind today."

"My pleasure." Chelsey glanced around the room thoughtfully. "Have you seen Thorny?"

"No," Mary confessed, "but he must be around here somewhere."

Not being able to readily locate Thorton Bradford made Chelsey a little uneasy. She called to Henry Rothman, "Henry, may I speak with you a moment?" Chelsey waited as a slight, wiry gentleman made his way to the front of the room.

"Yes, Ms. Stevens?"

"Did you happen to notice when Thorny left?" Chelsey knew that if anyone would know if Thorton attended the meeting, it was Henry. He was to Rosehaven what a gossip columnist was to the public.

"Well now, I really couldn't say," Henry hedged. Chelsey was reluctant to believe him. She strongly suspected he *could* say. By the guilty look on Henry's face, she doubted that Thorton had been anywhere near the meeting, but Chelsey knew Henry liked Thorny, and if Thorny hadn't wanted to come to the meeting, then it was okay with Henry. He didn't want trouble.

"Why don't you ask Fern Silsby?" Henry prompted.

Fern Silsby was Rosehaven's unofficial mayor. She knew everything about everyone. If a person wanted information, he went to Fern.

"Oh, Fern! Ms. Stevens wants to talk to you!" Henry turned tail and left, fleeing before Chelsey could question him further.

"Excuse me, Chelsey. I have to speak to Margaret Winslow before she leaves," Mary said apologetically as Fern broke away from her small group and approached Chelsey hesitantly. "You wanted to speak to me, Ms. Stevens?"

Strong bifocals made Fern's wavering blue eyes seem enormous as she peered at Chelsey expectantly.

"Yes, Fern. I was wondering if you happened to see Thorny leave the meeting?" Chelsey wasn't sure why it mattered if Thorny attended the meeting, but it did.

"Did that darn Henry tell you!"

"Tell me?" Chelsey felt herself tensing.

Fern's eyes swept the room warily. Leaning close, she whispered in a hushed tone. "Thorny wasn't here."

"Excuse me?"

"Thorny...he wasn't at the meeting." Fern's eyes grew as large as a hoot owl's.

"He wasn't? That's strange. I thought he would come directly from basket weaving...." Chelsey's voice trailed off as she saw Fern shake her head sagaciously.

"He wasn't there, either, Ms. Stevens. And neither was Otto, Lars or Ian." Fern grinned knowingly. "They went swimming."

"They what?"

"They went swimming. Over at the Bradford place. You know, where Thorny's son lives?"

Chelsey felt her stomach plummet. "They left the grounds and went to Mr. Bradford's estate?"

"Well, Thorny told me not to tell anyone where they were going...." Fern paused and her brow furrowed as she concentrated. "Come to think of it, it was real strange the way Thorny sought me out and told me about his swimming plans. Thorny has never told me anything like that before...but then maybe he's finally beginning to notice me," Fern reasoned. Chelsey could tell Fern felt flattered and just a little bad about tattling on him.

"Thank you, Fern." Chelsey began to gather her purse and folders.

"That's all right, Ms. Stevens. I guess they're all in trouble again, huh?"

"Well, Thorny knows he's not supposed to leave the grounds without asking." Chelsey tried to sound noncommittal.

"I told him that. I also told him they were going to get in a lot of trouble. And they are, aren't they?"

Ida Munsington timidly eased her way over to where Chelsey and Fern were standing and interrupted before Chelsey could answer Fern. "Hello, Ms. Stevens. Nice day, isn't it?" Ida greeted.

"Hello, Ida." Chelsey wrapped her arm around Ida's stooped shoulders. "It's lovely. Have you been enjoying the sunshine?"

"Oh, yes...yes..." Ida said softly. Ida and her husband, Guy, had lived at Rosehaven for four years. Ida was a retired librarian, and Guy a postal worker. Guy had died a year ago, and Ida was pathetically lonely now.

Noticing the small gathering, Louella Lassiter began to edge forward. Chelsey smiled as she noticed the tiny woman slowly making her way toward them. Chelsey knew Louella never missed an opportunity to socialize. A retired Broadway actress, Louella had confided that she missed the hustle and bustle of her former life since coming to Rosehaven. With a stream of smoke trailing from her cigarette holder, Louella turned to Ida, Fern and Chelsey.

"Dear, dear ones," she said theatrically. "How are you lovelies today?"

"Oh, for heaven's sake, Louella! Me and Ida's just talkin' to Ms. Stevens." It was a well-known fact that Fern did not take kindly to anyone imposing on her time, and Louella knew full well she was treading on sacred ground by butting in on Fern's conversation.

Even shy Ida gave Louella a hurt look and stepped closer to Chelsey as the insouciant Louella ignored the warning signals and smiled pleasantly.

"My dear, Chelsey, how simply divine you look today."

"Hello, Louella. You're looking well, too."

Fern's feathers were clearly ruffled. She cast a disdainful glance at Louella and continued her conversation with Chelsey as if Louella weren't there. "Well, Ms. Stevens, if there's anything else you want to know—about you-know-who—just let me know."

"Thank you, Fern. You've been very helpful."

Chelsey tried to involve the three women in friendly conversation, but Fern eventually grew petulant again and wandered away. A few minutes later, Ida followed suit.

"I really must be going, Louella," Chelsey apologized. "I have another matter to attend to."

"It's quite all right, my dear. I have a pile of scripts to read." Louella's stage voice took over completely. "It's been marvelous chatting with you. Do stop by my room, and we'll share a glass of that simply divine Dom Perignon my agent brought me."

"I'd love to." Chelsey's heart went out to Louella when she saw her drifting into her private dreamworld.

"Ciao, dahling."

Chelsey was still smiling as she exited the meeting room. Grace was forever scolding her for spending too much time with the residents, but Chelsey took pleasure in seeing to their needs personally. Other than the aging film agent who visited Louella twice a year, Chelsey knew Louella had no one.

Chelsey sighed as her thoughts returned to business. Now she had to perform the unpleasant side of her duties.

Find Thorton Bradford and his three aquatic accomplices.

THE BRADFORD ESTATE was all Chelsey had heard it was. After slipping through a hedge, she approached the main house. Nestled within towering sequoias, the old mansion was in immaculate condition. The three-story brick dwelling had fluted columns, dentil moldings, and sweeping verandas. It was a family home, rich in heritage and elegantly tasteful. The manicured lawns and numerous flower beds overflowing with vivid colors added a genteel warmth to the grounds.

Chelsey found the sight breathtaking. As a child, she used to dream of living on such an estate with a handsome prince and dozens of servants at her disposal. There would be family, and the sound of children's laughter floating from the nursery, the smell of spice cake baking in the oven, and the prince returning to enfold her in his arms and whisper his undying love....

Chelsey shook away her whimsical thoughts as she hurried around the corner of a wide veranda.

Within moments, she found the missing four; they weren't hard to locate. It was almost as if they wanted to be discovered the way they were whooping and shouting in the water like young boys at play.

Chelsey parted the thick hedge surrounding the pool area and peered through the foliage stealthily. Thorny was just positioning himself to do a cannonball off the diving board. Chelsey clamped her eyes shut and prayed his heart could stand the shock.

She heard a loud splash, and Chelsey opened her eyes in time to see a giant plume of water shoot into the air. The other three gave a rousing round of applause. Thorny began to swim the length of the pool in long, easy strokes as Otto bemoaned the fact his bursitis prevented him from accomplishing such a feat. A man with bursitis didn't do cannonballs, either, Otto complained. Ian sympathized, declaring that he wouldn't even try if he were Otto.

Chelsey shook her head in disbelief and stepped through the hedge. Lars saw her first. His eyes grew round and he nudged Otto, who was floating by on an air mattress. "Ole blabbermouth Fern has done her job," he whispered urgently.

"What?"

"Ms. Stevens—she's here."

"Who?" Otto opened one eye and nearly toppled into the water as he looked up and saw Chelsey peering down at him. "Oh, hi there, Ms. Stevens!" Otto scrambled off, paddled the mattress to the pool's edge and when he stood up, water streamed down the sides of his face.

"Hello, Otto. How's the water?" Chelsey bent down and dipped the tips of her fingers into the sparkling pool.

"Fine . . . fine. . . ."

"Good." Chelsey glanced at Thorny who was casually backstroking his way toward her. "Hello, Thorny."

"Good afternoon, Ms. Stevens." He lapped by without pausing.

Chelsey stiffened resentfully and stood up. "Gentlemen, I hate to interrupt such fun, but it's getting late. Dinner will be served in thirty minutes."

"Oh. Do you want us to come home?" Lars prompted agreeably.

"If it's not too much bother."

"No bother at all. I've about had enough swimming! How about you men?"

Ian and Otto nodded mutely.

Chelsey smiled. "Thank you, Lars."

By this time, Otto, Ian and Lars were hastily drying off with towels. Chelsey walked over to them casually. "I missed seeing all of you at the meeting this afternoon."

Lars hung his head sheepishly. "Well..."

"We didn't want to come," Otto excused.

"Well, there's certainly no rule that says you have to," Chelsey allowed.

"We know that." By this time Thorny had left the pool and had come to take his place on the firing line. "We thought it was just too nice outside to weave baskets or sit in a meeting," he offered easily, "so we decided to go swimming."

"I agree it's a lovely day." But by the look on her face, Thorny knew Chelsey was making a conscious effort to avoid a scene. She was annoyed by their disappearance, and Thorny knew it. Well, fine. He liked a woman with spunk. No doubt about it, she'd make Greg a dandy wife.

"Would it be convenient for you gentlemen to meet with me in my office after dinner?" Chelsey asked.

Ian, Otto and Lars glanced at Thorny expectantly.

"We could do that," Thorny acknowledged pleasantly. "What time?"

"Six?"

"We'll be there."

"Thank you." Chelsey turned, then paused and turned back. "You *are* through swimming for the day?" she asked pointedly.

"Are we?" Thorny glanced at his comrades casually.

"Yes." When Chelsey answered for them, her tone held a note of finality.

"Oh. Then I suppose we are. Uh, did you want to speak to my son before you leave?"

Chelsey looked puzzled; she had assumed Greg Bradford knew nothing of his father's misconduct. And the last person she wanted to encounter now was Greg Bradford. "No... why? Is he here?"

"No, but he will be soon if you want to stick around."

"I don't think that will be necessary, Thorny. I'll see you at six."

"I'll be there."

"WELL, WE'RE KNEE-DEEP in it this time," Lars predicted glumly. The hands on the clock rested at exactly six o'clock as the four men sat in Chelsey's office awaiting her arrival.

"No, we're not. What can she possibly do? Nail us to the floor?" Thorny sat on the sofa calmly thumbing through a magazine while Lars paced the floor restlessly.

"She didn't seem all that mad," Otto consoled.

"No, I thought she acted right nice about it... considering." Ian shifted around in his chair nervously.

Thorny glanced up. "Considering what?"

"Considering the way we climbed over your son's fence and all." Ian had a scratched shin, and a nagging glitch in his back from the unnerving episode.

"Lars, Lars, Lars," Thorny said, and clucked his tongue benevolently. "You worry too much, my friend. We just went for a swim in Greg's pool. You act as if we jumped ship and swam back to England."

"There must be a simpler way to get Greg to notice Chelsey," Lars complained. "I'm not gonna like it when she lets us have it with both barrels."

"Gentlemen," Thorny cast his magazine aside impatiently, "just stop worrying. I'll be our group spokesman. All you have to do is sit here and look suitably repentant. I'll do the rest."

"She was mad, I tell you. Real mad," Lars warned.

"And she'll be glad, real glad, when we land her a rich, good-looking husband," Thorny predicted. "Just let me handle this."

The door opened, and the men snapped to attention as Chelsey entered the office. They watched expectantly as she walked to her desk and sat down. Placing her glasses on the bridge of her nose, she peered over the rims at them judiciously. "Gentlemen."

Four lame smiles greeted her.

"It seems we have a disturbing problem on our hands."

Again, four weak smiles and a couple of shame-faced nods confronted her.

Chelsey sighed. "I'm sure Bristol-Myers is immensely grateful to you. For the past three weeks, you've been directly responsible for the way their stock is skyrocketing." To emphasize the point, Chelsey reached into her desk drawer and withdrew a large bottle of Excedrin. Pouring water into a glass, she downed two pills before she continued. "Would anyone like to explain why you decided to go swimming today?"

"It was hot?" Otto ventured.

"We didn't see any harm in it?" Ian gambled.

"It was Thorny's idea!" Lars got down to brass tacks.

Chelsey leveled her eyes on Thorny patiently. "Thorny?"

"Yes, ma'am."

"Is this true?"

"That it was my idea to go swimming?"

She nodded.

"Yes."

"Have you forgotten that your son requested that you not leave the grounds without supervision?" she prompted gently, knowing full well that his memory wasn't the problem. Thorny was sharp as a tack; he never forgot a thing.

"No, ma'am. I didn't forget."

"Then why did you, Ian, Otto and Lars leave the grounds?"

"Because you wouldn't have let us go if we'd have asked you."

"That's precisely the issue." Chelsey sighed and removed her glasses. With slow deliberation, she folded and placed them on the desk and rose to stand by the window. Her expression grew softer. "Gentlemen, I don't like to play the ogre. You are four highly intelligent men, and I can understand how hard it is to go from lives of unlimited freedom to a more controlled environment. You're bright, sensible adults, and I certainly don't mean to treat you like children, but because of various ailments you each have, your families have requested you not leave Rosehaven without written permission. As unpleasant as it is for me, one of my duties is to see that those wishes are carried out. Now, why do you want to make my job harder?" She smiled at them patiently.

"We don't. We just wanted to go swimming," Thorny said.

"But Thorny, you are making things difficult. You see, I'm the one accountable to your families. They're going to think I'm not capable of performing my job, and I wouldn't like that."

"We just went swimming," Thorny said reasonably, "in my son's pool. Greg doesn't care if I swim in the pool. In fact, it used to be *my* pool until I retired and gave the house and grounds to Greg."

"That may very well be, but surely you can see my dilemma. What if everyone at Rosehaven decided they wanted to go swimming in Greg's pool?"

"Greg wouldn't care."

Chelsey wanted to throw up her hands in despair. "Perhaps I've missed something. Does Greg know you were swimming in his pool this afternoon?"

"No, but he still wouldn't have cared," Thorny maintained.

"Nevertheless, I must insist that from now on you, Ian, Lars and Otto not go to Greg's pool without first obtaining permission from him to do so."

"Now, ma'am, I just can't promise you that," Thorny said honestly.

"Why not?"

"Because I probably wouldn't keep the promise."

Chelsey sighed. Clearly she was up against a brick wall on this subject. "Lars, Otto and Ian," she said with a sweeping glance that included each of them, "do you feel the same?"

"Uh, well—" Otto poked Lars in the ribs warningly, and Lars fell silent for an instant before he continued nervously, "We all sort of agree it don't hurt to take a swim once in a while, and it was Thorny's pool at one time. . . ."

"Well then, it looks like we have a real problem on our hands, doesn't it?" Chelsey was at a loss for a way to deal with such open rebellion.

"Looks that way," Thorny admitted.

"All right, gentlemen, I think we have the battle lines drawn. I want to think this through, and then we'll discuss the problem and the solution further."

"Sounds all right to me." When Thorny gave a nod, the men rose to their feet politely as Chelsey stood.

"Good evening, gentlemen."

Thorny tipped his hat. "Good evening, Ms. Stevens. Oh by the way, I seem to have misplaced my billfold. I might have lost it when I went swimming today. Do you suppose you could see about getting it back for me?"

"Of course. I'll take care of it."

"Thank you, ma'am, much obliged."

"NOW WHAT'S GONNA HAPPEN?" Lars was still complaining as the four men walked down the hallway.

"I think we should go in and see if Mildred Hoskins is sittin' in the lounge tonight," Thorny suggested.

"Oh, no," Lars griped. "I don't want to sit and gawk at Mildred Hoskins again." A resident for about two years, Mildred sat in the lounge every night with the grace of a football quarterback. "I mean, what do you think Ms. Stevens is gonna do? Call our families? Lordy, that's all I need. If my daughter gets wind of this, she'll drive down from San Francisco and jerk a knot in my tail. I wish I'd never agreed to this silly plan. With my luck, I'll live to regret it."

"Relax, Lars. Nothing's going to happen to us. Ms. Stevens will hightail it over to Greg's looking for my billfold. While she's there, she'll most likely start complaining about my being a ringleader and her having no control over me," Thorny soothed.

"You think so?" Ian was a little worried himself. "My family won't take kindly to my stirring up a bunch of trouble, either."

"I know so. She'll say, 'They might get hurt or have some sort of attack swimming over there by themselves.' Then Greg will fall all over himself agreeing. He'll offer to fix her a drink, and she'll smile and turn those big green eyes on him. He'll be a goner for sure. You wait and see, it'll all work out just like we planned," Thorny predicted.

"Well, it's a good thing you lost your billfold. It might help hurry things along," Otto said.

"I didn't lose my billfold!" Thorny groaned impatiently. "I deliberately left it lying on the table next to the pool. I just said I'd lost it to make sure Ms. Stevens went over there."

"Oh . . . yeah . . . smart. Real smart."

"After Chelsey tells Greg what's happened, he'll come running straight to me and say I have to start obeying the rules," Thorny predicted.

"And if you don't agree?"

"Well, you see, that's where I figure we've got the upper hand in this situation. If we don't behave, what are they going to do to us? Greg isn't about to let me get kicked out of Rosehaven, because that would upset Camille, so naturally he'll soothe Ms. Stevens's pinfeathers in an effort to keep that from happening."

"Well . . . maybe," Lars fretted.

"Your families aren't gonna be thrilled about having to find a new home for any of you, either," Thorny reasoned. "So they're going to be in there in Ms. Stevens's office insisting that you'll behave better and begging her to give you another chance—" Thorny's voice changed to a falsetto as he quoted "—'because it just isn't like you at all to act this way.'"

Otto and Ian chuckled and nodded.

"While all that ruckus is going on," Thorny confided in a low tone, "it's going to be hard for Greg to ignore the fact Chelsey is a damn good-looking woman, whether he wants to or not. If he's got any brains at all, which he does 'cause he's my boy, then our job will be done. Then I can start obeying the rules, 'cause it will only be a matter of time until I move back home."

"Sounds sensible to me." Otto nodded.

"Me, too," Ian agreed.

"Well, I think we've all lost our minds," Lars grumbled. "My daughter's going to kill me when she hears what I'm doing."

"Ah, you worry too much," Thorny whispered as they approached the lounge. "Hey, look..." He let out a low whistle, and the four men came to a sudden halt, their eyes widening with growing interest. "Sure enough, there's ole Mildred...."

Chapter Five

The crisp, late-evening air was invigorating as it swept over Chelsey's flushed cheeks. She sped lithely along the jogging path as the last rays of sun dipped below the horizon. As her tempo continued to increase, she reminded herself she was running for therapy, not for competition. Gradually slowing her pace, she noticed she was approaching the black wrought-iron gates of the Bradford estate.

A pair of lions stared ominously down at her from atop their lofty concrete perches. Chelsey's nose wrinkled as Greg Bradford's face took the place of the lions' in her mind.

The thought of Thorny's son made her pause to catch her breath. Dropping down beside one of the statues, Chelsey gazed along the shady, tree-lined drive that stretched intriguingly beyond the double gates toward the mansion. The quiet, majestic beauty made Chelsey want to linger.

Who was this man, Greg Bradford, and what was he really like? she found herself wondering, though she couldn't imagine why. The few times she'd encountered him hadn't been at all pleasant. There seemed to be an undefinable defensive wall between them, one Chelsey was beginning to admit she found regrettable. She couldn't deny she found Greg attractive. Even with his annoying way of catching her off guard, there was still something about him that struck a chord of interest.

Perhaps it was his eyes that fascinated her. Their dark, mysterious hue teased her warmly one minute, then outrageously taunted her the next. Or maybe it was his smile that captured her imagination. His soft-eyed expression could make her knees grow weak, and then with a flash of his youthful grin, he could bring her temper to the boiling point.

Chelsey's gaze was drawn back to the wrought-iron gates and her curiosity grew. What lay behind those gates? She knew after this afternoon what the house looked like, but the long, winding drive beckoned to her this evening. She moved to examine the entrance more closely. As expected, the gates were locked tightly.

After assessing the considerable height of the iron fence, she decided it would be possible to climb to the top and drop to the other side. Of course, it would be a foolish thing to do and she would be trespassing, she realized, yet something in her longed to see what lay beyond.

What if Greg Bradford discovered her breach of his privacy? The mere thought made her turn guiltily away from the gate. But he wouldn't, a tiny voice coaxed. If he were home, which he most likely wasn't, he would be in the house, and the house was a good distance from the gate. What could it possibly hurt if she slipped over the fence and walked a few feet up the drive just to satisfy her curiosity?

Before she could talk herself out of it, she hurriedly climbed the fence and dropped lightly to the other side. For a moment she held her breath, listening, afraid an alarm would sound. But the only sounds she heard were the occasional chatter of squirrels and the rustlings of a bird taking flight, so she began to relax.

She wouldn't push her luck, she promised. She'd just walk up the drive a little way and turn around and come back. The thought had no sooner crossed her mind when she saw two huge Dobermans bounding down the path with their eyes riveted aggressively on her.

Chelsey's heart began to pound as she inched her way backward, reaching blindly for the safety of the fence. She hadn't considered the possibility of guard dogs.

The animals bore down on her, their clamorous barking echoing loudly across the quiet countryside. She whirled and tried to climb back up the fence, but panic made her clumsy. She dropped back to the ground and pivoted around to see how close the dogs were getting. Cold metal rails dug into her back as she recoiled in terror just before one dog lunged and clamped his mouth on her ankle.

GREG SWORE SHARPLY and jammed his smarting thumb into his mouth. Why couldn't they invent a hammer that would hit the head of a nail without mangling a man's thumb! He swore again as he heard the dogs set up a howl.

Dropping the hammer on the workbench, Greg walked out of the garage and listened as the barking grew frantic. It took him a moment to determine that the Dobermans must be at the front gate. He shrugged, wondering what was making them raise such a racket this time.

As he climbed into the Jeep, he checked for the rifle. It was there, resting on a rack right behind the front seat.

The engine rumbled and, pulling out of the garage, Greg wheeled around the circular drive and headed for the entrance, anticipating trouble.

The dogs could have an animal treed, but it seemed unlikely. They rarely barked unless there was good cause. The neighborhood had experienced a series of robberies lately, but it wasn't quite dark yet, so he dismissed that possibility.

What Greg least expected when he reached his destination was the sight of Chelsey Stevens pinned against the gate, her slender ankle held immobile by one of his Dobermans.

Pulling the Jeep to an abrupt halt, Greg bolted from the driver's seat and snapped a brisk command to the dog. "Rabbi, stay!"

Chelsey stood frozen in horror. So far, the dog hadn't increased his pressure on her ankle, but he'd left no doubt that he had the advantage here.

Greg approached the dogs quietly. "Easy, boy, steady now." When he reached Chelsey's side, Greg said, "Rabbi, let go."

The dog immediately obeyed.

"Rabbi, Ria, sit."

The dogs sat obediently, but their serious gazes remained on Chelsey.

"Good dog." Greg reached down and smoothed his hand across Rabbi's ebony head. Ria, the smaller dog, nudged his hand, seeking the same show of affection.

"Good girl," Greg said, patting Ria's head. Then pointing down the drive, he commanded, "Go."

The dogs trotted off, and Greg turned back to see a white-faced Chelsey. His hands rested on his hips, and he shook his head sympathetically. "Well, well, if it isn't Ms. Stevens."

"The . . . dogs . . ." Chelsey barely found her voice before her hand came up to cover her mouth. She was starting to feel light-headed.

Greg's grin quickly evaporated as he realized Chelsey was going to faint. Stepping forward, his arms shot out just in time to catch her as she wilted. He lifted her slight weight with ease and held her close. Staring down at her unconscious features, he shook his head slowly in helpless frustration. "Now what did I say to offend her?"

CHELSEY HEARD a man's voice coming from somewhere far away. "Here, take a sip of this, and you'll feel better." Something liquid entered her mouth and made a stinging foray down her throat. She sputtered and gasped for breath as the man's voice continued to soothe her in low, easy tones. "Take it slow now... one small sip at a time."

Again the liquid trickled down her throat as Chelsey struggled to knock the cup aside and sit up. When her eyes finally opened, her confused gaze met Greg Bradford's concerned one. "Are you okay?"

Trying to recover her dignity, Chelsey pushed away the cup in Greg's hand and nodded. "I'm fine. What... happened?"

"You fainted." He flashed her one of his contagious grins, and she found herself sheepishly returning it.

"I did?"

He nodded. "Apparently you and Rabbi didn't see eye to eye on the subject of trespassing."

"Oh, you're wrong. I'm certain I looked him straight in the eye for at least twenty-four hours," she said in a shaky voice.

"It only seemed that long," Greg sympathized. "Actually I was there within five minutes after the dogs started barking." He held out his hand and helped her to her feet. Brushing her hands over the back of her sweatpants, she smiled at him gratefully. "I'm sorry. I feel ridiculous."

"For climbing the fence, or for getting caught?"

"Both."

Greg threw back his head and laughed, a deep masculine sound that made Chelsey want to smile. She began to feel at ease, even though he'd caught her in a foolish act.

"I really am sorry, but I'm afraid my curiosity got the best of me. I wanted to see what the rest of the Bradford estate was like." She self-consciously reached up to try to recapture her hair into a neat knot. Stray wisps of golden blond hair fell appealingly over her shoulders.

Without answering, Greg turned and picked up a bottle of brandy sitting on a large workbench and began to pour the contents into two white paper cups. Chelsey glanced around her and realized they were in a garage. The large area contained a Mercedes convertible parked in one stall, a white BMW in another, and a black Cadillac sedan in a third.

"Did you ever consider ringing the bell beside the gate?" he inquired casually.

"Oh...no...I didn't think of that."

"Well," Greg extended one of the paper cups to her. "You should have." He touched his cup to hers lightly. "I would have been happy to show you around, Ms. Stevens."

Their gazes met for a moment as Chelsey lifted the paper cup to her mouth and took a cautious sip. "Brandy?"

Greg nodded, his brown eyes quietly assessing hers. He wasn't sure why, but she got better looking every time he saw her. He set his cup on the workbench and picked up a hammer. If he turned his attention back to building shelves, he figured Chelsey would have some time to recover from her harrowing experience.

"The dog's name—Rabbi? That's rather unusual."

"The dogs were given to Thorny by his closest friend many years ago. His friend is a rabbi."

"They're lovely names."

"How's Pop today?" he asked casually when a few moments had passed.

Chelsey's eyes were drawn to the strong corded muscles in his forearms as Greg lifted a sheet of plywood and laid it across two wooden sawhorses. She was preparing to answer him when he switched on a circular saw. The loud whine assaulted the air, followed by a suffocating cloud of sawdust.

After a while, the noise abated. Greg lifted the long shelf into place and began hammering.

"Your father is well. I understand you've been traveling again." Chelsey knew she should be leaving, but she found herself lingering to watch him work.

"I've been in Switzerland." Greg noticed there hadn't been the customary accusation in her voice this time. "Hope Pop's been behaving."

"Well..." Chelsey hadn't planned on mentioning Thorny's newest escapade, but since she was here, and Greg would be informed of the disturbance anyway, she might as well get it over with. "There was a small incident this afternoon."

"Oh?" Greg turned toward her slightly, and his forehead wrinkled into a frown.

"It seems Thorny and three of his friends wanted to go swimming."

"And?"

"And so they climbed your fence and swam in your pool."

"My pool?"

"Yes."

"Well, damn." Greg reached inside his nail apron and absently retracted a handful of nails. "He actually climbed the fence?"

"Yes, but he wasn't hurt—although I believe I detected a slight limp in Ian," she said.

Greg shook his head and sighed. "This is exactly what I'd hoped to prevent when I sent Thorny to Rosehaven. He can't be allowed to roam like this. Can't you do something?"

"Rosehaven is not a penal institution, Mr. Bradford—"

He paused and flashed her that million-dollar smile again. "Hey, look. Don't you think it's about time you started calling me Greg?" The offer was made with such apparent sincerity, Chelsey could hardly refuse.

"Well . . . yes, Greg . . ."

"And may I call you Chelsey?"

She met his gaze and smiled. "Of course."

"Good." He winked at her. "Now, Chelsey, you were saying?" Her name sounded lyrical when he said it.

"Uh, yes, I was saying, Rosehaven isn't a penal institution. As I've explained before, we have no authority over our residents other than that designated by the families."

"I've designated that I want Thorny to remain on the grounds unless either I or my sister accompany him somewhere," Greg reminded her.

"I know, but your father seems to have a will of his own. . . ."

"Tell me about it."

Chelsey smiled again. "I'm aware of your concern. That's why I thought it best to mention the incident. Of course, this will have to go on Thorny's record."

Greg sighed again. "Great. And Camille will get on her high horse again."

Chelsey couldn't help but grin at his pessimism.

"Don't laugh." He eyed her sternly. "Your life isn't going to be a bed of roses, either, once my sister gets wind of this."

Her smile quickly faded. "Yes, I know." She'd met Camille Weatherford once. Camille had spent an afternoon at Rosehaven recently, and Chelsey had found her overly protective where Thorny was concerned. Chelsey had spent two hours going over Thorny's daily routine, assuring Camille Thorny was happy and adjusting well to his new environment.

"Other than this afternoon, how's Pop been acting?"

"Well, there have been other minor episodes, and the kitchen has reported several sticks of butter missing. Of course, just because your father was caught raiding the kitchen once, doesn't mean he was the one who did it this time. . . ."

They both knew Thorny was Rosehaven's butter thief, but Greg appreciated Chelsey's effort to be fair-minded about it.

After discarding the hammer, Greg picked up his paper cup and took a drink. His brow furrowed thoughtfully. "I don't know. I warned Camille that putting Pop in Rosehaven wouldn't work, but she insisted." He sighed as he gazed far away. "I think he's out to get us now."

"Out to get you?"

"Yeah, I think he's bored and he's lonely. What else has a seventy-three-year-old man got to do all day but think of ways to get even with the two ungrateful kids who stuck their own father in an old folks' home?"

"We try to make Rosehaven more than an old folks' home," Chelsey patiently reminded him again. "And you're being much too hard on yourself. Thorny appears to be quite happy, and I've never heard him speak badly of his children."

"Then why is he going out of his way to cause trouble? He never has in the past."

"I'm not sure. Perhaps it's just a matter of adjustment."

"I don't think adjustment has a thing to do with it. Thorny has always been easy to get along with. It's not like him to do some of the things he's doing." Greg frowned. "You think he's getting senile?"

Chelsey laughed. "No, Thorny's sharp as a razor."

"I don't know . . ."

"You know, you surprise me. You sound as if you really care." She was shocked to hear herself commenting on such a personal matter, but he was acting as if he were genuinely concerned about his father.

"What a hell of a thing to say. Of course I care!"

"I...I didn't mean to be rude," she apologized. "It's just—"

"Look, Chelsey." Greg's brown eyes met hers solidly. "I know what you think. I saw it in your eyes the first day we met in your office. You assume I'm an irresponsible playboy trying to get his aging father out of the way."

Well, she thought, *if he wants me to be honest, I will..* "Yes, it has crossed my mind."

"Well, you're wrong. If it weren't for Camille on my back, Thorny would still be with me. Hell, I don't care what Pop wants to do! The man is old enough to do anything he wants," Greg said. "It's Camille who insists Pop has to be watched like a two-year-old."

"I can understand your sister's concern. Your father is older, and he needs the proper care."

"Well I happen to think I was giving it to him. Camille should have left us alone. We were managing okay." Greg missed his dad, especially their late night pepperoni pizzas and the times they spent watching old movies together until the wee hours of morning. He and Thorny used to have a great time together.

Chelsey finished the rest of her brandy and handed her empty cup to him. "I'm sure, given time, Thorny will adjust to his new life. Thank you for the brandy, but I really must be going."

Greg looked at her, and Chelsey could see his expression begin to change. For the moment, the trouble with Thorny was forgotten, and she could see a familiar teasing light begin to surface in his eyes. "So soon, Ms. Stevens?"

"Yes, Mr. Bradford." She reverted to formal terms again, but this time she wasn't annoyed with him. He was different tonight, almost likable.

"Have you had dinner?"

"Yes."

"Oh." He smiled. "Then perhaps you'd be interested in viewing my etchings?"

"No, I wouldn't."

"Are you sure? You wouldn't have to climb the fence."

"I'm positive." She knew he was baiting her, and she suspected he'd probably run like a rabbit if she actually took him up on his offer. She'd overheard Grace telling another Rosehaven employee how Greg had lost his wife in an auto accident and how, supposedly, no woman would ever win his heart again. "I really do have to be running along."

"You're always in a hurry," he remarked.

She smiled. "It would seem that way."

"Well, hop in the Jeep. I'll take you home."

"That won't be necessary. I don't live that far."

She walked outside, and he trailed along. "Exactly where do you live?"

"Just over the fence in the cottage beyond the south end of your property."

"No kidding?" Greg was surprised she lived so close. He'd seen the small, vine-covered cottage many times. "I didn't realize the cottage was occupied."

"It comes with my job." She gazed toward the south. "It's comfortable." She paused as the thought of Thorny's lost wallet surfaced in her mind. "Oh, by the way, Thorny's wallet is missing. He mentioned he might have left it by the pool this afternoon."

"I haven't checked the pool today. Let's take a look." Greg placed his hand on the small of her back and guided her in the direction of the house.

Finding the missing wallet was easy. It was lying on a patio table in plain sight.

"Here it is." Greg handed the wallet to Chelsey and smiled. "I can't imagine Pop losing his billfold. You sure he's not going bananas?"

"He's fine, and I'm sure he'll be relieved to have this back again."

Greg offered to accompany Chelsey back down the drive she'd found so irresistible earlier. Feeling insecure where the dogs were concerned, she gratefully accepted.

The moon drenched the couple in its mellow glow as they walked, and Greg pointed out various points of interest. The Bradford estate was all Chelsey had imagined, and more.

When they reached the main gates, Chelsey turned and extended her hand to him. "Thanks for the rescue, Greg."

Greg took her hand in his, and his gaze met hers warmly. "My pleasure, Chelsey." And to his surprise, it *had* been a pleasure. He found himself disappointed that she was leaving so soon. "You must come again sometime."

"Thank you. I'll try a proper entrance next time."

They both chuckled.

The moonlight played across their features as they stood looking at each other for a moment.

He really is quite handsome, she thought.

She's damn good-looking, he thought.

"Well, I must be going," she said in a voice that held a hint of regret.

"I'll see you Friday night. Maybe I can buy you a cup of coffee?"

"Oh? Are you coming to the festival?"

Thorny had called that morning and insisted Greg attend the fund-raiser. Greg had been evasive, but the idea suddenly appealed to him.

"I sort of promised Pop I'd be there."

"Good. We're hoping for a large turnout." She smiled. "Maybe we'll bump into each other."

"I'd like that. And if we do, how about that coffee?"

She grinned and turned to slowly jog away, not quite sure if she wanted to make such a commitment.

"Yeah, how about that coffee," she whispered to herself.

Chapter Six

"Yes, I received the lovely roses, Neil. Thank you, but you really shouldn't have." Chelsey glanced up as Grace entered the room. "Yes?"

"I'm sorry... I didn't realize you were on the phone."

"No problem... no, not you, Neil. Hold on a moment." Chelsey placed her hand over the mouthpiece. "Do you need something, Grace?"

"The foreman of the construction crew would like to speak to you."

"I'll be off the phone in a minute, then you may send him in."

Grace quietly exited as Chelsey returned to her conversation. "I'd love to have dinner Friday evening, but I must be here during the marathon."

"Then let's make it Tuesday night," Neil Matlock coaxed. "How about it? Candlelight, wine, moonlight and dancing? It's yours for the taking."

Chelsey smiled and idly fingered the delicate petals of one of the perfect red roses in the large vase on her desk. Dr. Neil Matlock couldn't take no for an answer. "Candlelight, wine, moonlight and dancing? How can anyone refuse?"

"I'm hoping you won't."

"Then I won't," Chelsey said lightly. "When does the magic begin?"

"I'll pick you up around eight."

"I'll be ready."

The door opened again, and Grace ushered the construction foreman in.

Chelsey frowned. "Neil, I have to be going. I'll see you Tuesday." She replaced the receiver and glanced at Grace expectantly. Chelsey thought Grace understood to wait before she sent the foreman in.

"Will that be all, Ms. Stevens?"

"Yes... thank you, Grace."

Grace closed the door and went back to her desk, smiling. As she'd explained to Thorny this morning, getting rid of Neil Matlock wasn't going to be easy; but she could do it.

FRIDAY EVENING Rosehaven was alive with activity. Chelsey made her way through rows of rocking chairs already in motion, powered by smiling residents willing to do their part for charity.

Dodging Frank Parson's frisky antics in his wheelchair, she shook her finger at him playfully. "Watch it, Frank, or I'll lock your gears."

"Sorry, my gears locked years ago," Frank complained good-naturedly. When he spotted Violet Appleton, he rolled merrily away to harass her.

Chelsey noticed Ida had come to watch the activities, but she wasn't taking part. She sat in a corner, alone and lonely.

Chelsey walked to her and knelt beside her. "Ida, won't you change your mind and take part in the festival?"

"Oh, no, thank you. I'll just watch." Ida managed to summon a polite smile for Chelsey's benefit.

"We could use your help."

"Thank you, but I really don't feel up to it, Ms. Stevens." Chelsey sensed today had been hard for Ida. She'd clearly felt Guy's loss more acutely than she normally did.

Rising, Chelsey patted Ida's blue-veined hand encouragingly. Her heart went out to this woman suffering such overwhelming loneliness. There was so little anyone could do to alleviate the pain. "If you change your mind, I'm sure Mary Beasley will be happy to put you to work in one of the booths."

"Ms. Stevens? Oh, Ms. Stevens!" Mildred Hoskins's harried voice reached Chelsey as she made her way across the crowded room.

"Yes, Mildred?"

"The volunteer who's supposed to work in my booth hasn't shown up yet!"

Chelsey glanced at her watch. "I understand Mary has several volunteers due. The moment one arrives, I'll have her send one over."

"I hope it's soon. I'm getting desperate!"

Chelsey was about to check on the progress of the cake walk, when Greg Bradford walked in. She saw him from across the room, and for a moment she watched as he glanced around the crowded room trying to locate a familiar face. She realized she had been watching for him—almost eagerly.

He was dressed in casual clothes tonight, instead of his usual, conservative business suit. Dark brown slacks and a beige pullover fit his trim frame beautifully.

Chelsey! He's just a man, she reminded herself, and one who took delight in annoying her, so why should his arrival set off such feelings?

Greg caught sight of her and waved. She returned his greeting with a friendly smile and moved through the sea of rocking chairs to join him.

"Good evening, Mr. Bradford."

He lifted a reproachful brow. "Now what happened to Greg and Chelsey?"

"I'm sorry. Good evening, Greg," she amended.

"Good evening, Chelsey." His eyes twinkled as they met hers.

"I'm happy to see you decided to come."

"I wouldn't have missed it for the world." The sparkle in his eyes turned devilish. "I was dying to see you again, and I promised Pop I'd be a volunteer."

"Oh?" Chelsey's eyes twinkled this time. "How flattering." She leaned closer. "If you'll just come with me, I have the perfect booth for you." His after-shave teased her nostrils pleasantly.

"I'm all yours," he whispered back conspiratorially, falling into step with her as they moved across the room. "I'm not late, am I?"

"You're right on time."

"Pop around?"

"I haven't seen him, but I'm sure he's here somewhere."

"I hope you're not going to make me sell those sock monkeys I've seen the women making," Greg warned. "I'd feel silly selling those."

"No, you're not selling sock monkeys," Chelsey assured him. "You know, Mary Beasley usually places the volunteers, but I want to take care of you, personally."

"Oh, special attention, huh?" He winked at her knowingly. "Well, I have to tell you, Ms. Stevens, this gives me hope. I was beginning to get the impression you didn't like me."

Chelsey paused. "Now whatever gave you that idea?"

"You—every time we meet."

"Well, you couldn't be more wrong. I care for you so much I've handpicked the booth you'll work in this evening."

Greg seemed genuinely surprised by her change of attitude. "No kidding? I appreciate that. Then I suppose I'm in the kissing booth," he bantered, falling back into his old teasing pattern. Though he tried to capture her gaze, she kept her eyes firmly fixed ahead.

Before leaving earlier, he'd tossed around the possibility of reneging on his promise to Thorny and staying home this evening. It had been a hectic day, one problem after another at the office, and the thought of sitting back and taking it easy tonight had been tempting. But now he realized he was glad to be here. Being with Chelsey Stevens rejuvenated him.

"It's not the kissing booth." Chelsey paused in front of a gaily decorated stand where a large line was already beginning to form. She turned and finally met his capricious smile with one of her own. "Here we are."

"Oh?" Greg glanced around.

"Mildred, I have your volunteer."

"Wonderful! Send him in!"

"If you'll just step behind the booth, Mildred will show you what to do."

"Okay. We're still on for coffee later?"

"Well . . . we'll see." She smiled. "I hope you enjoy your evening."

Greg stepped behind the counter. A stunned look crossed his face as Mildred quickly grabbed his arm and pulled him behind the curtain.

Chelsey shook her head regretfully. She really should be ashamed of herself. This was really a dirty trick.

"STEP RIGHT UP, folks! Hit the clown in the face with a wet sponge! Only fifty cents, one thin half dollar, and the money goes for an excellent cause!"

Greg's head spun, and he saw stars again as another soggy sponge splatted against his gaily painted face.

He would get Chelsey Stevens for this. He'd tell her he didn't find this the least bit amusing.

To Greg's dismay, the sponge-toss booth was proving to be the most popular attraction at the carnival.

His face felt like dishpan hands. Though he might have provoked an underhanded tactic, he was stunned that Chelsey so deliberately set him up.

Still, an unwilling smile played at the corners of his mouth as he prepared himself for another messy onslaught.

Mary Beth would have done the same thing.

THE COLORFUL BANNER read: Rosehaven Calaboose.

Greg sat with a large towel wrapped around his neck, shivering as he drank a cup of hot coffee. He watched as various residents around him were being "arrested" and taken to a mock jail located just outside the door to the kitchen.

Enjoying a blissful fifteen-minute break before he was due back at his post, he kept a watchful eye out for Chelsey.

Not surprisingly, she'd disappeared immediately after she'd delivered him into the hands of Mildred Hoskins.

Once he found Chelsey, Greg planned to inform her that he wasn't happy with her choice of volunteer work for him. He'd rather have sold sock monkeys.

His thoughts were interrupted as the tip of a wooden cane soundly tapped his shoulder. "Care to have someone arrested, sonny?"

Greg glanced up to find ninety-three-year-old Leonard Woodson standing next to him. Woody, as he was called by his friends, had been playing honorary sheriff at tonight's festivities.

"Hi, Woody. How's it going?" Greg removed his large, inflatable clown's nose and laid it on the chair beside him.

Woody cupped a hand to his ear. "Eh?"

"How's it going?"

"Oh, okay, I guess. I woke up this morning. For a man my age, that's something."

Greg smiled. *"I guess so."*

"Want to have someone arrested?" he invited again.

"No thanks."

"It's for charity...and you don't have to yell. I'm not deaf, sonny!"

Greg reached in his back pocket and withdrew a twenty-dollar bill. "Here, consider this my donation, and I'll save you the trouble of arresting someone."

"Suit yourself." Woody stuffed the money into the donation box and moved on. His next stop was Thorny, who was standing with Ian, Otto and Lars, as they waited to take their turns in the rockers.

"Want to have someone arrested?" Woody asked.

"Don't know. How does that work, Woody?" Thorny was game for anything.

"What's everyone yelling for? I'm not deaf!"

"Sorry, Woody. How does it work?"

"Eh?"

"How does it work, having someone arrested?"

"Well, you pick out someone, and I arrest them. Bail is set, and then the person is taken to jail where they stay until someone posts their bond."

"Which is?"

"Oh, it varies. Usually five dollars or so."

"And where's the jail?"

"Eh?"

"Where's the jail?"

"Out back. We're putting the prisoners in an old horse trailer."

"A horse trailer?" Thorny glanced at Ian, Lars and Otto thoughtfully. "Well, I don't know. We might think of someone to have arrested."

"Fine with me. Just say the word."

Thorny leaned forward, and the four men huddled together for a brief discussion. Thorny turned back to Woody.

"What if we wanted to arrest someone and wanted the bond set higher than five dollars?"

"Well—" Woody scratched his head "—I suppose you could set it at anything you wanted. Did you have someone in mind?"

"Chelsey Stevens." Thorny grinned, and Ian and Otto punched each other.

"Yeah, let's have Ms. Stevens arrested," Lars joined in, but Thorny was sure he had completely missed the reason the others had for her seizure.

"Okay." Woody held the donation box out. "How much do you want me to set bond for?"

Thorny glanced around to see if their conversation was being overheard. Satisfied it wasn't, he instructed in a low tone, "Five hundred dollars."

Lars gasped and turned pale.

"But we don't want Ms. Stevens to know who's had her arrested," Thorny cautioned. "You're not to reveal our identities, but we do want you to imply that a man is responsible."

"But who'll bail her out for five hundred dollars?" Woody asked, wide-eyed. He didn't know a soul in his right mind who'd pay that much, even for charity.

"Now wait a minute!" Lars protested. "I thought we were going to have her arrested for five dollars, not five hundred dollars!"

Otto poked Lars in the side. "*We* aren't going to pay five hundred dollars, you old fool!"

"Then who is?"

"Well—" Otto glanced at Thorny lamely "—I'm not exactly sure. Who *will* pay five hundred dollars to bail her out?"

"Greg will."

"How do you know?"

"Because I'll give him the money if I have to, and tell him to go bail Ms. Stevens out of jail."

"Don't you think he's gonna wonder who put her in jail and set such a big bond?" Otto added cautiously.

"I'll take care of that. I'll just tell him I don't have any idea who put her there, but I want to get her out," Thorny replied. "Greg's a good sport, so he'll do what I ask. Since he'll be spending an exorbitant amount to bail her out, Chelsey will assume he must be the one who had her arrested in the first place. Naturally, she'll be flattered. He'll suggest they have a cup of coffee. One thing will lead to another, and then bingo! They'll finally notice each other."

Otto grinned. "I like it. Kind of like in the movies."

"Something like that."

"Sounds sensible to me," Ian said.

"I don't like it," Lars warned. "Too risky. What if something goes wrong? We could be out five hundred dollars."

Thorny could see Woody was tempted to offer an opinion, but he had no idea what they were talking about.

"Nothing will go wrong, Lars. And I already said I'd be responsible for the five hundred dollars," Thorny said. "We'll have Woody arrest Ms. Stevens, then I'll have Greg post her bail." Thorny looked at his fellow conspirators. "Agreed?"

"Greg will never go for it," Lars predicted.

"You just leave my son to me, Lars. Woody, arrest Chelsey Stevens."

"Whatever you say." Woody hurried off to carry out his duties. Five hundred dollars was a hefty donation, and Rosehaven could make good use of the money.

Fifteen minutes later Chelsey was being ushered into the hastily swept horse trailer serving as a jail. She had no idea who'd had her arrested, and she was amused more than concerned over the minor inconvenience.

Settling herself on a folding chair, she crossed her arms and dutifully proceeded to play the part of the injured party. "I'll be happy to pay the five dollars and donate another five if you'll forget about locking me up," she bargained.

It would be worth the donation to be able to finish the paperwork awaiting her, and the barnyard aroma of the mock jail was beginning to get to her.

"Nope, can't let you do that, Ms. Stevens." Woody slammed the tailgate closed and snapped a large lock in place.

Chelsey decided to increase her bribe. "Okay, I'll up it ten more."

"Nope, you're way off base."

"Okay. How much? Who had me arrested? Henry Rothman?"

Woody grinned. "Nope, not Henry."

"Then who?" She was still smiling.

"Can't say, except to tell you that it was a man who had you incarcerated."

"A man?" She was pleasantly amused. Neil Matlock? No, she hadn't seen him around tonight. "All right. Precisely what is my bail?"

"Precisely? Five hundred dollars."

Her smile began to wilt. "Five . . . what?"

"Five hundred dollars." Woody sighed. "So, might as well make yourself comfortable. You may be here awhile."

As the full implication of his words began to sink in, Chelsey was on her feet, peering between the slats expectantly. "Woody! Come back here!" She found herself talking to thin air as Woody bolted away to safety. She grasped the gate and rattled it loudly. "Woody!"

By eight o'clock the Rock and Roll Marathon was in full swing. Donations were coming through in satisfying numbers, and the crowd seemed to be having a good time.

Thorny approached Woody around eight-fifteen with a worried frown on his face. "Did you arrest her?"

"Yep. She's locked up tight as a tick."

"Well, I've got a problem. It's my turn to rock, and I can't find Greg."

"He's in the sponge-toss booth."

"He was, but he isn't now. Mildred said he asked to be relieved for a few minutes, and I can't find him anywhere. I was wondering if you could do me a favor?"

"Sure thing."

"Find Greg and tell him I want to see him before he goes back to his booth. I've agreed to rock for the next couple of hours, but I need to make sure he'll bail Ms. Stevens out promptly."

"Okay," Woody agreed before the two men went their separate ways.

It was close to ten o'clock before Greg was finally relieved of his duties. Thorny came rushing up as his son dried his hair with a towel and slipped into dry clothing.

"Hi, son."

"Hi, Pop. Where've you been all evening?"

"I've been in that blasted rocking chair! Where have you been?"

Greg looked at him wryly. "Where have I been? Look at me. Does my face remind you of something? A dried prune, maybe? Don't volunteer my services again, Pop. I'll be glad to make a donation, but I won't come over here and be slapped in the face with a wet sponge for three hours, not for any cause."

"Didn't Woody tell you I was looking for you?"

"Woody? No, why?"

"That cotton-pickin' Woody can't remember his own name, let alone pass on an important message!" Thorny groaned before mumbling, "Ms. Stevens must still be in jail."

"I don't know where Ms. Stevens is, nor do I care," Greg muttered under his breath as he finished buttoning his shirt. "So long, Pop. I'm going home." Greg turned to leave.

"Wait a minute." Thorny reached out and took his arm. "I need you to do something before you leave."

"What's that?"

"I think they might have Ms. Stevens in jail. You know, for donations?"

"So?"

"So, I thought maybe it would be real nice if you and I could bail her out." Thorny was sure Chelsey Stevens would think it was nice, too, after sitting in that smelly horse trailer for three hours.

"Pop, if you want to bail her out, go right ahead. I'm going home."

"Now wait a minute, son." Thorny raised his hand to cover his heart. "I think you're gonna have to do it for me."

Greg viewed his father suspiciously. "Why?"

"Because I'm old and tired. I rocked for two hours, you know."

"Why did you do that?" Greg noticed Thorny had a way of always bringing up his age when he didn't want to do something.

"Because half the volunteers pooped out, and Mary Beasley was in a real bind."

Greg sighed. As far as he was concerned, Chelsey Stevens could stay in jail after what she'd pulled on him tonight, but it was clear Thorny had his heart set on getting her out. "Oh, all right." He reached for his wallet. "How much is the donation? Ten, fifteen dollars?"

"It's gonna take five hundred."

Greg's mouth dropped open. "Five hundred! Dollars?"

"That's right."

"What do they figure she's worth? Her weight in gold?"

"No, but Rosehaven needs the money and we can afford it," Thorny coaxed.

"Pop! We give at the office...."

"But I want to do this, Greg. I like Ms. Stevens. Don't you?"

"Not for five hundred dollars."

"She's a nice-looking woman, don't you think?"

"Pop, what do Chelsey Stevens's looks have to do with this?"

"Oh, nothing. Just making conversation. You don't have to be so confounded touchy. Just write the check, boy. I'll reimburse you." Thorny's hand returned to rest feebly upon his chest as he took a deep, labored breath. "And hurry, please."

Greg eyed his father critically. "You sure you're feeling okay?"

"Fine... just fine. Write the check and see that Ms. Stevens is taken care of. I'm going to my room. Oh, uh, after she's released, it would be considerate if you walked her safely home—she lives in a cottage at the far end of Rosehaven, you know."

Greg glanced up from the checkbook again. He was becoming increasingly puzzled by Thorny tonight.

Although his father had never made any bones about his expectations for Greg remarrying someday, Thorny had never played matchmaker as obviously as he was now.

And Chelsey Stevens was his target? Greg had to work to keep a smile from surfacing. "Well, I'll write the check, but I'm afraid Ms. Stevens will have to see herself home." He'd admit Chelsey was attractive and he'd admit he was pleased to discover she had a sense of humor, but he was still smarting from the way she'd set him up tonight.

And like an idiot, he'd fallen right into her trap.

"Oh... well, walking her home was just a thought," Thorny said.

"I'll take care of the donation," his son said, "and you go straight to your room and get to bed." Greg proceeded to write the check. "And forget about pairing me with Chelsey Stevens."

Otto, Ian and Lars were waiting for Thorny when he turned the corner five minutes later and started down the corridor to his room.

"Did it work? Did you get Greg to bail out Ms. Stevens?"

Thorny paused, hating to relay the bad news. "We've run into a little snag, gentlemen."

"The plan worked, didn't it?" Otto asked.

"All I can say is, it's a darn good thing she doesn't know who put her in jail."

Ian grinned. "Why? I thought that's what we wanted—to make her think Greg was responsible."

Thorny shook his head worriedly. "No, I don't think we'd better do that."

"Why not?"

"Because she's still sitting out there."

"Still?" Their stunned voices ricocheted off the corridor walls. "What happened?"

"Shhh. I got delayed in the rocking chair, and Woody was supposed to tell Greg I wanted to see him right away. I waited and waited for Greg to come so I could tell him about paying her bail and getting her released, but Woody forgot to tell him."

"You trusted Woody with a message like that?" Otto exclaimed. "I thought everyone knew you can't trust Woody with an important message!"

"I knew I was taking a chance, but I'd looked all over for you fellows. Woody was the only one I could find before I had to take my turn in the rockers." Thorny sighed. It looked like his chance for getting out of Rosehaven and back to Greg's house was growing slimmer every day.

"But he *is* going to bail her out, isn't he?"

"Yeah. I had to pretend I was on my last legs, but he bought it. He's taking care of the bail right now."

"Then maybe the plan will still work," Ian said hopefully.

"Somehow I don't think Ms. Stevens is gonna be in the mood for socializing," Thorny admitted glumly. Their faces fell with disappointment.

"What a shame," Otto said.

"I thought for sure it'd work," Ian said.

"I told you it wouldn't," Lars said.

"At least she doesn't know who was responsible for letting her sit in a horse trailer all night," Otto added.

Thorny winced. "Thank God," he murmured, fervently hoping she would never find out.

"Tomorrow's another day," Ian predicted. "We'll go to Plan Three."

"Yeah, tomorrow's another day," Thorny agreed, determined not to become discouraged.

Some things just took time.

Chapter Seven

It took another fifteen minutes for Greg to locate Woody and deliver his check for five hundred dollars.

"Oh, I think I was supposed to tell you Thorny's looking for you," Woody relayed, as he absently stuffed the check into the donation box, which now bulged with coins and bills.

"Yeah, thanks for the message, Woody. I just talked to Pop, and he wanted me to post Chelsey Stevens's bail."

"I'll go release her." Woody wandered out as Greg headed for the front doors, unaware that Chelsey had been locked up for close to three hours.

Fern Silsby caught sight of him, and Greg was delayed awhile longer before he finally made his escape.

Outside he inhaled deeply of the fresh night air, then headed briskly toward the parking lot. Rounding a corner, he caught sight of Chelsey hurrying out of the building.

Greg put his fingers to his lips and whistled. "Hey, wait a minute!" He suddenly found he wanted to talk to her.

Surprise registered on Chelsey's face as she recognized the familiar voice. She began to seethe anew. The nerve of the man! Having her locked in a smelly horse trailer for hours, then calling out to her as if nothing unusual had taken place.

"I'm in a hurry, Greg!"

"So am I, but I want to talk to you, lady!"

"I said I was in a hurry," Chelsey repeated as she pivoted on her left foot and headed in the direction of her cottage.

Determined now more than ever to confront her for setting him up in the sponge-toss booth, Greg quickened his steps and in a few moments had overtaken her.

"I said, I want to talk to you, Chelsey."

She turned and faced him coolly. "And I don't want to talk to you, Greg. I didn't find your childish antics tonight the least bit amusing."

Calmly Greg met her defiant stare. "I wasn't aware I'd done anything amusing."

"Good, because it wasn't." Chelsey started off in the direction she'd been heading before he'd stopped her.

"Now just a minute." Greg was tired of her mood swings. He had no idea why she was on her high horse again, but this time he planned to find out. "What *is* bothering you?" He fell in step behind her, his long legs barely keeping up with her swift, angry strides.

"You don't know?" she tossed sarcastically over her shoulder.

"I haven't the vaguest idea."

Chelsey stopped and faced him. "You really have no idea?"

"No." His hands came to rest impatiently on his hips. "What's your problem this time?"

She swallowed hard, forcing herself to remain civil. "Where have I been all evening, Mr. Bradford?"

"I have no idea where *you've* been, Ms. Stevens, but you certainly know where *I've* been."

Chelsey could feel a blush creeping up her neck. "You offered your services as a volunteer," she reminded him.

"I didn't offer to be hit in the face with a wet sponge all night," he corrected her.

"You've had your revenge. Let's call it even." Chelsey turned and started walking again.

"I have?" It was news to him. "Tell me. Did I think of something equally devious to do to you?"

"Very funny."

"I didn't find my remark funny at all."

"Stop following me!"

"Am I trespassing?"

"No, you're annoying me."

"It seems I have a habit of doing that, doesn't it?"

Chelsey refused to answer as her cottage came into view. If he thought he could keep her locked in that horse trailer for three hours and expect her to laugh about it, then he was sadly mistaken! She stepped onto the vine-covered porch and began rummaging through her purse for her key.

Greg watched for a moment, debating whether or not to pursue the subject. Obviously she had the mistaken notion that he'd played some prank on her. Well, if she wanted to act like a spoiled child, then let her.

Heaving a sigh of disgust, Chelsey sank down on the step and buried her face in her hands. Greg watched for a moment, determined to hold his ground. She was the one who was in the wrong this time. But when the moments lapsed into minutes and she made no move to resume her search for the key, he finally relented.

"Good grief." Stepping up on the porch, he knelt beside her to find the key himself.

A few moments later he dangled the elusive object from his finger. "Is this what you're looking for?"

Chelsey snatched the key and stood up. She was about to insert the key in the lock when he blocked her hand. "Will you hold on a minute?"

Their eyes met and fixed solidly.

"Why do you insist on hassling me?"

"I'm not hassling you—at least not at the moment."

"You will admit you've been guilty of it in the past?"

"I'll admit I like to tease you," he conceded, then his tone softened as her hand dropped wearily to her side. "Look, can't we discuss this like two reasonable adults?"

She sighed, wishing his eyes weren't so beautifully expressive. It was clear that for once he was trying to be nice.

"All right." She turned from the door and sat down again on the porch step. The moonlight played across the shadows, bathing the cottage in its intimate glow.

Greg sat down beside her. Both were silent for a moment as they gathered their thoughts. Greg wasn't sure what to say. Chelsey was certain she deserved an apology.

"Would you mind at least giving me a clue? Just what is it that I've done to you?" he asked with a sigh.

"You don't know?"

He turned to face her. "Hey, just tell me."

"You had me locked in that horse trailer for three hours!"

Greg blinked. "I what?"

"Don't act the innocent with me. You had me arrested and locked in that horse trailer, just to soothe your bruised ego."

"That's ridiculous. Where'd you come up with that harebrained idea?"

"You're saying you didn't arrange it?"

"That's right." Their eyes locked obstinately again.

"Then why was your check for five hundred dollars in the donation box?" The moment she'd been released, Chelsey had made Woody let her examine the donation box. When she'd discovered Greg Bradford's name scrawled across the signature line of the check, she'd started to boil. He could certainly dish out the jokes—until he got a dose of his own medicine. Then he couldn't handle it.

"Pop asked me to write the check. He wanted you bailed out. I didn't even know you'd been arrested."

Chelsey's eyes narrowed with disgust. "Greg, are you trying to lay the blame on your own father?"

"Look, I said I wrote the check, and that was because Pop told me you were in jail and needed to be bailed out. I don't have the slightest idea who had you locked up."

"Of course not." And the state of Texas had just been moved to Alaska, she thought. "And you really don't care," she added, before he could.

"You said that, not me."

Their eyes met again.

"Do you really think I'd pay five hundred dollars just to get even with you?"

"The evidence certainly points to you."

"Don't kid yourself."

She didn't know why, but his insistence that she wasn't worthy of such a hefty donation only served to sting her injured pride more.

"I didn't think you made that donation out of generosity," she said. "I think you did it—had me arrested and posted such high bail, which no one would want to pay—to get even with me for leaving you in the sponge-toss booth."

"I didn't set you up, Ms. Stevens, quite the opposite. I think you just happen to feel guilty about setting me up in the sponge-toss booth, which, by the way, I found disgusting. Nevertheless, do you hear me accusing you of dirty pool?" Greg straightened his shoulders defensively. "I took my humiliation with a little dignity. I suggest you do the same."

"Well, what's done is done, and I prefer to forget it." Chelsey gave him a cool glance and rose to her feet. "It's been a trying day, and I have a splitting headache."

Greg stood and took the key from her hand and turned to unlock the door for her. "I'm sorry you've had a rough day. Is there anything I can do to make it end on a nicer note?"

His sudden kindness caught her off guard.

"No...I...thank you."

Turning, he paused and looked down at her. As she glanced up, moonlight played across her delicate features. He realized, though he tried to convince himself otherwise, he regretted she still thought he'd been involved in her incarceration.

Her perfume filtered softly through the air, teasing his senses to painful awareness. Suddenly he had the damnedest urge to kiss her. Though he was still stung by her unfounded accusations, feelings that had lain dormant for years were blooming again. He wasn't sure he liked it. Forcing his gaze from hers, he pushed open the cottage door.

"I gather the festival was a success," he commented, striving to keep their conversation impersonal.

"It appears to be."

"Well...I hope you feel better in the morning."

"I'm sure a hot bath and a good night's sleep will work wonders."

Their gazes met again, and Greg became irritated as he realized he was actually searching for reasons to linger.

"Look, Chelsey, if it helps any, I'll say I'm sorry." Reaching to the flower-covered trellis, he picked a fragrant bloom and handed it to her. For the first time, he managed a small smile.

She accepted the simple offering, breathing deeply of its intoxicating fragrance. "For having me thrown in jail and forgetting all about me for three long hours? You dirty rat."

"No, because I'm not mad at you anymore for using my face for a target, you conniving little witch." He grinned. "I didn't have you thrown in jail; I'm just sorry you're convinced I did."

Chelsey felt her pulse quicken. It seemed he had an uncanny knack for doing that to her. A few minutes ago she'd been angry enough to strangle him. Now all she could think about was the way his mouth looked so inviting.

He smiled, the way a man smiles when he wants to melt a woman's outrage. "Truce?"

Chelsey felt a tug at her heartstrings, and finally she returned the smile. "Truce."

If she hadn't moved away just then, Greg knew he would have followed his surging desire to put his arms around her and kiss her.

His frank admission bothered him long after they'd said goodnight and he'd retired to his lonely bed. He had wanted to take her in his arms and kiss her, and he had the unsettling certainty he would have enjoyed every moment of it.

"WELL I'LL ADMIT it's not working out the way I thought it would, but we can't give up yet." Thorny, Otto, Ian and Lars were knee-deep in pumpkin seeds as they sat outside the service porch on Monday morning, carving jack-o'-lanterns for a local business that lined its walks with the colorful pumpkins.

The sunshine was warm, promising a pleasant evening for area children to trick-or-treat.

"I think we should just leave them alone," Lars voiced again as he cut another triangular nose. He held the large pumpkin at arm's length to view the finished result. A happy, but fantastically distorted jack-o'-lantern grinned lopsidedly back at him. "Apparently, they don't want to get to know each other."

"We don't know that for certain," Thorny persisted as he reached inside his pumpkin to withdraw a large handful of pulp. He winced in disgust. He was sick of pumpkin seeds and sicker of cutting out silly faces.

The way he had it figured, he would not only be doing himself a favor, but he'd be doing the residents of Rosehaven a kindness if he married Greg off to Chelsey Stevens.

The woman was a real Dudley Do-gooder. It seemed to Thorny she volunteered the residents' help for every Tom, Dick and Harry who wanted something done for nothing, all in the name of a "good cause."

"I got my billfold back, didn't I?" Thorny reminded them. "So they must have seen each other."

"Apparently that's all that happened," Otto observed. "Why, Ms. Stevens wasn't even concerned enough about our swimming to mention it to your son, was she?"

"No..." Thorny had to admit Greg hadn't said a word about the incident.

"Having her arrested didn't work, either," Ian added. "Why, I bet they didn't even see each other after Chelsey left the sponge-toss booth."

"They probably didn't," Thorny agreed reluctantly. He was not only disappointed about the outcome of the evening, but he was out five hundred dollars to boot.

"Well, I say we stop acting like matchmakers." Lars stood up and brushed pumpkin seeds from his pant legs. "Greg will notice Chelsey without our help, if he wants to. If he doesn't want to, then we're wasting our time."

"Can't agree with you, Lars," Thorny said as he carefully carved another crooked nose. "I have to see this thing through. I say we proceed to Plan Three."

"Plan Three?" Otto glanced up in surprise.

"Yes, I made my decision last night. Are you gentlemen in the mood for a game of pool?"

"Sure, but we still have twelve more pumpkins to do," Ian complained. "Besides somebody is always using the pool table when we want it."

"Rosehaven's pool table maybe, but I happen to know where there's another pool table, one ten times better than the one in the rec room, and it's just begging to be used."

Otto perked up. "Where's that, Thorny?"

"At Greg's, of course."

Lars's eyes grew round. "Oh now, come on. We can't go back there so soon! That would be too daring, especially since Ms. Stevens has directly asked us not to leave the grounds again!"

"We have to go back. If we're going to accomplish anything with those two, we have to keep the heat on." Thorny shoved aside his finished pumpkin and stood up. "Right after lunch, we'll scale the fence again."

"I don't know...." It was clear Lars didn't like the sounds of this at all.

"Well, I'll go," Otto declared.

"I will, too." Ian laid down his knife and got to his feet.

Thorny looked at Lars. "Are you in?"

"I don't want to be."

"But you are?"

Lars groaned. "I'm going to get an ulcer."

"NOT THIS TIME." A pretty hand prevented the passage of an illicit salt packet beneath the table. "I know it's tempting, Otto, but your blood pressure is too high," Chelsey reminded him in a gentle tone as she stood beside the dining table where Ian, Otto, Lars and Thorny were eating. Otto reluctantly passed the salt back to Ian.

"And I really think you should give the sugar packet back to Otto," she said to Lars, who tried to look innocent while he spooned soup into his mouth.

Lars glanced up sheepishly. "Aw, one little package won't hurt."

"I'm afraid your blood sugar will indicate differently in the morning." Chelsey waited until Lars relinquished the sugar. "I'll have Martha bring you an extra custard for dessert," she bargained, sympathizing with Lars's daily battle with his sweet tooth, but knowing he was severely diabetic.

"Custard, custard, custard. That stuff's like eating cold rubber."

Chelsey moved on and let the four men continue eating their lunch.

Lars was so nervous thinking about their impending plans he could barely eat. When the meal was finally finished, Thorny looked at his comrades and nodded.

Climbing over the fence a few minutes later was easy. Ian made it without skinning his shin this time, and the men decided they were as agile as anyone twenty years younger. Striding four abreast up the drive, they drank in the exhilaration of freedom.

"We should've brought some women along," Otto said.

"Yeah," Ian agreed. "Violet Appleton likes pool, and so does Margaret Winslow. I bet they would've come with us."

"That's unusual coming from you, Ian." Thorny glanced at his friend. Ian rarely mentioned women. Instead, he lived in the past, speaking of his deceased wife, Elda, as if she were still alive.

"I know. I just thought it might be nice. Elda loved to play pool, you know. I miss that."

"Don't you think we're gonna be in enough trouble without dragging women in on this?" Lars complained.

"I swear Lars, you're a wet blanket if ever I saw one," Thorny accused good-naturedly. "Wouldn't you enjoy an afternoon with Fern Silsby?"

Lars looked aghast at the suggestion. "That's not funny, Thorny. What would I want with a man-crazy woman like Fern Silsby?"

Ian grinned. "Someone want to explain it to him?"

Everyone laughed, and Lars chuckled at himself. It helped to release some of his tension.

"Relax, my friend," Thorny advised, giving Lars an encouraging slap on the back. "We're just going to have a friendly game of pool."

"I've never been one for taking chances." Lars shrugged sheepishly.

"Well," said Thorny with a wink, "it's high time you started."

They reached the house and climbed the steep steps to the back door. At the top, they paused to catch their breath as Thorny rummaged through his pants pockets.

"What's taking so long?" Lars glanced around furtively, hoping they wouldn't be noticed by the gardener they'd seen weeding a nearby rose bed.

"Hold your horses; I'm looking for my key."

A careful search of every pocket failed to turn up the missing item. "Darn, I'll just have to ring the doorbell," Thorny said in disgust.

"But I thought your son would be gone," Lars whispered.

"He is, but he mentioned he's trying out a new housekeeper. She'll let us in." Thorny pressed the bell, and, in a few moments, a large, forbidding-looking woman opened the door.

"Yes?" Her voice was brusque and gravely.

"Hi, there. I'm Thorton Bradford, your employer's father."

The woman didn't even crack a smile. "Yeah?"

"I'm Greg's father—the man who owns this house," Thorny repeated a little louder.

"So?" The woman crossed her arms, reminding Thorny of a linebacker. This wasn't going to be as easy as he'd hoped.

"Me and my friends here have come over to play pool."

The woman's eyes narrowed. "Mr. Bradford didn't say anything about anyone coming over to play pool."

"Well, he must've forgotten." Thorny turned to the other three for help. "Tell her who I am, gentlemen."

"He's Greg's son all right," Otto offered.

Even Lars could participate in the conversation without fearing his nose would grow longer. "That's for sure, ma'am. He's Greg Bradford's father."

The housekeeper's brows drew together stubbornly. "That may be, but I can't let you in without Mr. Bradford's permission."

"She's a tough cookie," Thorny confided out of the corner of his mouth to the other three. Summoning up a pleasant smile, he took a different approach. "Ma'am, if you'd be so kind as to let me use the phone, we can clear up this little misunderstanding in no time at all."

"Well..." Thorny could see she was at least considering the suggestion.

"Please, just let me use the phone in the hall. I'll call Greg, and you'll see that everything is just fine."

"Well..."

The four men surged through the open doorway before the housekeeper could protest further.

"You can use the phone," she said, pointing to a hall table, "but make it snappy. I've got my work to do."

"Yes, ma'am." Thorny picked up the receiver and dialed the number for the Time and Temperature recording.

"The time is one-ten p.m. The temperature is..."

"Greg, this is your father."

"...seventy-eight degrees..."

"Yeah, I hate to bother you, son, but you forgot to tell the housekeeper we were coming over to play pool today— Oh, yeah, sure...I don't want to keep you. The housekeeper was a little leery about letting us in. Sure...sure thing— You hurry on to your meeting."

The housekeeper stepped forward. "I want to speak to Mr. Bradford."

"Oh Greg...Greg! The housekeeper wants a word with— Oops. Sorry, ma'am." Thorny replaced the receiver and smiled apologetically. "I barely caught him. He was just going into a meeting."

"Oh?" She looked confused about what she should do next.

"Yes, but he said it was perfectly all right for us to stay here. He said for us to make ourselves at home."

"Well..." It was clear she still wasn't sold on the idea. "If that's what he said..."

Thorny glanced at the other three men who were watching the exchange with bated breath. "That's sure what he said, ma'am."

"Well, don't be messin' up things. I've already cleaned the pool room," she said hesitantly.

"No, ma'am, we won't."

Thorny waved his friends into the hallway and, on second thought, drew the housekeeper aside. "Listen, honey. See if you can rustle up some snacks and cigars, will you?" He extracted a twenty-dollar bill from his billfold and slipped it inside her apron pocket.

"Now see here! I have work to do!"

"It won't take long, and Greg said he'd pay you a little something extra," Thorny fabricated.

"Oh, brother! No one said anything to me about having to play hostess to four old men!" The woman pivoted and started toward the kitchen as Thorny reached out and pinched her fanny. She whirled around and shot him a scathing look. "Watch it, buster!"

Thorny did a little hop as he went to join the others. Hot dog! It felt good to be able to do that again.

Thirty minutes later the four were happily engrossed in their game. Thick smoke stung the air from the Honduran cigars they were puffing. Steaming slices of pepperoni pizza were arranged on the buffet, along with chips, assorted dips, cheese, crackers and thick slices of summer sausage. It was a gastronomic delight that would be sure to haunt them later. At the moment they were having too much fun to worry about their dietary restrictions.

Even Lars was forced to agree it was the best idea Thorny had come up with yet.

CHELSEY WAS MEETING with Harriet Bishop, a senior member of the staff, when Grace pecked lightly at her office door.

"Yes, Grace?"

"I'm sorry to interrupt you, Ms. Stevens, but it's important."

"Come in, Grace."

"This is personal. Would you mind joining me out here?"

Chelsey smiled apologetically at Harriet. "Excuse me. I'll only be a moment."

Puzzled, Chelsey stepped into the outer office. It wasn't like her assistant to interrupt a meeting. "What is it, Grace?"

Chelsey noticed Grace made sure the door to Chelsey's office was securely closed. It was no secret at Rosehaven that Harriet Bishop's husband, Walter, had been seriously considered for the position as chief administrator of Rosehaven before Chelsey had been awarded the job. Walter was still on staff at Rosehaven, but in a lower administrative position. Word was, Harriet hadn't handled Walter's not being hired for the top job well. It was rumored that she kept her ear tuned for trouble and relayed even the slightest infraction of the rules to the regional director. Though the woman had nothing personal against Chelsey, Chelsey knew she was convinced that Walter would run Rosehaven with a better hand.

"I'm sorry to disturb you, Ms. Stevens, but I thought you ought to know."

Chelsey experienced an intuitive quirk in the pit of her stomach. "What is it?"

"Thorny, Ian, Otto and Lars were seen climbing the fence into the Bradford estate about half an hour ago," Grace confided in a low whisper.

"Oh, dear. Are you sure?"

Grace nodded. "Fern spotted them."

"Oh, dear," Chelsey repeated. She knew if Fern reported it, it was true.

"Do you want me to go get them?"

"No, I can't ask you to do that. Let me finish with Harriet, then I'll go over and see what they think they're doing."

"You better not let Ole Nosy get wind of this," Grace warned, nodding toward the door. "She'll run straight to Walter."

"I know. I'll try to get rid of her without arousing her suspicions."

"Good luck. That woman is a bloodhound when it comes to trouble."

Chelsey returned to her office, and a few minutes later a puzzled Harriet emerged. Chelsey overheard Harriet whispering to Grace, "What's the emergency?"

"Emergency? Oh . . . nothing really, just a little something that requires Chelsey's personal attention," Grace said.

"I know, but what?"

The phone rang and Grace smiled. "Excuse me?" She snatched up the receiver and pretended to become engrossed in what appeared would be a lengthy conversation.

Harriet walked into the hall and paused. Chelsey opened her door a crack, and she could tell by the look on Harriet's face that her suspicions had indeed been aroused.

A few moments later Chelsey left her office and hurried toward the service entrance. Harriet trailed behind her a safe distance and watched as Chelsey slipped out the back door and headed for her car.

Rumor had it that Chelsey was having difficulty controlling four of the men at Rosehaven. Thorny Bradford and three of his friends had left the grounds and trespassed on the Bradford property without authorization once. Harriet had a hunch another such incident might have just occurred.

"May I help you, Mrs. Bishop?" the head cook asked as he approached the woman peering out the kitchen window.

"No, don't let me disturb you, Frank." Harriet watched Chelsey get into her car and start the engine. Moments later the car left Rosehaven and turned onto the road leading toward the Bradford Estate. A smile spread slowly across Harriet's stern features.

So, the emergency did have something to do with the Bradford Estate. Her smile widened. Walter would be interested to hear it.

Most interested.

Chapter Eight

Chelsey pulled her car up to the wrought-iron gate of the estate and stopped. She rolled down her window and called to the gardener working nearby. "Excuse me?"

"Yes?"

"My name is Chelsey Stevens. I'm the administrator at Rosehaven, and I'm looking for Thorton Bradford. Is he here?"

"No, ma'am, I haven't seen him."

"Are you sure?"

The sound of an approaching car captured Chelsey's attention, and she glanced in the rearview mirror. A black Cadillac pulled up behind her and stopped. An audible groan escaped her as she recognized Greg behind the wheel; her timing couldn't have been worse.

Greg got out of his car and walked to her window. A smile began to form when he discovered who was sitting behind the wheel.

"Well, well, Ms. Stevens. What a pleasant surprise. I see you decided to use the gate this time."

"This isn't a social call, Greg. I'm looking for your father." Chelsey hated to face it, but Greg had to be informed soon that Thorny had disappeared again.

Greg's smile began to recede. "Pop?"

"It seems he's . . . wandered again."

Greg swore softly. "And you think he's come over here?"

"I have reason to believe he has."

"I'll follow you." Greg walked back to his car and pressed a button under the dash.

The large gates swung open, and Chelsey eased her car through. She drove to the house and parked.

The house was quiet, with no sign of unusual activity. In the late-afternoon sun, the swimming pool sparkled like a polished jewel. The grounds looked deserted, except for one other gardener, who was engrossed in trimming a hedge.

What if Fern was mistaken? The thought belatedly sprang into Chelsey's mind. What if Thorny and his three friends hadn't climbed the fence? What if they were in their rooms this very moment taking an afternoon nap?

Chelsey realized it hadn't occurred to her to question Fern's information. But Grace had made sure the men were missing, hadn't she?

Greg pulled his Cadillac into the garage as Chelsey's doubts continued to build. What would Greg think of her if Grace's information proved to be false? He would think she was a complete fool, she agonized. A complete fool who was incapable of running a large establishment like Rosehaven.

And Harriet Bishop. If she ever found out that Chelsey had resorted to chasing down four residents like they were truant children, Chelsey had no doubt that a report of the event would be on the regional director's desk by tomorrow morning.

Emerging from the garage, carrying a brown leather briefcase, Greg motioned for Chelsey to join him. Falling into step beside him, Chelsey thought she should at least offer Greg some sort of explanation for her suspicions. "I hope I'm wrong, but my secretary was informed that Thorny, Ian, Otto and Lars were seen climbing the fence shortly after lunch."

The gentle breeze carried a faint whiff of Greg's after-shave, and Chelsey found the familiar smell diverting.

"I don't know what's gotten into him," Greg said abruptly. It seemed there was a new headache daily since Thorny had entered Rosehaven. "He's never acted this way before."

"Perhaps it isn't entirely his fault," Chelsey suggested, recalling that while Lars was a follower, Otto and Ian had minds of their own.

"Maybe not, but I have a feeling Pop's the ringleader. I just don't know what he's trying to prove."

They approached the back door, and Greg quickly admitted them through the kitchen entrance. A faint aroma of cigar smoke, along with the sound of men's voices in the background caught their attention.

Greg looked at Chelsey and said dryly, "It sounds like Goldilocks and the three bears are here all right."

Chelsey followed him as they stepped up three flagstone stairs and entered the kitchen. Her eyes scanned the marble walls, stainless steel counters, and rich mahogany cabinets. A quaint, stone fireplace dominated the west wall. Brass pots and utensils were hanging over the grate where logs were laid, ready for use. A butcher-block table stood to the left of a commercial stove with a brass range hood. Chelsey decided this had to be the most attractive kitchen she'd ever seen.

"They must be shooting pool," Greg said as he put his briefcase on the counter. He shrugged out of his jacket and tossed it over a nearby stool. Loosening his tie, he walked to the large industrial-size refrigerator and opened it. "How about a beer?"

Chelsey shook her head. "No, thank you."

Greg glanced at her. "You don't care for beer?"

"I'm here to retrieve the men," she reminded him.

Greg selected a can before nudging the door closed with his shoulder. "I wouldn't think that would be a chief administrator's job," he remarked casually as he pulled the tab and dropped it in the waste can. His gaze met hers, and the sudden realization she was growing very fond of him hit her with the subtlety of being struck by a truck. She was powerless to explain the effect he was beginning to have on her.

Neil Matlock came to mind, and she couldn't help but compare the two men. They were both educated and successful. Both dressed well, drove expensive cars and had affluent life-styles. But that's where the similarities ended. While Neil was smooth and sophisticated, often to the point of seeming aloof, Greg was outgoing, warm-hearted and, for the most part, unassuming. He was even a little rough around the edges at times, but Chelsey found she liked it—in him. The difference in the two men's personalities disturbed her. Normally Neil was the sort of man who drew her attention. But she had to admit that Neil had never made her feel the way Greg did with one simple smile.

Chelsey knew, if she let herself, she could fall in love with Greg, even though it would be foolish. He obviously wasn't in the market for a second wife.

"Normally it isn't an administrator's job," she said. "But this isn't a normal situation."

"Oh?" Greg waited, expecting her to elaborate on her answer, but she didn't. Instead she glanced at her watch guiltily. "If you don't mind, I need to ask the men to return to Rosehaven. I'm still officially on duty."

She noticed Greg seemed in no hurry to get on with business.

"Why so edgy?" He leaned on the counter and winked at her. "You're the boss, aren't you? And Pop and his friends aren't hurting anything."

Chelsey watched as he picked up her hand and gently began to massage it as he talked. "They're not children. Why don't you relax, enjoy a cold drink and let them have their fun." His voice was deep and smooth and persuasive.

Greg hadn't realized he'd taken her hand, until he noticed she was looking at him strangely.

The gesture was an unthinking but intimate one he'd adopted with Mary Beth. When he realized what he was doing, he quickly released her hand and placed it back on the counter gently.

"It's my responsibility to see that the residents of Rosehaven are properly supervised," Chelsey said quietly, wishing he hadn't released her hand. She had liked the feel of her hand in his, and now she missed the contact. "And I take my responsibilities seriously."

"Killjoy." His eyes still twinkled with amusement, although he felt uncharacteristically shaken by their innocent encounter. He'd enjoyed holding her hand! It was feminine and soft . . . and nice.

"You and your sister placed Thorny in Rosehaven's care. I would be doing you an injustice if I took the same attitude, don't you think?"

"Not particularly. After all, this is Pop's home too. I don't care if he and his friends come over and shoot a game of pool occasionally." It was difficult for Greg to follow the conversation. He kept thinking about holding hands with her. He wondered how it would feel to hold her in his arms and—

"Your sister might object."

"What?" He didn't see how his sister could object if he took Chelsey in his arms. Greg winced as he remembered Thorny was the topic of their conversation. A vision of Camille's angry face appeared in his mind and snapped him back to reality. "Yeah, Camille might."

"Then please, help me do my job."

Greg's brow lifted. He sensed a thinly disguised note of pleading in her voice. "Is someone implying you don't do your job?"

"If the wrong person finds out about these unauthorized excursions by your father and the others, there could be trouble."

"Tell whoever it is to kiss off. You're good at your job, aren't you?"

Chelsey was relieved to find that the tone of his voice implied that she was. "It isn't that simple." She only wished it were. She would love to tell Harriet and Walter Bishop to kiss off as Greg put it. Harriet made Chelsey's life miserable by constantly hovering, waiting for Chelsey to make that one fatal mistake so that Walter could become Rosehaven's new chief administrator. Chelsey shook away the perturbing reminder; she was just as determined not to make a mistake.

Greg's features tightened. "Someone is giving you a hard time."

Would it matter? Chelsey found herself wishing she had someone like Greg in her corner. But he was just making conversation, she told herself. He wasn't offering to fight her battles.

"It's not important." There was no point in discussing Walter and Harriet Bishop with him. It was *her* problem. She nodded toward the muted sound of the men's voices. "I really must take care of this quickly and return to work."

"All right." Greg set his beer down on the counter, oddly disturbed by her answer. Somebody was harassing her. He'd bet on it. He was surprised to find the thought so troubling. "Follow me."

When Greg and Chelsey entered the pool room, the party was in full swing. Chelsey's heart sank when she saw the array of assorted junk foods and sweets. Ian and Otto would both be sick the following day.

Thorny glanced up and smiled. A large cigar protruded from the corner of his mouth. "Hi, son. Want to take me on?"

"No, but I think Ms. Stevens will be tempted," Greg warned.

"Oh?" Thorny looked at Chelsey expectantly. "How about it? Want to play a game of eight ball?"

Chelsey smiled lamely. "I think I'd better pass."

Thorny knocked the eight ball into the side pocket, then slowly straightened. "I suppose you're here to take us back?"

"I am." Chelsey nodded at Ian, Otto and Lars who stood in the background, sheepishly watching the exchange.

"Okay," Thorny said, then glanced at Greg to gauge his reaction to discovering his father and three of his friends in the pool room. He was relieved to find no visible sign of disapproval on his son's face. "Are you in a hurry, Ms. Stevens, or do we have time to shoot one more game?"

"I'm in a bit of a hurry," Chelsey acknowledged. "You see, I have these annoying little payments facing me each month—utility bills, car loan, groceries—and I'm afraid if we all don't return to Rosehaven promptly, my regional director might feel obligated to deprive me of my ability to pay them."

"Oh...well, we weren't planning on staying much longer," Thorny said. "We were going to play just one more game...."

Chelsey nodded sympathetically, knowing she should point out that what they had done was wrong, and that it would reflect badly on her. But she couldn't. She found herself, horror of horrors, almost agreeing with Greg, though she would never want him to know it. What had it hurt that the men enjoyed themselves this afternoon? They were in their seventies; their bodies were failing them; most of their loved ones were either gone or had grown indifferent, so why shouldn't they be allowed to enjoy the rest of their lives without a bunch of depressing no-no's?

For a moment there was an uneasy silence in the room, then Ian quietly laid down his cue and reached for his coat. Lars and Otto meekly followed suit. It was evident the thought had never occurred to them that their well-intended antics to bring Greg and Chelsey together might endanger her position at Rosehaven.

"Well, I suppose you're right." Thorny obediently replaced his cue in the rack. He'd had enough pool for the day, and his stomach was rolling like the Red Sea from all that butter pound cake he'd eaten.

He glanced at Greg again, hoping to detect one positive sign of how his relationship with Chelsey was progressing, but there wasn't any.

Greg was sitting on the edge of the sofa with his arms crossed, his face noncommittal, but Chelsey looked downright worried.

"Now, don't you be worrying about your job, Ms. Stevens. It's not your fault we've been difficult to control," Thorny said. "We'll take full responsibility for our actions if anyone tries to give you trouble."

One by one, Otto, Ian and Lars added their soft-spoken support.

"We'll stand behind you, Ms. Stevens."

"We don't aim to get you in trouble."

"No, we sure don't."

"Then I suggest the four of you try to make her job less complicated," Greg suggested, and Ian, Otto and Lars avoided his stern gaze.

"Pop, you and I need to talk." Greg began collecting the dirty plates and cups.

"Sure, son. I'm available anytime."

"I'll call you later this evening."

Thorny knew he was in trouble, but he wasn't worried. He had accomplished his main goal: Greg had spent some time with Chelsey. He'd hoped today might have been more productive, but he'd have to remind Ian, Otto and Lars that Rome wasn't built in a day. Although, judging from the expressions on their faces, they were ready to give up everything, including Roman construction.

"NOW, WHO DO YOU SUPPOSE wants Chelsey Stevens's head?" Thorny asked the others over breakfast the next morning.

"What makes you think someone does?" Otto asked, glancing around furtively as he hurriedly sprinkled a package of salt over his poached egg.

"The way she acted yesterday tells me something's up," Thorny admitted, chewing his whole wheat toast thoughtfully. "She's worried about her job, and I'd like to know why."

"I don't know why she'd be worried," Lars offered. "She appears quite efficient to me."

"*We* know that, but I'd lay odds something fishy's going on behind the scenes." Thorny saw Fern Silsby sitting at the next table. Leaning toward Otto, he whispered, "There's old blabbermouth. I'll bet she knows."

"She would, if anyone does." Ian mechanically spooned oatmeal into his mouth.

"I think I'll ask her to sit with us so we can find out what's going on," Thorny whispered.

Chair legs scraped loudly against the floor, and coffee wobbled precariously in cups as Ian, Otto and Lars hastily collected their plates and left the table like rats deserting a sinking ship.

Thorny sighed; they just couldn't be counted on in a crisis. If this thing was going to get done, he'd have to do it himself. Taking a deep breath, he looked at Fern and winked.

"Hi, sweetie."

Fern looked up from her plate.

"Want to come over and sit at my table?"

Fern glanced around to be sure Thorny was speaking to her. There wasn't anyone else around, so it was possible.... She glanced back at him and pointed to herself questioningly.

Thorny nodded.

Chair legs squeaked, and coffee sloshed onto clean tablecloths. Moments later, Fern was wedged in tightly next to Thorny. "Why, thank you, Thorny. I'd be delighted to join you."

Since Thorny didn't want Fern to discover the true reason for his sudden interest in her, he chatted for a while before gradually bringing up the subject. "What do you know about someone wanting to oust Chelsey Stevens?"

As Fern absently spooned a prune into her mouth, she sorted through the well of information inside her head. "I know Harriet Bishop was mad as a hornet when they gave the administrator's job to Chelsey Stevens instead of her Walter."

"Is that a fact?"

"And I know Walter wasn't any too pleased when the promotion he'd expected was given to a woman."

"Do you think Walter would adjust to being passed over in favor of a woman?"

Fern looked at him dubiously. "Would you?"

Thorny thought about it for a moment. "If the woman was more qualified than I was, yes."

"Then you're a generous man, Thorny Bradford, because most men would resent a woman moving in on them. Walter has been with Rosehaven for twenty-five years, and Harriet felt the promotion should have been his."

"Sounds like Harriet is more concerned over the outcome than Walter is."

"They both resent it," Fern said. "Harriet watches Ms. Stevens like a hawk. She's hoping to prove to the board that they've made a mistake. She figures they'll fire Ms. Stevens and give the position of chief administrator to Walter. Want half my prunes?"

"No," Thorny said absently, the wheels in his mind turning again. "That's too bad about Harriet wanting Ms. Stevens fired."

"Yeah, I don't like Walter. I can't talk to him like I do Ms. Stevens." Fern finished her coffee, then dabbed her napkin around her mouth daintily. "Will you sit with me at happy hour tonight?"

"No."

"Why not?"

"Because I probably won't go."

"If you do go, will you sit with me?"

"We'll see, Fern. We'll see." Thorny stood up, thinking, give the woman an inch, and she takes a mile.

At least he'd found out what he'd wanted to know. Harriet Bishop wanted Chelsey Stevens fired.

It wasn't Walter's inability to relate to the residents of Rosehaven that bothered Thorny, it was the man himself.

"HAPPY HOUR? Gee, Pop, I'd love to, but I've already made plans for tonight."

"Well, if you're too busy..."

"It's not that, Pop." Greg wished he didn't feel so guilty. If Thorny had wanted him to attend happy hour, he should have mentioned it earlier.

Greg had spent two hours on the phone the night before talking to Thorny, trying to explain the necessity of following rules. Thorny had skirted the issue, choosing instead to discuss Chelsey Stevens and how scuttlebutt around Rosehaven had it that Walter Bishop was after her job. The conversation had left Greg feeling uneasy. He'd lain awake most of the night, believing that Thorny was partly responsible for Chelsey's problems. If Thorny, Ian, Otto and Lars hadn't given Chelsey such a hard time, her job wouldn't be in jeopardy.

But by morning Greg had decided Chelsey's job wasn't his concern. He had his own problems trying to keep Thorny under control.

"Well, I suppose if you can't come, I'll just stay in my room and go to bed early," Thorny said despondently.

"Come on, Pop. Why should you do that? Go to happy hour with your friends."

"I can't. Ian isn't feeling well, and Otto's daughter is going with him." Greg thought he heard a whine in Thorny's voice. Thorny had never whined before.

"What about Lars?" Greg prompted.

"He hates happy hour."

Greg sighed. "All right." He could see his plans going straight down the tubes. "When does it start?"

"Now, don't worry about me, son. I'll be all right. I don't want to spoil your evening. It wouldn't be the first time I've had to sit here alone. You go have fun. Don't worry about me."

"Oh, shoot! I'll come. When is it?" Greg hated it when Thorny pulled his "woe is me" act.

"I don't want to be a burden...."

"Pop, I haven't time for this. Just tell me what time happy hour begins, and I'll be there."

"What about your plans?"

"They can be altered. I'd promised friends I'd have dinner with them. I'll phone and tell them I'll be a little late."

"Great! It starts at six. Wear a nice suit." Greg was startled by the sudden surge of life in Thorny's voice.

"A suit?" His plans had been for an informal evening.

"Yeah, that blue one you just bought. I have to go. Here comes Gilda the Masher with my heart medicine." The line suddenly went dead.

Greg replaced the receiver, shaking his head. He couldn't figure Thorny out at times, but if attending happy hour with him meant that much, Greg wasn't going to disappoint him.

That evening while he showered and dressed, Greg told himself he was glad he'd rearranged his plans. After all, he hadn't spent enough time with Thorny lately. He shaved and absently splashed on a new cologne that claimed to "stimulate a woman's senses." Greg promised himself to stay for about thirty minutes, then he'd join his friends.

Chelsey Stevens popped into his mind once or twice, and he found himself smiling. The suit had to be for her benefit. He was beginning to strongly suspect that Thorny had selected Chelsey as a prime candidate for the new Mrs. Bradford.

Dropping his hairbrush on the counter, Greg glanced at himself critically in the mirror. Well, at least his old man had good taste in women, he thought absently.

Damn good taste.

When Greg arrived at Rosehaven, Thorny was waiting at the door to greet him.

Thorny surveyed Greg's suit critically. "You look nice," he said.

"Thanks, but why the suit?" Greg reached up to loosen his tie. He planned to run home and change clothes before meeting his friends.

"Everyone dresses up for happy hour," Thorny explained as they walked toward the recreation room.

"Oh, look." Thorny paused in front of the door marked Administrator. "Here's Ms. Stevens's office. Want to stop in and say hello?"

Greg kept on walking. "No thanks."

Hard-headed kid! Thorny fell back into step with his son as they entered the rec room a few moments later.

The room was crowded. Someone was playing soft music on the piano, and there were fresh flowers on the tables. Thorny ushered Greg to the bar and ordered two soft drinks.

Greg lifted his brow. "Cola?"

"The other stuff isn't good for you. Besides, you're driving, aren't you?"

Greg smiled. "Are you going to make me eat my brussels sprouts, too?"

"I might." Thorny's glance kept returning to the doorway.

Greg turned. "Expecting someone?"

"No."

Fern Silsby spotted Thorny and rushed to his side. In a few minutes, Louella, Fern, Mildred and Violet were gathered around the men, chatting. Woody and Henry joined the small group, and the noise level in the room grew.

Greg was speaking to Woody when he paused in midsentence. His eyes darkened as he watched Chelsey walk through the doorway. He knew she was the real reason he'd appeased Thorny tonight and agreed to attend happy hour. He'd been hoping all along to catch sight of her, and here she was, every bit as lovely as he remembered.

She was wearing a soft, peach-colored dress, and her hair, swept to one side behind a sprig of baby's breath, floated softly over her shoulders.

Greg's gaze refused to leave her as she made her way across the room. He thought she looked positively stunning. All eyes turned to Chelsey as she paused beside Ida Munsington's table and leaned to whisper in her ear. Even from this distance, Greg thought he could detect the scent of her perfume.

Thorny came back from the bar with a second round and handed Greg a drink. "Here you go."

"Thanks, Pop."

Thorny was about to take a sip when he suddenly noticed Chelsey had arrived.

"Oh...uh...look who just walked in!"

With considerable effort, Greg turned his attention in the opposite direction to the captivating Ms. Stevens. "Who?"

"Ms. Stevens...my goodness, does she look good tonight," Thorny whispered in awe.

"Really?" Greg sipped his drink and set it on the table. Thorny was about as subtle as a blinking neon sign. "Well, I have to be going, Pop."

"Turn around and look at her, Greg."

"Pop," said Greg sternly, "I won't ogle Ms. Stevens. Now cut it out."

"Cut what out?"

"Quit trying to set me up with Chelsey Stevens."

"Whatever makes you think I am?"

"I'm not an idiot. Now cut it out," Greg repeated.

"You don't like her?"

"That has nothing to do with it. I just don't happen to want you to pick out the women I date. And you're going to embarrass *her* if you keep this up."

"You're making a mistake." Thorny's tone was almost sullen. "Where could you find a prettier, more suitable woman? Why, she could run your household, have your children and balance your checkbook." *And get me out of here,* Thorny added silently. "Wouldn't that be nice?"

"No, and I want you to stop this, okay?"

"You're being downright pig-headed, boy."

"Maybe so, but I just don't want you running my personal life. I don't try to run yours...." Greg's voice trailed off guiltily. "At least I don't try to match you up with Fern Silsby," he amended. "But I just might, if you don't stop this."

"Oh, good Lord," Thorny groaned. "Chelsey Stevens and Fern Silsby aren't even in the same ballpark!"

"So let's both forfeit the game, okay?"

"Well, at least say hello to her before you leave."

"No! Has it ever occurred to you that *she* might not be interested in me?"

"A woman her age not interested in a wealthy bachelor? Pickleloaf. You're going to mess around and lose her," Thorny warned. "I know for certain she's got a date with that snappy heart surgeon tonight. The man has money, looks, and apparently he has a brain larger than a pea—he must, because he's smart enough to take her out. What do you think about that?"

Greg heaved a sigh and ran his hand through his hair. "I don't think about it. Not at all."

"I swear sometimes Elizabeth and I were handed the wrong baby at the hospital. Come on."

Greg stiffened as Thorny grabbed his arm and began dragging him through the crowd.

Chelsey straightened from her conversation with Ida and smiled as she watched Thorny pull Greg along behind him. Thorny had stopped by her office twice this afternoon to make sure she planned to put in an appearance at happy hour this evening. She had a hunch she was about to find out why.

"Hi, Ms. Stevens."

"Hello, Thorny." Chelsey's gaze met Greg's, and her eyes filled with discreet amusement. It was obvious he'd been roped and hog-tied into making an appearance.

"You remember my son, Greg?"

She smiled. "Yes. Hello, Greg."

"Hello, Ms. Stevens." Greg nodded, and a faint smile played on his lips.

"You certainly look beautiful tonight, Ms. Stevens. Doesn't she, son?"

"She certainly does." Greg found it hard to keep his tone neutral.

Their gazes met, and this time there was no laughter in Chelsey's eyes.

"Well, what are you up to tonight, Ms. Stevens?" Thorny tried to make it sound like a casual inquiry.

"Not much." Chelsey laughed softly. "I was supposed to go out for dinner and dancing, but my date had an emergency come up, so I'll probably go home, have a peanut butter sandwich, a glass of milk, and go to bed early."

"Oh, what a shame. Well, no sense in doing that. You could wine her, dine her and dance with her, couldn't you, son?"

Greg shot Thorny an incredulous look. "Well, I—"

"I really don't mind the change in my plans," Chelsey intervened quickly. "I'm exhausted; I'd welcome an early evening."

"Well, it seems a shame—you dressed up and all." Thorny looked to Greg pleadingly.

"Pop, she said she was tired—"

"Thanks for your concern, Thorny, but I should mingle for a while before running along." Chelsey began moving away.

"It was nice seeing you," Greg said as he edged Thorny back into the crowd.

"Very nice to see you," she returned, her eyes bright again with amusement.

Greg's gaze followed Chelsey as she walked away. She had enjoyed every moment of his embarrassment, and he knew it.

"Well, if that doesn't take the cake! You just missed the perfect opportunity," Thorny accused. "I don't know what's wrong with you!"

"Pop, lay off!"

"All right, but if you die old and alone, don't blame me."

"I'll make a note not to."

With a heavy heart, Thorny watched Greg leave a few minutes later. He'd been nearly certain that once Greg got a load of Chelsey all dressed up, he'd be a goner for sure.

But she could have been a cheese ball for all the notice he paid her.

Thorny was beginning to think his boy had gone soft in the head.

GREG WAS WALKING out the front door just as Chelsey was leaving.

"Heading home?" He held the door open for her.

"Yes, how about you?"

"I'm supposed to meet some friends for dinner."

"That's nice."

They stepped out into the crisp night air and paused.

"You do look lovely tonight, Ms. Stevens," Greg said.

"Thank you, Mr. Bradford. You look exceptionally nice yourself."

"Pop insisted I wear a suit."

Chelsey smiled knowingly.

"And you know what he's trying to do, don't you?" Greg prompted.

She nodded. "I wondered if you did."

He nodded. "Does it bother you?"

She shook her head. There was no point in denying she felt a growing attraction to him. She did. And she had admitted to herself that she would welcome more of his company.

A slow, almost devilish grin spread over his handsome features. "Would you happen to have enough peanut butter for two?"

"Yes."

"Can you keep a secret?"

"I've been known to."

Greg glanced around, then leaned closer. "Now listen carefully, Ms. Stevens. We're both dead ducks if Pop finds out about this."

She grinned. "You don't want your father to know?"

"Are you kidding? It would only encourage him."

"And you don't want that?" she asked, feeling an unexpected prick of disappointment.

Greg's eyes softened. At this point, he wasn't sure what he wanted. He just knew that he had a sudden craving for peanut butter. "I don't want Pop to think he can manipulate me. That would be dangerous."

"Yes, that would be dangerous." The smile returned.

He reached out and cupped the side of her face thoughtfully. "So? How about it, Ms. Stevens? Care to split a peanut butter sandwich with me?"

"What about your friends?"

"They'll probably be through eating by now."

"I heard you didn't date."

"I don't, but I do like peanut butter sandwiches."

"I believe I said peanut butter, milk and early to bed. I hope you don't expect all three." Chelsey knew why she was accepting his invitation and she thought she knew exactly what she could expect: a pleasant evening with a man who was still in love with the memory of his deceased wife—and peanut butter sandwiches. She just wanted to make sure his expectations were no different.

"Ms. Stevens, I'm shocked." He looked properly offended. "What kind of man do you think I am?"

"Normal."

"Well, at least that's encouraging," he said as he draped his arm around her shoulders and they proceeded down the steps, "but peanut butter is all I had in mind."

He paused and pulled her ear to his mouth and whispered softly, "But if you ever wear that dress in my presence again, I may be asking for jelly next."

Chapter Nine

Peanut butter sandwiches paved the way for hamburgers and fries at a local fast-food place a couple of nights later.

Chelsey was surprised, but not shocked to find Greg waiting for her as she emerged from Rosehaven Friday evening. The time they'd shared together after happy hour had been enjoyable and relaxing, and Greg had hinted he might be around the coming weekend.

She was just inserting the key in her car door when a masculine hand reached out to relieve her of the task.

"You know what?"

Her hand paused and she smiled. "What?"

"I have this sudden, uncontrollable urge for junk food. How does a malt, a large order of French fries, and a double cheeseburger sound to you?"

"Like two more unwanted pounds." Chelsey usually tried to stick to a light fare in the evening.

"Aw, come on." Greg's gaze traveled over her with appreciation. "Two pounds on you looks good, but I'm easy to get along with," he said. "I'll make you a deal. You come with me, and I'll eat the French fries, double cheeseburger and chocolate malt, and you can graze at the salad bar."

Chelsey pretended to weigh the suggestion thoughtfully, even though she had every intention of accepting his invitation. The meal sounded disastrous, but the company was tempting. "Well, I don't know.... A chocolate malt, you say?"

"Yes, rich, thick, creamy...but I hear they have great garbanzo beans."

"And a *double* cheeseburger?"

Greg winked. "With lettuce, tomato, pickle, two kinds of special sauces on a sesame seed bun."

Chelsey shrugged. "Lead the way."

Greg grinned and opened the car door for her. "What happened to prudence?"

"I believe it passed away somewhere between the malt and cheeseburger or just after the garbanzo beans."

"I'm beginning to believe there might be hope for you yet, Ms. Stevens," Greg said. "Get in. I'll drive."

The next two hours were the most pleasant Chelsey could ever recall spending with a man.

After dinner they decided to take a walk along the shore of the Pacific. Like two small children, they laughed and removed their shoes and waded knee-deep into the water, letting the surf wash over their legs and taking pure delight in the simple, uncomplicated pleasure.

As they parted at Chelsey's door later that evening, Greg leaned down and kissed her. The gesture was brief, but no less disturbing than if it had been longer and more sensual. His kiss was different from others she'd shared though she couldn't begin to say why. She just knew she welcomed it.

"I've had fun tonight, Chelsey." His clear gaze met hers and his eyes expressed a deeper sentiment than his words. He couldn't tell her that he hadn't had fun with a woman in a very long time and that now it felt good. It was becoming evident with each passing hour that they had more in common than either of them had originally thought. While Greg made it clear that he enjoyed beer and football more than he enjoyed champagne and the ballet, Chelsey was pleased to discover he did possess an extensive knowledge of the arts, along with a fine appreciation for them. To her surprise, she learned he was well acquainted with the finer things in life. He just chose to live his life in a simple fashion.

Chelsey, on the other hand, proved she could share a double cheeseburger and walk along the shoreline barefoot with her hair whipping about in the wind as easily as anybody.

"I've had fun, too, Greg." The taste of his after-shave lingered lightly on Chelsey's lips, tempting her to hope for another embrace.

But Greg chose not to offer one. He turned and stepped off the porch, then paused.

"Do you like seafood?"

"I love it."

"I hear there's a nice place up the coast. Want to try it tomorrow night?" The invitation was issued casually, as if it were of no importance whether they actually went or not.

"Sure, why not?" Her acceptance was given in the same nonchalant manner.

He flashed her an infectious grin. "Yeah, why not? Six o'clock be okay?"

She'd had more romantic invitations, but none she would look forward to as much as this one. "Six will be fine."

The following morning Chelsey cleaned house, then spent the afternoon doing her hair and nails. The day seemed to drag, and Chelsey checked the clock periodically to make sure it was still running.

When the phone rang around four, she picked it up and was surprised to hear Greg's voice.

"Chelsey, hi."

"Hi."

"I'm afraid I'm going to have to break our date. There's an emergency here at the plant that requires my personal attention."

"I'm sorry. I hope it isn't anything serious," she said, wondering if there really was an emergency or if Greg was just having second thoughts about their date.

"No, it's just one of those headaches that'll take awhile to straighten out."

"I hope you get it worked out okay. Thanks for calling." Chelsey tried to persuade herself that she wasn't disappointed, that she was used to having dates broken at the last minute whenever an emergency arose, but she wasn't convinced. The nagging question remained whether Greg's emergency was real or contrived.

As she replaced the phone in its cradle, she was engulfed by restlessness. The night stretched ahead of her bleakly. The sound of Greg's voice had served to remind her of how much she had been looking forward to seeing him. And now that wasn't going to happen.

The phone rang again and she absently picked up the receiver. "Hello."

"Chelsey?" It was Neil Matlock's friendly voice this time.

"Yes?"

"Good, I'm glad I caught you in. I know it's late, but I was wondering if you were free tonight?"

Part of her wanted to say no, yet another side said why not? It seemed senseless to sit at home alone, wondering about Greg Bradford, especially when she could enjoy the company of an exciting man like Neil. True, she'd prefer to be with Greg, but since that wasn't possible, Neil was a good second choice.

"As a matter of fact, I am free tonight, Neil."

"Wonderful! Maybe we can finally have that dinner and dancing I've been promising you. Mark Grayson has agreed to take my calls tonight, so we shouldn't be interrupted," Neil promised.

Chelsey smiled. She would have to see that to believe it. She couldn't recall a time when she and Neil were together that he hadn't excused himself at least twice to answer his beeper.

"Wear something pretty, and I'll pick you up around seven."

"I'll be looking forward to it, Neil."

Replacing the receiver again, she decided she'd done the right thing. If Greg Bradford had invented an excuse to break their date, then she would never let him know it had disappointed her.

The evening turned out to be delightful. Neil had made reservations at his country club, one of Chelsey's favorite places to visit. The dining area jutted out over the ocean, and the food was excellent.

The night was beautiful and uncharacteristically balmy for the first of November.

The chateaubriand was excellent, the salad delectably crisp, and the cherries jubilee prepared in kirsch was exquisite.

After dinner they danced on the small balcony overlooking the ocean, against the backdrop of surf breaking against the shore and the sweet filtering strains of violins. It was a near-perfect night, except for one minor annoyance. Chelsey's mind refused to release the image of Greg.

"Have I told you how beautiful you look tonight?" Neil's voice was low against her ear as they glided smoothly across the balcony. "Not that you aren't always gorgeous, but that particular shade of blue you're wearing is exceptionally becoming."

"Thank you, kind sir. But it surely must be the lovely gardenia you gave me that makes this dress seem special."

"Ahhh, my sweet. If I heaped a thousand gardenias at your feet, they would pale and become transparent in the midst of such overwhelming beauty."

"True," Chelsey accepted his lavish praise with mock seriousness and a brief nod of her head. "But it is you I'm concerned about. Have you had your glasses checked lately?"

They both chuckled, enjoying the easy sense of camaraderie that had always existed between them.

"I was delighted to hear you were free tonight," Neil confessed as the music tempo changed and he waltzed her gaily around the floor. "I was sure when I called you so late that you'd already have other plans."

"I did," Chelsey admitted, "but they were changed at the last moment."

Neil looked down at her expectantly. "Are you sorry?"

Chelsey smiled. "No, I'm having a marvelous time. It's so good to see you again."

It was very late when Neil walked her to the door of her cottage. Chelsey knew he expected to be invited in for a nightcap.

Although the evening had been wonderful, for some reason she found herself reluctant to extend him the invitation.

"I hope you'll forgive me, Neil, but I'm very tired."

"I'm sorry." He gazed down at her in the moonlight. "I hope not too tired to have some coffee before I go?"

"It's tempting, but I'm afraid I wouldn't be able to keep my eyes open." Chelsey knew he would find her refusal unusual. She'd always invited him inside after their dates for a cup of coffee and idle conversation. But tonight she wasn't in the mood. Her thoughts kept straying to Greg, and she was annoyed at herself for letting them do so. Was she going to permit thoughts of Greg Bradford to begin dominating her social life? She forced the worrisome possibility aside. "I hope you understand."

Neil, ever the gentleman, accepted the disappointment gracefully. "Of course." He stepped back and inserted her key into the lock, then gave her a smile.

"It's been fun, Chelsey. We must do it more often."

It's been fun, Chelsey. Greg had spoken the same words to her the night before, yet coming from him they had sounded different . . . more meaningful.

"Goodnight, Neil."

Thirty minutes later Chelsey turned out the light by her bed, thinking she would drop off to sleep immediately, but it wasn't to be. Thoughts of Greg Bradford raced through her mind, and she discovered that instead of comparing Greg to Neil, as she should be doing, she was doing exactly the opposite.

She was comparing Neil to Greg, and Greg was proving to be her first choice! With a low groan, Chelsey rolled out of bed and began pacing the floor. How had she let this happen to her? When had it begun to happen? She wasn't sure, but she was sure of one thing. Beginning tomorrow morning, she was going to avoid Greg Bradford. It was the only solution at this point. She was becoming much too involved with him, and it was up to her to put a stop to it.

Next time he called—if he called—she would simply refuse his invitation.

Satisfied she had the matter well in hand, she drifted off to sleep just as the sun was peeping over the hilltop.

The jingling phone awakened her at six-fifty. Groping for the receiver, she tried to orient herself, but she couldn't think clearly.

"Hello." Her voice was barely above a whisper.

"Hello. I'm free now," Greg announced in a breezy voice.

"What?"

"The problem's been handled, and I'm ready to pick you up. How soon can you be ready?"

"Greg!" Chelsey rolled over and fumbled for the clock on her nightstand. "Do you have any idea what time it is?"

"Yeah." Greg glanced at his watch. "Six fifty-one."

"Six fifty-one." She groaned. "What are you doing up so early?"

"Up? I've never been to bed."

"Why not?"

"Because I worked all night."

"All night?"

"Yes, but the problem is solved, and I'm ready to relax. How about having breakfast with me?"

"Don't you want to go home and go to bed?"

"No, I feel great. I've had three pots of coffee, a hot shower, and a change of clothes. I'm good for another twelve hours."

Chelsey wasn't as optimistic about herself, but she said, "I can be ready in thirty minutes."

"Good. I'll see you then."

Chelsey struggled out of bed and pulled on her robe as she walked to the bathroom. *Well, so much for refusing his invitations, Chelsey. Way to go, Ms. Stevens.*

IT WAS THE BEGINNING of another gorgeous day. The sky was a captivating blue, the temperature promised to be in the high sixties, and there was very little breeze as Greg and Chelsey walked to the car. He was driving the Mercedes convertible, and the top was down.

Chelsey reached into her purse for a scarf, then changed her mind. She'd decided to wear her hair down today, and it would feel good to let the wind whip through it. She could brush out the tangles later.

Greg started the car and pulled away from the curb while Chelsey was still buckling her seat belt.

"I tried to call you a couple of times last night," Greg remarked as he absently adjusted the rearview mirror.

"I wasn't home."

"I discovered that."

Chelsey hoped he wouldn't pursue the subject, and he didn't. The car sped along the roadway as Chelsey leaned back to enjoy the scenery.

"Where do you plan to have breakfast?" Chelsey had to raise her voice above the rushing wind to be heard.

"San Francisco!"

"San Francisco?" Chelsey looked over and mouthed the words mutely as Greg flashed her a roguish grin.

"Hope you didn't have anything special planned for the day."

"No." Chelsey laughed. "Nothing special." San Francisco! He had to be kidding, she thought.

But he wasn't. The two-hour drive passed as if it were minutes instead of hours.

As they drove through a small coastal town, Greg suggested they stop at a fast-food place and purchase coffee and cinnamon buns. Chelsey was not accustomed to eating breakfast in a car, but like most things he was associated with, Greg made it fun.

When they arrived in San Francisco, they left the Mercedes in an underground parking garage and rode a cable car down to Fisherman's Wharf. Chelsey was well acquainted with the picturesque city, but today she sensed she would discover it again in a new and different light.

"I love this town," Greg confessed as they clung to the side of the crowded car. The sights and sounds of the city were unique. He looked at Chelsey and smiled. "I want to show you the San Francisco I love, Chelsey." The bell on the cable car clanged loudly as it passed through the intersections, warning the cars of its passing.

"I can think of nothing I'd like better," she returned, and the glow in her eyes assured him she was willing to share his excitement.

When the car stopped in Chinatown, Greg suddenly took Chelsey's hand and they hopped off the car. For the next couple of hours they wandered up and down the streets, taking time to browse through the colorful shops and make outrageous purchases that neither of them would ever use.

"What am I supposed to do with a teapot shaped like a woman's leg?" Chelsey complained as they emerged from a gift shop.

"How should I know? I just thought it looked like you," Greg teased.

They climbed onto a cable car and continued their journey to Fisherman's Wharf. Once there, they ate their fill of fresh shrimp, boiled in large, steaming vats along the sidewalk and devoured thick, hot slices of sourdough bread.

"Would you like to try sushi?" Greg offered his serving for her to sample.

Chelsey turned away in disgust. "No thank you."

Greg grinned. "It's great!"

"I would say that's definitely a matter of opinion."

Pitching his empty plate in a trash receptacle, Greg draped his arm around Chelsey and leaned over to kiss her briefly. "You're okay, Ms. Stevens, even if you do get a little prudish at times."

It was she who winked at him this time. "There's just something about you, Mr. Bradford, that brings it out in me."

"I'll buy you a kite, anyway," he returned generously.

"Great. It will look wonderful displayed next to my teapot."

The kites were a colorful sight with their ferocious dragon faces breathing fire and their triple tails whipping freely about in the breeze. Vivid reds, breathtaking blues and stunning yellows dipped and swayed against the backdrop of the sky as skilled hands worked the aerial toys through intricate flying patterns.

Greg wanted to browse through the selection carefully before purchasing, so they spent the next hour examining kites in the shapes of birds, fish and dragons. There were kites with tails, box kites, oval-shaped kites, octagon-shaped kites, round ones, square ones and oblong kites. In the end, it was a yellow-eyed, ferocious-looking dragon kite that won Chelsey's heart. The colors were brilliant, and the tail was long and streaming.

"Honestly, Greg. What am I going to do with this!"

A windy boat ride across the bay was next on their agenda. Chelsey leaned against the width of Greg's chest as he stood holding her in his arms, protecting her from the elements as they watched the island of Alcatraz slowly slip by.

"You're wearing the perfume you wore the day we first met, aren't you?" Greg nuzzled her ear, then the warmth of her neck.

She smiled and snuggled closer in his embrace. "Passion?"

"I'd say I'm getting close."

"That's the name of the perfume."

"Oh."

The shadows were lengthening as they strolled arm in arm along the piers, feeling incredibly comfortable with each other.

A tall, well-dressed man emerged from one of the shops, carrying a large package. Chelsey's footsteps slowed as the man walked toward them. "Oh, good heavens. Look."

"What?"

"It's Clint Eastwood," she whispered under her breath. Chelsey had never met the handsome actor, and mayor of Carmel, even though she lived in the same town. Nor had she ever caught even a brief glimpse of him on the streets.

"So?"

"So?" Chelsey looked at him incredulously. "It's Clint Eastwood, Greg. *Clint Eastwood!*"

Greg looked back at her. "You want to meet him?"

"Meet him?" He must be joking.

Greg stepped forward as the mayor of Carmel approached them. "Hello, Clint."

"Greg!" Clint extended his hand. "Nice to see you again. Taking in the sights today?"

"Yes. Clint—" Greg drew an astounded Chelsey close to his side "—I'd like you to meet Chelsey Stevens. She's chief administrator at Rosehaven."

"Rosehaven, oh yes. Fine establishment." Clint reached out and took her hand. "It's an honor, ma'am."

"Thank you. I've seen all your pictures...." Chelsey knew she sounded inane, but the surprise introduction had left her nearly speechless.

"Well, if you'll excuse me, I have a dinner engagement." Clint flashed a melting smile in Chelsey's direction. "Nice to have met you, Ms. Stevens. Greg." He nodded.

"So long, Clint. Take it easy."

Clint walked off, and Chelsey turned to face Greg in disbelief. "How do you know Clint Eastwood?"

"We've attended several of the same functions."

"But he's so...so nice."

"Do you think he goes around gunning down people on the streets?"

"Well, no...." She was clearly in awe of the handsome celebrity.

Greg shook his head and drew her back into the groove of his arm as they began to walk again. For once, he thought, he'd managed to impress her.

As dusk descended, they stopped to eat dinner in a restaurant along the waterfront. It was a long, leisurely meal shared over candlelight and easy conversation. Their hands touched often, and they smiled at each other easily.

Chelsey raised her wineglass in a quiet toast to the man sitting across from her. Her eyes were luminous as she gazed at him. "I love your San Francisco," she complimented softly.

Greg lifted his glass and touched it briefly to hers. "You've made it even more beautiful than I remembered. Thank you."

Their gazes met and held for a moment. "Greg, I feel I owe you an apology," Chelsey began.

"Why?"

"I confess that in the beginning I made some snap judgments about you, judgments I realize now were not entirely fair."

"And what were those judgments?" Greg leaned back in his chair and sipped his wine.

"Well, for one, I thought you were trying to get rid of your father."

"Yes, I sensed that."

"And I thought you were an irresponsible playboy who was born with a silver spoon in his mouth."

Greg shrugged. "I'm not irresponsible, and I'm not a playboy, but I confess to being wealthy—thanks to Thorny. You know, Pop doesn't have much education. My grandfather was killed in a logging accident when Pop was still in school. The family was left in pretty dire straits. There was just enough insurance money to cover the funeral expenses.

"Afterward, Thorny had to drop out of school and take a job in order to keep the family intact. A kind man by the name of Willard Newton owned a small electronics company in Seattle where Pop lived. When Thorny came to him at the age of fourteen and pleaded for a job, Willard heard him out. Thorny was hired as an errand boy, and by the time he was thirty, Pop not only owned the company, but he was a millionaire. Pop doesn't have a lot of education, but he's got good business sense. He made sure Camille and I went to the best of schools and had all the advantages he missed out on." Greg smiled. "Thorny's dream had been to become a doctor. Can you imagine that?"

Chelsey smiled. "I can imagine Thorny being anything he wanted to be."

"Yeah, he's that type."

Chelsey reached out and placed her hand on top of his. "I'm sorry I misjudged you, Greg. A man could ask for no finer son."

"Apology accepted... if you'll accept mine. You're not exactly what I had you pegged to be, either," Greg confessed.

"You were not exactly nice," she asserted.

"But you're fun to annoy." He grinned. "You always get this cool, glacial look on your face when I say something to annoy you. It became a challenge to see if I could get you to loosen up."

"Well, I'm ready to call another truce if you are."

"Sure." He winked and lifted his glass to her again. "Here's to good times and a permanent truce."

She smiled and joined him in his toast.

"Are you tired yet?" he asked.

She knew she should be. She'd only had a couple of hours' sleep the night before, but she didn't feel the least bit fatigued. She shook her head. "What about you?"

"I've never felt better. Would you like to take in a show?" he asked.

"I'm not properly dressed."

"You don't have to be where I'm taking you."

They took a cab to Clement Street. They disembarked and Greg directed them to a small, out-of-the-way café.

The floor show was fun and boisterous but performed in good taste. Chelsey laughed, flushed, and was immensely relieved when she and Greg were not selected as audience participants.

Afterward, they danced until the wee hours on a small floor so crowded they could barely move, but neither of them seemed to notice. The music was inviting, and the opportunity to hold each other close without threatening their newly formed truce was enough.

"Do you realize it's close to two o'clock?" Chelsey murmured. By now her body was numb with fatigue, but she refused to let the magical day end.

"I know. We should be going." His embrace tightened, and he didn't need to finish his thought. Chelsey sensed he, too, had no desire to see their day end.

"We should," she admitted, "but I suppose another few minutes isn't going to hurt."

"By the way," Greg said, as he maneuvered Chelsey through the crowd. "There's something I've been meaning to ask you."

"What's that?"

"What about Neil Matlock?"

"What about him?"

"What's between the two of you?"

"Dr. Matlock is a very good friend. He's fun to be with. He has excellent taste in clothes, food and, naturally, women," she bantered.

"Might your relationship develop into something serious?"

Chelsey knew she could say that it wasn't any of his business, but she was delighted that Greg was interested enough in her to be curious about Neil.

"I suppose anything's possible, but if you're asking if there's anything serious between us at the moment, the answer is no."

Greg finally lowered his gaze to meet hers. "Why does that make me feel better?"

"I have no idea. Maybe because my face turned sort of glacial?" she said with a grin.

He threw back his head and laughed. "That must be it."

By three, they had managed to close the place, and they could tell by the pleading looks they were getting from the employees that it would be greatly appreciated if they left.

The sun was just coming up as Greg pulled up to the cottage and braked. "You realize it's Monday morning."

Chelsey winced. She had slept most of the way home. "Yes, and I have to be at work in a couple of hours. What about you?"

"I planned to take the day off."

"Some people have the luxury of doing that."

She sat up as Greg pulled her over to him. "Stop complaining, Ms. Stevens. You know you enjoyed every minute of it."

His mouth came down to meet hers, as her arms came up to fold around his neck. They kissed long and leisurely, forgetting the hour, savoring the taste and feel of each other.

When their mouths finally parted, Chelsey gazed up into his eyes thoughtfully. "Thank you."

"For what?"

"For today. I don't think I'll ever forget it . . . or you."

Greg placed his finger lightly beneath her chin. "I plan to see that you don't."

Their mouths melted together again, and Chelsey found herself hoping he would keep that promise.

Chapter Ten

The first indication Greg had that he was in any real trouble was when Chelsey Stevens began to dominate his every waking thought.

They'd seen each other almost every night since their day together in San Francisco. The days and hours had flown by, and each time they went their separate ways, Greg found it increasingly difficult to leave her.

He tried to convince himself that the attraction wasn't really all that serious. He reasoned that Chelsey was a lovely, intelligent woman whom any man would be pleased to have as a companion.

They were good friends; they had fun together. She could make him laugh, and he seemed to lighten her conservative outlook. They enjoyed old Spencer Tracy and Katharine Hepburn movies. They both shared a love for classical music and a penchant for Rocky Road ice cream. Chelsey confided she had no family and longed for one of her own; Greg agreed having a family was a gift most people took for granted.

Greg wasn't going to justify his growing feelings for her; he just planned to enjoy the unexpected ray of sunshine that had come back into his life.

The attraction would pass. He assured himself again and again that he didn't have anything to worry about. He was comfortable with his life, and this unexpected attraction was pleasant. The agony of Mary Beth's death had finally eased. Business was booming, and he'd formed some good, solid friendships over the past few years. He had everything he could ever want.

But the argument didn't hold water when he tossed in bed at night and thought about how feminine and warm Chelsey felt in his arms. Or how her mouth felt against his . . . or the intoxicating smell of her perfume . . . or her hair. . . .

Maybe he should start backing away from her. No, he didn't want to do that. He enjoyed being with her too much. He'd been without a woman's companionship for too long. That was precisely his problem, he concluded. Between the pressures of his job and worries over Thorny, he had avoided taking any chances. Perhaps if he would take their relationship a step further, it would solve his problem.

A brief, uncomplicated affair with Chelsey Stevens: that's what he needed and wanted. Maybe that would make him feel better.

He'd never forgive Pop for getting him into this mess.

"I'M OUT OF IT. I'm too tired and too old to be in hot water all the time." The four men sat on a park bench, feeding pigeons.

"I'll admit we've had a few setbacks, but I don't think we should give up." Thorny knew the men were discouraged; so was he. And if it didn't matter so much to him, he'd give up himself.

"Well, I hate to say it, Thorny, but I'm beginning to side with Lars."

"Why do you say that, Otto?"

"Because it's been several weeks since we started the campaign to get your son and Ms. Stevens together, and it appears to me they're further apart than when we first started."

"And you, Ian? Do you feel the same?"

"Well, it does seem like your son isn't the least bit interested in her. You'll have to admit that, Thorny."

Thorny didn't want to. Facing the fact that Greg wasn't going to take a personal interest in Chelsey was tantamount to admitting that he was stuck in Rosehaven for the rest of his life. He wouldn't accept that, at least not if he didn't have to.

No, he would just have to try harder, that's all. Although, Lord knew, he'd tried everything he could think of for the past month to bring the couple together. Greg's stubborn refusal to acknowledge that Chelsey was an attractive, bright, eligible young woman puzzled Thorny. He could have sworn he'd detected a note of interest in Greg's eyes the night Chelsey had appeared at happy hour, but as usual nothing had developed. Greg had left to join friends, and Chelsey had returned to a lonely jar of peanut butter.

"Well, I can understand if you three want out." Thorny wouldn't make their lives miserable by insisting that they stick with him. If he had to, he'd go it alone.

"I hate to desert you, Thorny, but my daughter has warned me that if they notify her once more that I've left Rosehaven without authorization, she's going to move me to Winterhaven," Otto confessed.

Winterhaven. The mere word struck cold terror in each man's heart. Winterhaven was a maximum-care nursing facility where residents were treated more like inmates. They were alive, but most of them weren't aware of it. None of the men wanted to go there.

"I think I'm going to have to throw in the towel, too," Ian admitted. "I haven't been feeling well lately."

"Oh?" Thorny glanced up. Ian wasn't a complainer, so his remark surprised Thorny.

"Yeah, nothing special wrong. Just feeling my age, I guess."

Thorny tossed a bread crumb to the boldest pigeon. "It's all right, men. You've done your best." The bird cooed softly as it picked up the morsel and waddled off.

"Thanks, Thorny. We sure tried." Thorny knew Ian, Otto and Lars felt bad about letting him down, but he supposed they'd done all they could.

"Maybe Greg will run across a nice girl one of these days and just up and marry again. Then you can move back with him," Ian said.

The men sat silently, huddled in their jackets. The sun disappeared behind a cloud, and the wind began to pick up.

Autumn was almost over; winter wasn't far behind.

"You know what your trouble is, Thorny?"

"No, what's my trouble, Lars?"

"You just need a little patience."

"You think so?"

Lars nodded and tossed another crumb to a pigeon. "Just a little more patience."

"Yeah, well, maybe you're right." The thought held little comfort for Thorny. When a man reached his seventies, patience was a luxury he could ill afford.

"MS. CHELSEY STEVENS?"

Chelsey glanced up from the corporate reports she was reading. A young man wearing a florist's cap stood in the doorway holding a large glass bowl.

"Yes?"

"More flowers for you, ma'am." The boy walked to her desk and set the arrangement beside two massive vases of red roses. He handed her the card.

Chelsey smiled. Neil Matlock must be feeling guilty for having broken their last two dates. It was the third time this week he'd sent flowers and his apologies.

Chelsey gave the boy a tip and sent him on his way before opening the card. Her smile widened as she read the message. "In Canada on business. Let's have dinner when I return. Greg."

Her gaze returned to the delicate lavender orchid floating in the bowl. It was lovely.

Touching her finger to the rim of the bowl, she wondered why he'd sent the flower. He'd called from Canada yesterday, and they had talked for more than thirty minutes. So why would he send her a flower and an invitation for dinner? They had already agreed they'd see each other the moment he returned. A smile played over her features as she recalled how Greg had been an almost regular visitor to her cottage lately.

From the first night they'd sat in her kitchen, making fold-over peanut butter sandwiches and talking until the wee hours of the morning, something began to change between them. The day they spent together in San Francisco sealed their new friendship.

Since then, he'd come over regularly. They'd laughed and carried on easy conversations about the day's events, and it was always late when Greg finally noticed the time and went home.

Chelsey was surprised to find how comfortable she'd grown with him. He was an excellent conversationalist—witty and highly intelligent. His goodnight kisses left her breathless, and with a longing she found hard to define. He was passionate, ardent, attentive, but becoming increasingly paranoid that Thorny would learn of their clandestine meetings.

Sighing, she went back to her reports, wondering why her eyes kept returning to the orchid, instead of Neil's roses. Chelsey had experienced a rush of delight when Greg had displayed mild annoyance that she had accepted two dinner dates with Neil this past week. Her smile deepened as she recalled how Greg had been unable to conceal his relief when those dates had fallen through because of hospital emergencies.

Careful, Chelsey, she warned herself. *Greg may be fun to be with, but he isn't in the market for a lasting relationship.* If he were, he wouldn't hesitate about letting Thorny know they were dating now.

She knew Greg said he didn't want Thorny to think he could suddenly start running his life, but Chelsey wondered if the real reason was that Greg didn't want her to think *she* could start running his life.

Either way, his attitude was beginning to hurt her feelings.

It was after six before Chelsey could get away. She left the building with an armload of reports. The night air felt blissfully cool against her flushed cheeks as she hurried down the steps.

Greg was just walking up the steps.

"Well, hello there." He reached out and prevented a bulging stack of folders from toppling to the ground.

"Thanks." Chelsey shifted the papers into order. "Greg! I thought you were out of the country." She had to restrain her excitement at seeing him.

"I wound up things early. My plane just got in, and I thought I'd stop by and visit with Pop before I went home." Seeing the open emotion in her eyes, his gaze grew tender. "How are you?"

"Fine." She smiled. "I believe I saw Thorny on the way to the dining room as I was leaving."

"Good. I'll catch him there." Greg's eyes traveled over her lightly. "Have you had dinner?"

"No." He had a special way of looking at her, one she was beginning to cherish.

"If you'll hang around a few minutes, we'll grab something to eat together."

Greg realized though he'd only been gone a few days he'd missed her. He'd missed her sunny disposition and her lovely smile. More and more he realized she was becoming an important part of his life. She would pop into his mind various times during the day—during business meetings, when he was showering, or as he was driving. She was his last thought at night, and his first each morning. He told himself he'd stop by Rosehaven to see Thorny, but deep down, he knew there was another more personal attraction that brought him straight from the airport.

"I'm sorry, but I can't have dinner with you."

"Seeing that heart surgeon again?" Greg irritably shifted his weight from one foot to the other.

She smiled, recognizing a hint of jealousy in his voice. "No, I'm not seeing Neil. And I'd like nothing better than to have dinner with you, but I really can't."

"Why can't you?" It suddenly dawned on him that he'd deliberately cut his trip short so he could see her this evening.

"I have to run to the pet store."

"Pet store?"

"I've ordered a kitten."

"A kitten? For yourself?"

She smiled again. "No, for Ida Munsington."

Greg experienced a flood of relief that her date was with a pet store, not the doctor. "Well, look. I'm good with cats. Why don't I go with you? We can still pick up something to eat on the way."

"Can you spare the time?" She was thrilled that he was offering to go along with her. The pet store was twenty miles away, and she hated to drive on the turnpike after dark—not to mention her pleasure in having his unexpected company for the evening.

"For you, I can. Give me a few minutes with Pop, then we'll be on our way."

"All right. I'll just drop off these files, change clothes and meet you back here in thirty minutes."

He winked. "Sounds good."

As Chelsey started past him, she remembered the lovely orchid he'd sent. "Oh, by the way, thanks for the orchid, Greg. It's beautiful."

Greg turned. "Orchid?"

"Yes, it's lovely. You shouldn't have."

"Oh . . . good. Glad you liked it."

She flashed him another sunny smile. "Well, see you soon."

"Yeah, soon."

What orchid? Greg wondered as he proceeded up the steps, and then it hit him.

Damn! Thorny had struck again.

"ALL RIGHT. Who sent Chelsey Stevens the orchid?"

"I did."

"And you signed *my* name?"

"I thought she'd like it better if it came from you."

"Pop," Greg took a seat opposite Thorny, "you have to stop this."

"What?"

"This ridiculous matchmaking! I want you to promise me you'll stop."

"I'm only thinking of our welfare."

"Our welfare? Our welfare! How does my marital status affect your welfare?"

"It just does. I don't want you to be old and all alone." *And if you were married, I wouldn't be stuck painting duck decoys for the rest of my life,* he added silently.

"Will you let me worry about that? I still have a few productive years."

"Not that many. Old age gets here faster than you think, believe me. You need children to care for you, children who will stick you in a retirement center the minute your arches break down and your cholesterol count goes up."

"Pop!" It wasn't like Thorny to be sarcastic. The deterioration in his disposition was growing worse.

Greg was doing everything within his power to keep his father happy, but Thorny wasn't willing to cooperate anymore.

"Come on, Pop, Rosehaven wasn't entirely my idea. You were the one who made the final decision. Aren't you happy here?"

"Oh, Rosehaven's all right." Thorny let a little wistfulness slip into his voice. "But maybe it would be better if I moved back in with you."

Since his plan to get Greg a wife wasn't working, maybe he'd resort to begging.

"Pop, you know it would be fine with me, but who would take care of you? Camille would never permit it."

"Yeah, I know." Thorny sighed. "What about that housekeeper you hired?"

"She quit."

"When?"

"The day after you were there playing pool. You didn't do something to offend her, did you?"

"Oh, no. No, not a thing." Time to change the subject, Thorny decided. "How was your trip?"

Greg wasn't sure whether to believe his father or not. "Fine. Has Camille called?"

"Four times this week." Thorny toyed with the television remote control, flipping absently through the channels. It'd been a long, boring day, and the evening didn't hold much promise for improvement. If he were at Greg's house, he'd fix some buttered popcorn. "Camille and Herb are going on another cruise."

"That's nice."

"Yeah, I'd like to go on a cruise." At this point, Thorny would settle for a float in a canoe.

Greg sat for a moment, debating the wisdom of admitting to Thorny that he was meeting Chelsey in a few minutes. While the news would undoubtedly raise his father's sagging spirits, Greg didn't want to raise his hopes, too. And it would if he told him, so he decided to compromise.

"Look, Pop." Greg moved to the bed to maintain eye contact. "Would it make you feel any better if you knew I'd been seeing someone for the past couple of weeks?"

Thorny glanced up. "You have?" Although the news should have encouraged him, Thorny felt strangely disappointed. He'd had his heart set on Chelsey.

"Yes."

"A woman?"

"No, a tractor. Of course, it's a woman!"

"Who?"

"Does it matter?"

"I guess not."

"Let's just say she's a lovely lady I know you'd approve of. I'm seeing her again this evening. If, and it's a big if, anything serious develops, you'll be the first to know."

"Well, I guess that's a start."

"I'm glad you think so."

"Are you seeing one of your secretaries?"

"No."

"Oh." Thorny was silent a moment, then, "Didn't you say you took Cindi Richards to lunch not long ago?" Thorny knew Cindi worked in Greg's office.

"Yes." Greg was preoccupied with a television commercial now.

"How was it?"

"How was what?"

"The lunch?"

Greg shrugged. "Okay if you like chicken salad. I have to be going, Pop. Can I get you anything before I leave?"

"No.... Did I mention that Walter Bishop's trying to get Chelsey Stevens's job?"

"I believe you mentioned it." Seven times in the past two visits, Greg thought. The news always served to annoy him. Why hadn't Chelsey discussed the problem with him? He made a mental note to ask her what was going on. "I have to be going."

"Thanks for stopping by."

"I'll give you a ring tomorrow...and, Pop, keep what I've said about my seeing a woman under your hat. Okay?"

"Okay. Say hello to Chelsey if you happen to see her on your way out. I think she works late once in a while."

Greg paused in the doorway. "Pop, you know what your trouble is?"

Thorny sighed. *I should by now,* he thought. *Lord knows, everyone else tells me often enough.* "What's my trouble, son?"

"You worry too much."

"Is that it?"

"It's the truth. You've worried about your kids all your life. It's time you sat back and let us do the worrying now."

"I guess you're right." Thorny supposed it wouldn't hurt to humor him. He still had a lot to learn.

"I know I am. So stop your worrying."

"Okay, but if you do happen to see Ms. Stevens on your way out, be nice to her."

Greg nodded. "If I see Ms. Stevens, I promise I'll be extremely nice to her."

The irony of his words made Greg wince.

THE TINY BUNDLES of fur tumbled and scrambled over one another happily.

Chelsey knelt and sat back on her heels, studying the kittens. Each one was adorable. It was impossible to make a selection. "I don't know. What do you think?" She looked to Greg, hoping he'd make the decision for her.

"I'm always partial to the underdog. How about the black one?"

Chelsey started to reach for the smallest kitten when another pushed the runt out of the way and scampered onto Chelsey's lap.

"Oh, dear. Sibling rivalry," Chelsey laughed softly as she scooped up the runt and hugged it to her bosom.

Greg watched, discovering he felt envious of the kitten.

"I just don't know which one to pick," she confessed. "I want them all!"

"Then take them all," Greg suggested.

"Six kittens! I'd love to, but I can't have any of them." Giving the runt one last hug, she set it gently back in the pen. "My allergies won't permit me to have pets." She studied the kittens for a few more moments before picking up a tiny calico. "I like this one."

Greg helped Chelsey to her feet, and they went to make the purchase. As they passed the bird cages, Chelsey paused to admire the colorful parrots and cockatoos.

"Aren't they pretty? Polly want a cracker? Polly want a cracker?" Chelsey leaned over, coaxing one of the birds to speak.

"Gregie wants a hamburger. Gregie wants a hamburger."

Chelsey glanced up and grinned. "Is this your way of telling me you're hungry?"

"Let's just say I'd arm wrestle the bird for a cracker," Greg said dryly.

They'd almost made it to the register when Chelsey paused again.

"Now what?"

"See that cute bird sitting on the orange roost?"

"Yeah, what about it?"

"It's a cockateel."

"Okay," Greg allowed. "It's a cockateel. Are they good with dumplings?"

"Greg. You don't eat them." She leaned closer to study the gray, yellow-headed bird. It was a cute, perky little thing. "Louella loves birds."

"Louella? The retired actress?"

"Yes, she'd love that bird."

"Where would she keep it?"

"In her room. It could fill a lot of lonely hours," Chelsey mused.

Greg watched as Chelsey summoned a clerk to retrieve the bird. This was a side of Chelsey he'd never seen. She actually loved all those old people. She was one of the few who really cared if they were lonely or hurting, so much so she'd spend her free time buying kittens and cockateels to brighten their days.

When they left the store an hour later, Chelsey carried the kitten and a basket, while Greg carried a bird cage, the cockateel, two boxes of birdseed, a litter box, and three cans of cat food.

Greg realized the relationship was getting serious.

Later, on the drive home, Chelsey was still protesting the fact that Greg had insisted on paying for all the merchandise. The total had come to a staggering amount, and Chelsey was embarrassed.

"You really shouldn't have."

"I wanted to," he dismissed easily, pulling into the line of traffic. "It will make up for the orchid I didn't send you."

Chelsey glanced over at him. "You didn't send me the orchid?"

Greg shrugged sheepishly.

"Oh, dear. Then who . . . ? Oh my." Thorny. Thorny had sent the flowers in Greg's name. She should have suspected.

"Pop sent the orchid."

"I see." Chelsey leaned her head against the seat back and stroked the kitten as they drove along the crowded turnpike. She felt a sting of disappointment that Greg wasn't the one who'd sent the flower, but then, why should he? "It was lovely, no matter who sent it."

"Are you upset?"

"Heavens no. Why should I be?"

"It wasn't fair of Pop to send flowers in my name," Greg said. "I like to send my own flowers."

"He meant well."

"He means for me to marry you," Greg stated.

She smiled. "Well now, he can't very well accomplish that without your knowledge, can he?"

Greg frowned. "I don't know. That's what worries me."

Chelsey chuckled.

The bird began making a terrible racket in the back seat. "Who did you say the kitten was for?" Greg asked a few minutes later.

"Ida Munsington. She's been miserable since her husband passed away. I thought having a pet might ease her loneliness."

Chelsey's features were illuminated attractively by the lights from the dashboard, and Greg found it hard to keep his attention on the road. "That's very thoughtful of you."

"It's nothing. I see so much loneliness." She sighed. "I suppose it goes with the job, but it always bothers me."

"The elderly don't have a patent on loneliness."

Chelsey thought Greg's voice suddenly sounded very tired. She ached to lay her hand on his shoulder and tell him how sorry she was that he'd lost his young wife. But she didn't. Greg had never mentioned his wife, and she knew he would when he felt the time was right.

"They certainly don't have," Chelsey agreed.

"Growing old must be hell. It never used to bother Pop, but lately he seems depressed."

"We're all getting older," Chelsey conceded, "but it doesn't have to be an unpleasant experience."

"I don't know how you figure that. I think it's awful," Greg admitted. "Your hair goes first, then your looks, then your health, then whatever is left deserts you. I dread it."

"I know, but I'm looking for a certain amount of contentment, too. You know, a job well done, maybe growing old with someone I love—that sort of thing." She glanced at Greg and smiled. "And there's still a lot of flirting going on among all those old people."

"You're kidding."

"I'm not! We had a wedding last spring. The groom was ninety-four and the bride was eighty-seven." She leaned closer. "It's no secret around Rosehaven that if Fern Silsby could manage it, Thorny would be the next one to walk down the aisle. Just think, Greg. Fern could be your new mother."

Greg winced. "I've warned Thorny that if he doesn't let up on trying to marry us, I'm going to encourage Fern to go for it."

Chelsey arched her brow defensively. "You're that desperate, huh?"

Greg reached over and pulled Chelsey close, and she laughed and snuggled contentedly into his side.

"I promised Pop I would be nice to you," Greg teased. He buried his face in her hair for a moment, inhaling its fresh scent.

"Do you find that so difficult?"

"Not in the least." They exchanged a brief kiss before Greg turned his attention back to his driving.

"How was Thorny?"

"Okay, I guess.... No, he wasn't," Greg amended after second thought. "He was in another one of his strange moods."

"Oh dear. I've noticed he hasn't been himself lately."

"I know." Greg thought for a moment. He hated to mislead Thorny, but maybe his father's mood would improve now that he knew Greg was seeing someone.

Seeking to lighten his mood, Chelsey leaned over and whispered into his ear, "About your being nice to me...when do you plan to start?" She kissed her way from his ear, around his cheek, and paused just inches from his mouth.

"Hello," she whispered seductively.

"Hello, you wicked woman."

His arm came around her, and he drew her close to give her another quick kiss. When he almost ran off the road, he scowled at her and said sternly, "You're too distracting."

She smiled and nuzzled his neck. "Wonderful."

Greg regained control of the car, but she noticed he kept her pressed closely to his side.

"I'll make it a point to let Thorny know whether you've kept your word. The kiss was nice—brief, but nice," Chelsey admitted.

He winked at her, knowing she had no plans to tell Thorny of their relationship. "You haven't seen anything yet. I can get a lot nicer."

"Yeah?"

"Yeah, the minute we get rid of the bird in the back seat and the— Damn!" Greg sucked in his breath as the kitten, who climbed out of its basket, dug its claws painfully into his leg in its attempt to scramble into his lap. Chelsey plucked the kitten out of his lap and hugged Greg. She couldn't remember when she'd been so happy.

An hour later, the car turned into the Bradford estate and headed up the drive, the animals having been tucked securely away at Rosehaven. Chelsey thought Greg had forgotten his invitation for dinner, but her stomach told her it hadn't.

Greg pulled the car into the garage, switched off the engine and punched the button for the door to close. A moment later the lights went out, throwing the garage into total darkness.

"Now let's see how brave you are, Ms. Stevens."

"Oh dear," she bantered, "is my virtue about to be in jeopardy?"

"It's entirely possible." Chelsey's breathing quickened as Greg turned and drew her into his arms.

"You sound as if that scares you, Greg."

"It does. It scares me to death." His voice had grown solemn now, all traces of the earlier playfulness gone.

"Would you like to talk about it?"

"I don't know.... I guess we should." He sighed and buried his face in the warmth of her neck. "You know I was married once."

"Yes."

"And my wife...died."

"Yes." She wanted to make this easier for him, but she didn't know how.

"That was five years ago. Since then I've dated, but somehow something has always been missing," he confessed.

"I'm sorry."

"You should be." His lips trailed feather kisses along the slender column of her neck. The darkness, the intimacy, his softly spoken words, all served to make her grow limp with longing. "When you came along, Chelsey, you made me feel alive again. I'm not sure I like your doing that."

His mouth sought and found hers. They kissed deeply for a long moment. The feel of his body pressing against hers teased and tormented, awakening her every nerve to tingling awareness.

"What was your wife like?"

Greg was silent for a moment before he replied softly. "Mary Beth? In many ways you remind me of her. The way you smile, your sense of humor, the way you're able to cope when most women would be throwing their hands up in despair..."

Chelsey knew she had just been given a beautiful, and sincere, compliment. "I think I would have liked her."

"You would have. She was some lady...." He was silent for a moment. "What about you. Any old loves that still haunt you?"

"No. I almost got married once, but he wanted me to stay home and raise avocados and children—in that order. He had a small farm about fifty miles from here."

"And you didn't want to?"

"I wanted a career more than guacamole dip and dirty diapers, so we agreed it would be a mistake."

He chuckled and pressed his mouth to her throat. "What was his name?"

"William Clapsaddle." She giggled.

"Damn."

"It's the truth. Horrible isn't it? That's another reason I changed my mind. Chelsey Clapsaddle somehow lacked something."

"Well, I feel sorry for poor old Willy Clapsaddle, but I confess I'm glad you changed your mind." Conversation faded as their lips melted together into another prolonged kiss.

"If Pop had any idea what I was thinking about you right now, he'd have no trouble sleeping tonight," Greg murmured as their lips parted long moments later.

Chelsey's fingers reached to gently explore Greg's face. He felt so good, so reassuring. His familiar scent engulfed her senses, and she realized just how deeply she was falling in love with him.

"And what about you?" she asked softly. "Will you have trouble sleeping tonight?" She knew she was baiting...teasing...tempting; but she didn't care.

"I don't know.... I suppose that will depend on you, my love." His mouth met hers again, hungrily exploring the sweetness.

My love. The words echoed enticingly in her ears. He'd never used such an intimate endearment before. Was he suggesting that she stay with him tonight? Her mind reeled at the tempting thought. She'd always considered herself a woman of the eighties, but she didn't believe in a dinner-then-off-to-bed sort of date. Chelsey wanted so much more from Greg. A commitment—but was he ready to give one?—an assurance he would return her love—could he?—the hope that she wasn't being a complete fool... But the deepening ache inside her reminded her of needs that cried out for fulfillment.

"Let's go into the house," Greg urged moments later, his own spiraling needs filling his voice with urgency.

Chelsey wanted time to think, but her mind refused to function. His heady kisses made her feel powerless to make a sound judgment.

"Greg, I don't think we should..."

Amid her whispers of indecision, Greg eased Chelsey out of the car and lifted her in his arms. Their mouths met again and again...and again. Hungry, sweet, mindless kisses that blocked out reason and the last shred of sanity.

"You realize this can only complicate matters," she implored. At this point, she could still walk away, unscathed. But if she allowed her heart to rule, she could be deeply hurt. She would want more than one night, but would he?

"Don't think about it," he whispered, his voice shaken by emotion as she trembled in his arms.

"It's foolish..." Their mouths blended again.

"Foolish," he agreed.

"Absurd..."

He nodded, but his mouth never left hers as he carried her out of the garage and strode purposefully toward the house.

Chelsey sensed that in the morning she'd be horrified that she was so weak...so timorous...so hopelessly in love.

It was too foolish...too soon...too uncertain...too inevitable...too overwhelming. And entirely too late to do anything about it.

Chapter Eleven

Later, Chelsey's face held the radiant glow of a woman who'd been thoroughly and exquisitely loved. On a cushy, floral-upholstered sofa, she sat with her knees pulled up to her chin, her hands clasped tightly around her ankles, watching the fire burn low in the grate.

The soft ray of a lamp bathed the Bradford living room in a rich, warm glow. The room was refined, yet comfortable with several intimate seating areas scattered about. Furnished in shades of regal red, royal blue and creamy ecru, the simple elegance of the room was breathtaking.

A full moon shone through the glistening French doors, casting its mellow pattern on the floor, as Chelsey tried to envision Greg as a young boy running through the house, his boyish shouts filling the now silent rooms with laughter and joy.

The image made her smile. What a wonderful childhood he must have had, growing up with a father like Thorny, a loving mother and a caring sister.

Chelsey snuggled more deeply within Greg's robe and breathed in his familiar scent. She couldn't recall ever feeling so content, so at peace.

They had talked of how their childhoods had been so different. Chelsey's early years had been a succession of foster homes. While she was never mistreated, she had yet to experience the exhilaration of close family ties. They were something she longed to have someday: a family, a home, someone who loved her.

Greg walked into the room carrying a large tray. Setting it down on the coffee table, he approached the sofa. Leaning down, he gave Chelsea a long, meaningful kiss. "You okay?"

She smiled. "I'm fine."

"I hope you like scrambled eggs. It's all I could find."

"I love scrambled eggs." He handed her a plate from the tray, then took his own and sat down beside her.

"What's this I hear about one of your coworkers trying to take your job?"

His unexpected, out-of-the-blue question caught her off guard.

"Where did you hear that?"

"From Pop, at least twice every time I've visited him lately."

Chelsey took a small bite to test the eggs, wondering if Greg really wanted to know or if he just wanted to make casual conversation. "I don't have concrete evidence that someone is actually after my job. You know how gossip is."

"But what do you think?"

"The eggs are very good," she complimented him.

Greg's gaze pinned her. "Stop evading the question. Is someone hassling you?"

"No one is hassling me," Chelsey denied truthfully. "It's more subtle than that."

Greg set his plate back on the tray and picked up a cup of steaming coffee. He sent her a level gaze. "Are you going to tell me about it or am I going to have to pull it out of you?"

"Really, Greg. There's nothing to tell." She felt foolish confiding in him. She'd always fought her own battles; she'd had to. And while they'd just shared a couple of the most meaningful hours of her life, she still saw no reason to involve him in her personal problems.

"Pop thinks there is." Greg's gaze grew infinitely more tender. "Come on, Chelsey. Tell me about it."

With a sigh, she set her plate down. Somehow she knew she could confide in Greg and he'd understand. "It's simply a case of male chauvinism."

"Wait a minute now. Not all men are chauvinists."

"Maybe not all, but Walter Bishop certainly fits the description."

"Walter Bishop? Is he the one giving you trouble?"

"Walter and his wife, Harriet. They both work in the administration at Rosehaven. And both deeply resent the fact that the job of chief administrator was given to me instead of Walter."

"Is Walter as qualified as you are for the position?"

"Yes, but it's his personality that hinders him. He doesn't relate well with the residents."

"Well, wanting your job and getting it are two different things," Greg said, dismissing the subject easily. "As long as you perform, you don't have a thing to worry about."

"Normally, I wouldn't worry, but I'm afraid that lately Walter and Harriet have lots of rope to hang me."

"Why?"

"Because—" Chelsey hated to name Thorny and the other three as the root of the problem "—I seem to have run into some difficulty controlling a few of the residents."

"Pop," Greg deduced glumly.

"Not just Thorny. There's Ian and Otto and Lars, too. Their families aren't too happy about my inability to halt unauthorized excursions. I'm not sure whether Walter and Harriet are aware of those escapades, but if my hunch is correct, they are."

"Which means your superiors will hear of them, too."

She sighed. "Yes."

"Chelsey, I don't know what to say." Greg set his cup back on the tray. "I'm sure Pop would be upset if he thought his actions were endangering your job. I'll talk to him first thing tomorrow morning."

"I don't blame him for getting restless." Chelsey rose and walked over to warm herself by the fire. "Darn it, Greg! I should be able to perform my duties more efficiently. Maybe Walter is right; maybe I don't manage Rosehaven the way it should be managed."

"That's crazy. Those people love you," Greg chided. "Would Walter Bishop care enough to buy a lonely widow a kitten or Louella a bird to brighten her days?"

"Walter may fall short on personality, but I believe he cares for the welfare of the residents, Greg. And he has a point. An administrator should have control."

"Then tell Walter he can have the job."

"And then what do I do?"

"Find another one."

"Of course. Just like that."

"It won't come to that," Greg reasoned. "When it comes down to the nitty-gritty, I guarantee your boss is going to realize that your work requires no apologies. If Walter Bishop were running Rosehaven right now, Thorny, Ian, Otto and Lars would still be breaking rules. Those men are over seventy, dammit, and they're bored out of their gourds. They aren't concerned about rules and regulations. What do they have to lose by stepping out of line occasionally? It can't hurt you. You have to maybe give a little."

"I don't know, Greg. . . ." Changing the status quo sounded too risky to Chelsey. She didn't have a security blanket to fall back on if her superiors didn't agree with such unorthodox care of the elderly.

"Look, trust me on this," Greg coaxed. "I've been in management for years, and I know what it takes to back me down. If I have an employee with your sort of leadership qualities, I'm not going to fire her because of situations beyond her control. Let me give you a piece of sound advice: stand up for yourself. If someone calls you on the carpet, call his bluff." Greg moved off the sofa to gather Chelsey up and into his arms. "And if anyone gives you trouble, you come to me."

Wrapping her arms around his neck, she gazed into his eyes adoringly. "And you'll do what?"

He tweaked her nose affectionately. "We'll both hop the first freight out of town."

NOVEMBER FADED UNEVENTFULLY into December. Greg and Chelsey were seeing each other constantly. When Greg was away on business, he phoned twice a day and sent orchids. When he was in town, he was a regular visitor at Chelsey's cottage and she often visited him at his house.

They rarely went to public places, choosing instead to spend their precious few hours together alone.

Had Thorny known of the ever deepening relationship, his attitude might have been different. As it was, he was discouraged.

Even reminding himself that Greg was dating someone, didn't help. Whoever she was, Thorny knew she couldn't be the right one. Thorny was convinced that Chelsey was the right one, if Greg would only wake up.

But gradually Thorny was beginning to accept the fact that wasn't likely to happen.

Thorny just hoped Camille was happy now, and that she'd soon have a family of her own so she would stop mothering him.

Chelsey's mood was the exact opposite of Thorny's. Other than Walter Bishop's continuing intimidation, her life couldn't have been better. Sometimes she wished Walter would disappear, but he was there every day hovering over her work with a fine-tooth comb. Their offices were close, and Chelsey found herself going out of her way to avoid him.

But she still couldn't remember when she'd been happier. There was a glow about her that almost all who knew her commented upon.

The only flaw in her happiness was the nagging question of why Greg insisted on keeping their relationship a secret. She'd agreed not to let her secretary or the residents of Rosehaven know that she was seriously involved with Thorny's son. She didn't act like she minded the secrecy, but she did.

She'd avoided Neil Matlock lately. She considered her involvement with Greg a serious one, whether he did or not.

She could recite Greg's reasons for the need to continue the secrecy by heart. He wanted to enjoy their relationship without pressure from Thorny to set a marriage date; he was teaching Thorny a lesson by showing him that he couldn't meddle in Greg's personal life.

But deep down, all his excuses were beginning to haunt Chelsey. Was there another reason Greg wasn't willing to declare his love? Chelsey wondered if Greg was so unsure of their fairy-tale involvement that he thought if he told the world his feelings for her would evaporate. Or was he just afraid that Chelsey would be unnecessarily hurt if he decided to end their involvement?

The uncertainty was always with her. But just when she'd decide to confront Greg and clear the air, the problem would slip her mind. Greg had an uncanny way of making her forget even her own name.

Take, for instance, the afternoon when she had been on her way to a meeting with marketing director Frank Williams. She hadn't slept much the night before, mulling the problem over in her mind. As she had rushed down the corridor, she'd seen a figure hurriedly approaching her. When she recognized Greg, she was stunned. She'd thought he was still in Japan and wouldn't be back for days.

"Hi," she'd said lamely.

"Hello, beautiful." Abruptly and automatically Greg had reached to hug her before realizing they were being watched. Just as abruptly he had let his hands drop limply back to his sides. "I have exactly two hours before my plane leaves for Washington," he had stated calmly, his eyes lazily relaying the message his kiss would have communicated. "Let's go somewhere where we can be alone."

"Oh, Greg... I'm sorry, but I have an appointment."

Leaning closer, his disquieting gaze had caused a familiar longing to wash over her. "Break it."

"Greg—"

"Break it, please. Two hours—two short hours—then I'm gone for another four days."

The four days had loomed as bleakly before them as four eternities.

A few moments later Frank Williams received a brief phone message from Chelsey, breaking the appointment.

Chelsey had noticed Walter glance up from his seat behind the nursing desk where he sat reading a chart. He'd frowned as he watched Greg and Chelsey exchange a few personal words.

A few seconds later Walter had handed the nurse the chart and stood up.

"Let's go." Greg had taken Chelsey's arm and they'd walked down the corridor together.

"Walter is watching us," Chelsey confided.

"Doesn't he always?"

Though Walter didn't seem to bother Greg, he was a nagging irritant in the back of Chelsey's mind the rest of that day.

Now it was Saturday. Thorny, Ian, Otto and Lars sat at the breakfast table wistfully looking out the window. On a day as sunny and brisk as this one, there should have been something to do besides sit around and grow older, but they couldn't think what.

Rosehaven's corridors and lobbies were decked out in their Christmas finery. "Silent Night" filtered sweetly over the intercom. But the gaily lit trees and snow-covered wreaths did little to boost Thorny's declining morale.

Ian had come down with a cold that he couldn't seem to shake. The change in weather had caused Otto's arthritis to flare up, and Lars's blood sugar was giving him trouble.

Thorny's health was good, except for the unprecedented boredom.

Grace Martin paused on her way into work, carrying a cup of hot coffee. "Good morning, gentlemen."

"Morning, Grace." Thorny spoke, and the others nodded their heads. "What are you doing here on Saturday?"

"Trying to catch up on a few things I've let slide." Placing a supportive hand on Thorny's shoulder, Grace leaned over and inquired softly, "Are we making any progress?"

Thorny knew what Grace meant. Early in his campaign to bring Greg and Chelsey together, he had elicited her help. He figured if Grace could undermine Neil Matlock's efforts to see Chelsey, then Greg would stand a better chance of capturing her attention.

Now, since Greg was seeing another woman, there seemed no purpose in continuing the maneuver.

"No, Grace, it doesn't look good," Thorny admitted.

"Well, I want you to know I'm doing all I can," Grace whispered. "But it's getting risky. Chelsey would have my head if she knew I was deliberately misleading Dr. Matlock."

"Does he call often?"

"Not as much as he did for a while." Grace glanced around to be sure no one was eavesdropping. "I've mislaid messages, 'forgotten' to tell Chelsey he'd called, and scheduled her for meetings when I knew he was going to stop by. I think he's getting discouraged.''

''Well, don't endanger your job, Grace. We've done all we can. I don't know what's wrong with Greg.''

''I hate to see you so down, Thorny.'' Grace could sense defeat in Thorny's tone, and her own spirits began to sag. A love match between Chelsey and Greg would have been exciting.

''Thanks, Grace, but it's no use.'' Thorny patted her hand absently. ''I have to face it. My boy's elevator just don't go all the way to the top.''

After breakfast, the day loomed bleakly before Thorny. Around nine, he decided to visit Ian and was surprised to find his friend still in bed.

Ian opened his eyes and smiled. ''Hi, Thorny.''

''How you doin'?''

''Oh, not so good,'' Ian admitted.

''Cold still bothering you?''

''Yeah.''

They sat in compatible silence for a while. Thorny thought Ian looked bad this morning. The wrinkles in his face were deeper than Thorny remembered, and his hands, clutching the sheet close to his neck, looked like the hands of a man much older.

''Can I get you anything? I have some new magazines Greg brought me. If you want, I'll let you read them first.''

''No, thanks, Thorny. My daughter brings me everything I need.''

Thorny viewed the tray of untouched food still sitting beside Ian's bed. ''I see you didn't eat anything.''

''No, haven't had much appetite lately.''

''What'd the doc say?''

''He said to just lie around and take it easy.'' Ian's voice didn't have the strength it usually had, nor the optimism.

''Well, you'll be fine in a few days.''

"Yeah, I guess so."

Thorny wished he hadn't made that observation. They both knew that at their ages, a simple cold could turn out to be life-threatening. Thorny never thought much about death. He neither feared it, nor welcomed it.

"The lobby looks real nice," he said. "They put the tree up yesterday."

"I always liked Christmas," Ian said. "Elda loved it, especially when the kids were little."

"Elizabeth was the same way. She always went all out. Baked for days." Thorny could almost smell the tantalizing aromas.

"Elda always made Christmas cookies." Ian sighed as memories of happier times tore at him. Tears began to gather in his faded blue eyes. "I want to go see Elda before I die, Thorny."

Ian's quietly spoken request took Thorny by surprise. "Come on, Ian. You're not going to die," he soothed gently.

"I want to visit her grave, Thorny."

"Well, maybe if we ask your daughter, she'll take you."

"No, she won't. She thinks it upsets me when I visit Elda."

Thorny patted Ian's hand reassuringly. "Well, maybe she's right, Ian. It doesn't help to keep visiting the grave." Thorny knew that from his own experiences. For the first year after Elizabeth's death, Thorny had visited her grave every day. But it didn't help. Usually, it made him feel worse.

"I want you to take me to see her, Thorny." As Ian looked at Thorny, his eyes filled with longing. "Please help me."

Thorny rose and went to stand at the window. He gazed out across the grounds, trying to collect his thoughts. "Ian, how could I do that? I can't drive anymore."

"I don't know. Maybe we could take a bus? Elda's not buried too far away. Maybe ten, fifteen miles." The new hope that had suddenly sprung to life in Ian's voice made Thorny realize he couldn't refuse him outright.

"But a bus may not go anywhere near the cemetery."

"It might not, but you could find out, couldn't you Thorny?"

"Even if one does, you're too sick to ride a bus," Thorny reminded him. "Why don't we take a cab?"

"No, that costs too much. I want to take the bus. I'll make it," Ian promised. "You just find out which one we have to take to get to Garden of the Saints Cemetery, and I'll make it."

"I don't know, Ian. . . ." Thorny didn't like it. Ian was in no shape to travel. He decided it would be best to stall, hoping this would be a passing whim.

"Well, I'll give it some thought, Ian."

"Thorny—" Ian's head came off his pillow, and his gaze met Thorny's solidly "—if you don't take me, I'll go by myself. I want to visit Elda one more time."

Talk like that depressed Thorny. "I'll see what I can work out, Ian. That's all I can promise."

Ian lay back on his pillow, and his eyes drooped wearily closed. "Thank you, Thorny. I know if anyone can do it, you can."

In the lounge later that morning, Ian's request still hung heavily in Thorny's mind. "You know what would probably make us feel better, Henry?" Thorny was staring out the window as he sat with Henry Rothman.

"No, what?"

"Playing a little golf." Thorny guessed he could find out easily enough which bus went by the cemetery where Elda was buried. He could do that much for Ian.

"Golf?" Henry hadn't played golf in years.

"Yeah, let's take a bus to Pebble Beach and play eighteen holes." By proposing a bus ride, Thorny could acquire the information he needed.

"A bus? Wouldn't it be easier to take a cab?"

"Maybe, but we haven't got anything else to do. Let's take the bus at least part of the way, then we can take a cab."

"Well, okay...but it's against the rules," Henry reminded Thorny.

"I know." Thorny didn't care if it was against the rules. He'd broken the rules more than once, and nothing major had happened. He remembered a sign he'd seen once that said it was often easier to get forgiveness than permission. Since he was going to be in Rosehaven from now on, Thorny chose that for his new creed.

"HAVE YOU TALKED to your father?"

"No, not lately. Is there something wrong?"

"No, he's fine, Greg, but I'm worried about him." Chelsey had met Greg at the airport this morning. Since it was Saturday, they'd decided to stop at a small café in Carmel for a late lunch.

Greg glanced up from his plate. "Worried? Why?"

"Because I sense a certain depression in him that wasn't there before, and I think you and I are partly responsible for it."

Greg had noticed the change, too, and it concerned him, but then who could figure Thorny's moods lately? "I don't know what to do for him."

"Do you really think it would hurt to let him know we're seeing each other?" Chelsey's heart was in her eyes. She hated to bring up the subject, but she hated the deception more. She'd promised herself she would talk to Greg about the matter the moment he returned from Washington.

Greg reached over and covered her hand with his. "You know what he'd do then," he said gently. "He'd be sending out wedding invitations behind our backs."

"I know, but maybe if he knew his efforts hadn't gone completely unrewarded, he'd feel better."

The reminder of how diligently Thorny had worked to bring them together brought smiles to their faces. It did seem a pity to continue to let him think all his efforts had been wasted. "Couldn't we explain that while we care for each other very deeply..." Chelsey hesitated to use the word love. She'd fallen deeply in love with him, but she wasn't sure he returned the feeling. She loved his sunny disposition, and the sweet sensitivity he tried so hard to conceal. She had come to know his moods, his strengths and his weaknesses, and they only made her love him more.

Mary Beth had been mentioned only once, but there had been something in Greg's voice that had made Chelsey believe the rumors might be true. It was unlikely that anyone could ever take his wife's place. So Chelsey proceeded cautiously. "We could explain to Thorny that we're perfectly content the way we are, and that we don't need a permanent commitment to make us happy."

Greg glanced at her. "Is that how you feel about us? You don't want a permanent commitment?"

Chelsey wasn't sure how to answer. Yes, she would rather be Mrs. Greg Bradford, but she thought it was too soon to push the issue. And she was smart enough to realize she loved him too much to walk away, so what other choice was there? If he needed more time, she would give it to him.

"I'm happy with what we have, Greg."

Greg was surprised, and a little stung, by her answer. For weeks he'd known he was falling in love with her. But the knowledge that she was comfortable with the relationship exactly the way it was didn't please him.

As for marriage, he wasn't sure where he stood on that issue, but it disturbed him to hear Chelsey say that she was content to let their relationship drift along aimlessly.

"Pop wouldn't understand such an arrangement," Greg said flatly. "He believes when a man and a woman fall in love, they eventually get married." There was an edge in his voice that puzzled Chelsey. Did he think she was trying to force a marriage proposal out of him? That was the last thing she wanted him to think.

"Well, things are different nowadays," she conceded, although she wished they weren't. Relationships would be much simpler if black was still black, and white was still white, rather than this murky "I might be here tomorrow, but then again, I might not" attitude. She wanted more from Greg Bradford. "I was just thinking of Thorny...."

"Well, I don't want him to know we're seeing each other," Greg said crossly. "At the moment, I see no point in it." Until Chelsey viewed their relationship with long-range possibilities, Greg wasn't about to tell Thorny.

"All right. Then we'll continue to sneak around." She could barely keep the sarcasm out of her voice as she quickly snatched up her cup of tea and took a swallow.

"Who's sneaking?" Greg challenged. Now he was the one who was puzzled.

"We never go anywhere public," Chelsey accused.

Greg glanced around the crowded room. "What's this if it isn't public?"

"A restaurant, that's what it is. Anyone could believe we just bumped into each other here." Just once she'd like for him to take her somewhere highly visible for a night of dinner and dancing, somewhere nice that said, "Look world! We're together and proud of it!"

"I thought we agreed we'd rather spend our time alone." Greg's hectic travel and business schedule made him long for serenity when he was home. He thought Chelsey felt the same way.

Was that the real reason they ate in dark cafés and split their time between her cottage and his house, or was he afraid someone would see them together, and the word would get back to Thorny? Chelsey thought resentfully. She didn't know what had gotten into her, but she felt very neglected. She suddenly threw prudence to the wind.

"I think you're deliberately avoiding having to make a decision, Greg."

"About what?"

"About us!"

"Good grief. How did we get on this subject?"

"Because you purposely keep avoiding it!"

"Would you like dessert?" Greg asked. A change of subject seemed in order.

"No, thank you." She put her cup back down and reached for her purse. "I want to stop by the Crossroads and do some shopping on my way home." She could barely keep her voice civil. His indifference was beginning to scare her.

"Now?" Greg looked at her as if she'd lost her mind. He'd just gotten home, and he'd assumed they'd spend the rest of the day together.

"Now." She reached for the check.

"Chelsey!" Greg slid out of the booth as she turned on her heel and started for the register. He snatched the check out of her hand irritably. "What's going on?"

"Nothing, I just have shopping I need to do." It was a transparent lie, but it was all she could think of.

Greg reached out and took her arm, gently restraining her. "I thought we'd want to be together for the rest of the day. Can't the shopping wait?" His eyes told her he was sorry. But his words didn't, and that annoyed her.

Their gazes met and held. Chelsey could feel her resolve weakening. "I need some space, Greg. And I think it wouldn't be a bad idea for you, either." Chelsey wasn't sure she could go on indefinitely in Mary Beth's shadow.

"Space? From me?" That hurt. His hand dropped away from her arm as if his fingers had been suddenly burned.

She nodded. She needed time alone to put things into perspective. Exactly where was she going with Greg Bradford? Exactly where did she want to go? At the moment she wasn't sure. "I'll call you later."

"All right...if that's what you want." Greg stepped back, and she slipped hurriedly past him.

He watched with growing bewilderment as she left the café. What happened? Why was she suddenly on the defensive with him? As he inhaled the faint, enchanting fragrance of her perfume that still lingered, a lonely feeling overcame him. Around him several couples sat in booths holding hands and speaking in low, intimate tones, painful reminders that a long, lonely day and night lay ahead of him. Chelsey hadn't been gone five minutes, and he already missed her.

Space? All of a sudden she thought they both needed space. Well, he thought, maybe it was time to give it to her. The relationship had developed so quickly that maybe they did need a cooling-off period to reassess their feelings. The realization only made him feel more miserable.

He'd give her exactly twenty-four hours of "space," then he planned to find out what was really going on.

IT WAS CLOSE to nine o'clock when Thorny and Henry returned to Rosehaven Saturday evening. They were sunburned and tired, but the day had been rewarding. Thorny had shot in the low seventies, and he'd found out what bus to take to Elda's grave.

Walter Bishop was waiting for the two men at the front door.

"Hello, gentlemen."

Thorny paused and glanced at Henry uneasily. He hadn't planned on Walter still being there.

"Hi, Walter. Working a little late, aren't you?"

"Yes." Walter's smile was cool. "I see you have a sunburn. You must have stayed out too long today."

"We played eighteen—"

Thorny punched Henry in the side to prevent him from revealing where they'd been all day.

"Oh . . . yeah. We stayed out too long," Henry amended.

Thorny watched as Walter surveyed the men's attire. They were wearing visors with Pebble Beach boldly inscribed across the front, and Thorny knew if Walter looked close enough he'd see they were still wearing golf shoes. The shoes had been on sale, a bargain both Thorny and Henry had found irresistible. Thorny wished now they'd not decided to wear them home.

"Well, guess we'll turn in." Thorny nudged Henry to move ahead of him. "So long, Walter."

"So long, gentlemen." Walter watched with a smug smile on his face as Thorny and Henry clanked their way down the corridor, the steel spikes on their new golf shoes reverberating loudly against the hushed walls.

Chapter Twelve

Monday morning began normally enough. Chelsey was at her desk earlier than usual. She'd just spent one of the most miserable weekends of her life, and she couldn't wait to get back to an organized routine.

Greg had taken her at her word. He hadn't called, so she'd had plenty of time to wallow in her self-imposed "space."

She realized now she'd been foolish to blow up the way she had. Greg had every right to be upset, but his benign acceptance of her spurt of independence nettled her.

Apparently the relationship meant so little to him that he wasn't concerned about reconciliation. The fact was hard to face.

Shortly before nine, a disheartened Chelsey told Grace to show her first appointment in.

AFTER CONSIDERABLE THOUGHT, Thorny had come to a logical decision. He owed Chelsey Stevens an apology. It hadn't been right to try to force Greg on her.

If they weren't attracted to each other, then they weren't. It wasn't the end of the world, and he realized he'd been wrong to interfere in his son's life.

Even though he had no plans to obey Rosehaven's rules on a regular basis, Thorny had decided he wasn't going to involve Chelsey in his schemes anymore. He didn't want to jeopardize her job, and he didn't want Greg upset with him, so he guessed he wouldn't leave Rosehaven again without permission until things settled down.

Directly after breakfast Monday morning, he went to Chelsey's office to make his apologies.

"Hi there, Grace."

"Hi, Thorny."

"Ms. Stevens busy?"

"She has someone with her right now. Is there something I can help you with?"

"No, I'll just wait. I need to speak to Ms. Stevens personally." Thorny picked up a magazine and took a seat.

Twenty minutes later Chelsey emerged from her office with a distinguished-looking gentleman. They were still engrossed in conversation. "I'm looking forward to meeting your mother, Mr. Keys. It would be a pleasure to have her with us at Rosehaven."

"Thank you, Ms. Stevens. I'm impressed with what I've seen. I'm sure Mother will be, too." The man smiled pleasantly as they shook hands. "I'll be contacting you later in the week to make the final arrangements."

"I'll be looking forward to hearing from you."

Chelsey was starting to go back into her office when she noticed Thorny. "Hi, Thorny. Are you waiting to see me?"

The sight of Greg's father tugged at her heartstrings. For the past hour, she'd been able to block out Saturday afternoon, but seeing Thorny brought the whole unpleasant scene with Greg rushing back.

Laying the magazine aside, Thorny stood up and doffed his new Pebble Beach visor politely. "Yes, ma'am."

"Come on in," she invited and Thorny trailed behind her into the office.

Taking her seat behind the desk, Chelsey smiled. "Is that a new hat you're wearing?"

"Yeah, sort of."

"Have you played Pebble Beach often?"

Thorny grinned guiltily. "Every chance I get."

"It's a lovely course." Chelsey folded her hands. "Now then, what can I do for you?"

"I came to apologize," Thorny began.

"Apologize?"

"Yes, I've been thinking it over, and I don't believe what I've been doing is right, so I thought I'd better make amends."

Chelsey wasn't exactly sure where this was leading, but she had her suspicions. "What is it you've done, Thorny?"

"Well, you see, Ms. Stevens, I've . . . well, not just me," he corrected, "but Ian, Otto, Lars and myself have been trying to pair you off," Thorny admitted.

"With your son, Greg," Chelsey supplied.

"Yes." Thorny raised his brows. "Then you know?"

Chelsey recognized the irony of his statement, and quickly suppressed a smile as she reached up to remove her glasses. "Yes, I know."

"I guess we haven't been too discreet, but the four of us figured you and Greg would make a real nice couple. That's why we've been doing all the things we're not supposed to. We thought if we could throw you two together often enough, something would eventually develop. But it didn't work."

"Oh, but it—" Chelsey barely stopped before admitting too much. "But it's so nice of you to feel that way," she finished lamely. "I'm flattered that you and Ian and Otto and Lars think I'd be a suitable candidate for your son's wife."

"Oh, you are," Thorny assured her, "but lately I've come to realize I shouldn't be trying to interfere in Greg's life. He doesn't like it."

Chelsey closed her eyes and absently rubbed the bridge of her nose as Greg's handsome image came into her mind. How easy it would be for her to confess her love for him to Thorny, but she knew Greg wouldn't approve. "Thorny—"

"Oh, I know what you're gonna say," Thorny interrupted. "You're going to tell me I shouldn't have done it, and you're right. I shouldn't have. That's why I'm here to apologize. I won't be buttin' in again," he finished sincerely. "I promise."

Chelsey's smile was infinitely affectionate. In spite of all the trouble he'd caused, she'd grown to love Thorny. In many ways, Chelsey thought of him as the father she'd never had. "No, I wasn't going to reprimand you, Thorny. I was going to suggest that maybe you should be telling Greg this, and not me," she said gently.

Thorny rolled his visor around in his hands nervously. "I'm going to tell him, but he's not going to take it as well as you are."

"I understand he's back from his recent trip." She reached for the phone. "Why don't I call and tell him you'd like to talk to him this evening?" Chelsey was willing to swallow her injured pride long enough to make the call. Perhaps with Thorny's admission, Greg would be willing to bring their clandestine relationship out into the open.

"That won't be necessary, but thanks anyway. Greg will probably call me sometime today. Then I can tell him."

"Well, I'm sure you'll feel better after you talk to him."

"Probably. I just wanted to let you know that Ian, Otto, Lars and I won't be causing you any more trouble."

Chelsey grinned. "I'm relieved to hear that."

Thorny sighed. "But I'd sure have been glad if our plan had worked out."

"Well, you never know. Greg and I still could make a compatible couple someday." She hated to continue misleading Thorny, yet she felt compelled to give him one small ray of hope that things could work out the way he'd hoped.

"Well, I guess I should just be happy the boy is finally seeing someone," Thorny admitted. "It gives me hope."

The smile on Chelsey's face began to lose some of its animation. "Greg's seeing someone?"

"Yeah." Thorny turned and started for the door as Chelsey rose to her feet on shaky limbs.

"Thorny, wait a minute." Her heart began to pound against her ribs.

Thorny paused. "Yes, ma'am?"

"Did you say Greg is . . . seeing someone?" It was all she could do to keep the hysteria out of her voice.

"Yeah. I think it's one of the secretaries at the office," Thorny confided. Actually he was only speculating, but he'd put it together when Greg had mentioned that he'd taken Cindi Richards to lunch. Greg didn't take women to lunch, so Thorny figured she had to be the one he was seeing.

A tight band had suddenly formed around Chelsey's throat, threatening to shut off her air supply. "Are you sure?"

Thorny looked at her, puzzled by her sudden interest. "Yeah, that's what he said." Thorny shook his head thoughtfully. "Cindi Richards is a nice-enough girl, I guess—a little bubble-brained at times, but nice."

Cindi's I.Q. and her bust measurement were close to the same number, Thorny was sure, but he was determined to let Greg make his own choices from now on.

"Cindi Richards?" Chelsey moved away from her desk woodenly. "Greg is seeing a woman by the name of Cindi Richards?" she repeated, trying to make the words sink in.

"Yeah. You know her?"

"No." Chelsey's reply was abnormally sharp as she snapped out of her stupor. The realization that Greg had been playing her for a fool threatened to bring scalding tears to her eyes.

"Well, I guess I'll be running along." Thorny placed his visor back on his head. "Oh, by the way," he said in a low, conspiratorial tone, "Greg told me not to mention that he was seeing anyone, so if you don't mind, just sort of keep it under your hat," he urged. Thorny knew he shouldn't have said anything about Cindi, but he thought it would probably make Chelsey feel better to know that she was off the hook. After all, it was the least he could do for his son. "You know how Greg is about his personal life."

The fire in Chelsey's eyes was hard to control as she slapped her hand down on the top of her desk angrily. "Yes, I think I do!"

Thorny blinked, stunned by her adamant agreement. "Well, I guess I've taken up enough of your time." He edged toward the door uneasily. "Thanks for hearing me out."

Chelsey sank weakly back into her chair as Thorny hastily exited the office.

All along, she thought, *Greg has been seeing another woman while he was pretending to fall in love with me.* The knowledge was like a hot knife slicing deeply into her heart. No wonder he'd insisted no one be told of their relationship. It would be difficult, even for Greg Bradford, to explain why he was seeing two women at the same time.

Chelsey was still reeling from Thorny's surprise announcement when the office door flew open. An irate Louella stood in the doorway, clutching her bird, Cecil B., protectively to her bosom. "You simply *must* do something about that obnoxious mouser!"

Chelsey stared at her vacantly. "Obnoxious mouser?" She had a sinking feeling that this wasn't going to be her day.

Ida Munsington angrily pushed her way around Louella's stalwart frame and barged into Chelsey's office in tears. "Don't listen to a word she says, Ms. Stevens," Ida cried. Ida was clenching her kitten that was shaking like a leaf in a hailstorm from all the commotion. "Cecil B. brought this all on himself!"

"Liar!" Louella shouted.

"Weirdo!" Ida returned defiantly.

"Ladies, ladies, please!" Chelsey was on her feet, plainly shocked by the women's display of tempers. Never had she heard nice, sweet Ida Munsington use such a belligerent tone. "What is the meaning of this?"

Louella narrowed her eyes and pointed an accusing finger at the cat. "That animal tried to eat Cecil B.!"

Ida gasped indignantly. "She did not! Cecil B. was taunting my little Pudmuffin!"

"Taunting? Taunting, indeed! How dare you say Cecil B. was taunting that nasty fur ball! He was only trying to get a little exercise when your hooligan tried to eat him!"

"Cecil B. should never have been out of his cage," Ida exclaimed, piously drawing Pudmuffin closer to her chest. "Ms. Stevens told both of us we were to keep the animals in our rooms."

"Then why was Pudmuffin," Louella asked, spitting the name contemptuously, "out in the hall?"

"I was tidying up, and she just roamed out of the room. After all, Louella, my baby likes exercise, too!"

"Ladies, ladies!" Chelsey tried again to break into their heated disagreement. "Can't we discuss this in reasonable tones?"

"I insist that you have that cat removed from the premises, or I will have my agent move *me* elsewhere!" Louella threatened.

"You don't have an agent, you fruitcake!" Ida glared at Louella boldly.

The ache in Chelsey's head began to throb like a war drum as she scrambled toward the door. The women's angry voices had caused a small, inquisitive crowd to gather.

Chelsey smiled lamely at Grace as she started to close the door. "Hold my calls."

Something told her this was going to take a while.

"WE HAVE FOUND that relieving the Alzheimer's patient out of the responsibility of having to make choices greatly reduces his anxieties," Meredith Rider explained.

Chelsey reached for the Excedrin bottle and poured a fresh glass of water. "So, by offering only one dish on the patient's meal tray, he or she is spared the agony of trying to choose what to eat?"

"Exactly. We find—" The intercom buzzed, interrupting the head dietician's next remarks.

"Excuse me." Chelsey flipped the intercom. "Yes?"

"Ferris Winslow is here to see you," Grace announced expectantly.

"Ferris Winslow?" Shaking two pills from the bottle and popping them into her mouth, Chelsey wondered why the regional director had to pick this particular day to visit.

It had taken Chelsey the rest of her morning to soothe over the business between Ida and Louella, and now she was hopelessly behind in her paperwork. "I'll only be a few minutes more, Grace." Chelsey chased the aspirins with half a glass of water and sighed. "See that Mr. Winslow is comfortable."

The meeting with Meredith was concluded as quickly as possible. As Chelsey accompanied the dietician into the reception area, she glanced around, expecting to find Ferris Winslow waiting.

He was waiting all right, but he wasn't alone. Walter and Harriet Bishop sat with him.

"Hello." Chelsey walked over and shook hands with Ferris, watching Walter and Harriet suspiciously out of the corner of her eye. "This is a nice surprise."

"Hello, Chelsey." Ferris stood up, and Chelsey recognized the strain in his features. "I hope we haven't come at a bad time."

"Not at all, Ferris." Chelsey glanced at Walter and Harriet again. "Are you together?"

Walter stood up, holding a bulging manila folder. "Yes, we were hoping you might spare us a few minutes of your time."

"Certainly. . . ." Chelsey paused as Harriet promptly got to her feet and the couple disappeared into her office.

Chelsey looked at Ferris and shrugged. "Come right in."

When they were all seated, Ferris began quietly, "It seems we have a problem."

"A problem?" Chelsey eased forward in her chair. What did Walter and Harriet have up their sleeves?

Though Ferris seemed hesitant, Walter wasted no time in stating the real purpose of their visit. "We think your inability to run Rosehaven in a satisfying manner has gone on long enough."

Ferris cleared his throat uncomfortably as Chelsey sat up straighter. "Perhaps we could state that in a more tactful manner, Walter."

"Say it any way you want. The fact remains that Chelsey Stevens is not running Rosehaven competently."

Walter's tactless remark left Chelsey stunned. "I beg your pardon?"

"This shouldn't come as a surprise to you, Ms. Stevens. Both Harriet and I have warned you for months that this was going to happen," Walter stated curtly.

Puzzled, Chelsey looked to Ferris. "Do you want to explain the meaning of this?"

"I understand there has been some trouble recently concerning a few of the residents," Ferris said.

Looking pointedly at Harriet, Chelsey asked, "And where did you get your information?"

"I don't think the source matters."

"It does if you're basing your opinion on hearsay."

Ferris shook his head worriedly. "I would hope you know me better than that, Chelsey."

"Then exactly what am I being accused of, Ferris?"

Ferris sighed and reached for the folder Walter had placed on the desk.

For the next ten minutes, Ferris read details about every incident that Thorny, Ian, Otto and Lars had been involved in since Thorny's arrival at Rosehaven. He included the anxious calls from Ian's family and Lars's daughter, and the formal complaints from Otto's family about the lack of supervision.

When Ferris revealed that Thorny and Henry Rothman had taken a bus to play golf at Pebble Beach last Saturday, Chelsey winced. She'd had no idea they'd pulled that one on her.

When Ferris finished, Chelsey sat silently for a moment, reviewing all that he had said. She didn't have to be clairvoyant to know where the charges of incompetency had originated, but she was surprised that Ferris had found them serious enough to warrant an investigation.

Ferris closed the folder slowly. "Is there anything you want to add?"

"No, I believe the information has been properly recorded," Chelsey replied. "I haven't been trying to hide anything."

"No one has accused you of hiding anything," Ferris remarked.

"Maybe not hiding," Walter observed, "but—"

Ferris held up one hand warningly. "Walter, if you don't mind, I'll be the spokesman here. It will make things considerably less complicated."

Walter glanced at Harriet, who seemed surprisingly subdued at the moment. "Whatever you think, Ferris," Walter said.

Turning back to Chelsey, Ferris asked again, "Is there anything you want to say in your defense?"

"Yes. I want to know what it is exactly that I'm being accused of."

"I thought that was obvious. While I know there comes a point when our supervision over the residents is sometimes limited, Rosehaven's reputation is founded on our ability to provide the best of care for the elderly. The families of these men have entrusted them to us. If we fail to meet their trust, they can easily have their relatives placed in other facilities. Now we all agree we wouldn't want that, would we?"

"No."

"I've also been led to believe you've been showing favoritism to certain women residents by buying one a cat and another some sort of a bird?"

"Favoritism?" Chelsey found the charge incredible. "I fail to see where buying two lonely women pets to keep them company could be considered favoritism. Each resident has special needs, and I try very hard to meet those needs, Ferris. Some adjust to their new lives rather easily; some don't. I had no idea anyone thought I was being unfair."

"It seems as if some view your intentions otherwise," Ferris noted apologetically.

Chelsey knew Ferris Winslow to be a kind and fair-minded person, yet that knowledge could not prevent the slow burn that was beginning to erupt inside her.

How dared he, or anyone else for that matter, march into her office and accuse her of playing favorites and not satisfactorily performing her job? Since being made chief administrator, she had diligently performed her duties to the best of her ability. Her job, and the residents of Rosehaven, had always come first with her, sometimes to the point of personal sacrifice.

If circumstances beyond her control caused her competence to be continually questioned, then she wasn't sure she even wanted to work for such a hard-nosed employer.

Greg's advice suddenly came to her mind, and she felt her spine stiffen with resolve. "Stop letting people push you around! Stand up for yourself! Have a little backbone. Call his bluff if he gives you trouble," Greg had once told Chelsey about her employer.

Did she dare take his advice and call Ferris's bluff on this one? She suddenly wished Greg was here to support her. He would tell her what to do. Her mind whirled with indecision as Ferris, Harriet and Walter quietly watched her.

"I don't know what to say, Ferris. Is my competence being questioned over incidents in which I have no control?" she pleaded.

Ferris shuffled in his chair uneasily. The accusations were difficult for him. He liked Chelsey Stevens. She was good at her work, pleasant, and the residents had a genuine fondness for her. But his job was on the line, too. Walter would see that his complaints were taken to the highest authority, and Ferris didn't want to be caught in the middle. The charges against Chelsey were serious ones.

"It's been suggested you have a personal motive for letting Thorton Bradford have unlimited freedom," Ferris confessed.

"Oh? And what might my personal motive be?" she asked coolly. Walter and Harriet couldn't know anything about her relationship with Greg . . . could they?

"Some suspect you might have a romantic interest in Mr. Bradford's son."

Chelsey felt her face flood with guilt. Apparently they did know! She couldn't honestly dispute the claim. There was no way Walter and Harriet could prove their suspicions, but if Chelsey admitted that she was in love with Thorny's son, the secret would be out, and the world would know what a blind fool she'd been. She couldn't bear that. Especially when she'd just found out that Greg was seeing someone else. But if she lied, and the truth came out anyway, then she could be dismissed for giving false information.

"Is that why you permit Thorton Bradford to do pretty well as he pleases?" It was a tough question, but Ferris felt compelled to ask it.

"I *don't* permit Thorny to do as he pleases!" Chelsey sprang to her feet angrily. She'd taken about all she was going to take. "Hell, Ferris! He's seventy-three years old! What does it hurt if he has a little fun occasionally?" Chelsey's eyes widened, and she clamped her hand over her mouth in mortification. She *never* swore, and yet she'd just repeated, almost verbatim, Greg's theory concerning Thorny.

Walter looked over at his wife smugly.

Summoning every ounce of courage she possessed, Chelsey met Ferris's stunned expression directly. Her eyes snapped at him defiantly, as the harrowing day finally closed in on her. "I have about had it with these insinuations that I'm not doing my job," she said in a determined voice. "For three years, I have given Rosehaven my best. If that's not good enough, then you'll just have to fire me!"

Chapter Thirteen

Greg entered his kitchen late Monday afternoon and threw his briefcase on top of the counter. The day had been depressingly long. He'd hoped Chelsey would call, but she hadn't. Nor had she called the day before.

Absently loosening the knot in his tie, he wandered through the empty rooms and eventually wound up in the den.

The house seemed colder today, lonelier than usual. When Thorny had lived with him, there had always been the smell of something tasty bubbling on the stove when Greg had gotten home. Thorny had loved to putter in the kitchen, and Greg had never minded. In fact, he missed Thorny's "wildcat" stew—even though after enjoying it, both of them had suffered heartburn for days. It was still one of Greg's favorites.

Dropping down on a leather chair, Greg admitted that it wasn't only Thorny he missed. Staring vacantly at the cold ashes in the fireplace, his mind replayed again the senseless disagreement with Chelsey. He hadn't known that keeping their relationship out of the public eye would upset her so. For that he was deeply sorry.

After two sleepless nights, he'd also decided that if she wanted Thorny to know that his plan had worked and that they'd fallen in love, then Greg was willing to swallow his pride and concede that point, too. He still didn't think telling Thorny was the smartest thing to do, but if Chelsey actually intended to break up with him over it, then he didn't figure he had any choice.

Somewhere in the wee hours of the morning, he'd come to a conclusion he'd suspected all along: he was deeply in love with Chelsey. It had taken him a long time to come to terms with his memories of Mary Beth. While he'd never be able to forget his wife, Greg knew he'd finally arrived at the point where he could put her death in the proper perspective. And he knew in his heart that Chelsey was exactly the kind of woman Mary Beth would have wanted for him.

Greg wanted to give Chelsey the family she'd never had. Not only did he want to surround her with his own love, he wanted to give her a houseful of children and share with her the joys of having a loving father like Thorny. It would make Thorny's life happier. Even Camille would welcome Chelsey into the family with open arms.

So, there really wasn't any point in keeping his relationship with Chelsey concealed any longer, Greg decided.

Having arrived at his weighty decision, Greg heaved a sigh of relief and stood up. He might as well drive to Rosehaven and tell Thorny right away. Greg's formerly disheartened spirits soared as he glanced at his watch: he had enough time to speak to Thorny, and then stop by Chelsey's office to bring her home.

Bring her home. That sounded exceptionally good to Greg.

THORNY DECIDED to visit Ian before heading to dinner Monday evening. The afternoon was overcast and dreary, the kind of day that always depressed Ian. Thorny had spent more than an hour trying to cheer him up.

"Too bad we don't live where it snows more often. I like snow," Thorny commented casually as he gazed out of Ian's window. It had snowed in Carmel once, several years ago, but only a scant amount had stayed on the ground. Thorny had thought about moving to Minnesota, but Elizabeth had told him he'd lost his mind.

"Elda liked snow," Ian recalled.

Wishing sincerely that Ian didn't relate every topic to Elda, Thorny braced himself for what he knew would be coming next.

"Have you decided when we're going to visit Elda?"

"Not yet," Thorny hedged. He'd hoped to steer Ian clear of the subject of visiting Elda's grave. "Wonder what they're having for dinner tonight?"

"I don't know. Did you find out what bus we'd have to take to get to the cemetery?"

"Yeah, but the weather's going to hold us up, Ian."

"We don't have to go today," Ian allowed. He looked out the window wistfully. "And we won't have to stay long when we go." Even Ian knew his health wouldn't permit a long outing. "I just want to know when you'll be taking me."

A soft tap on the door prevented Thorny from having to answer. "Must be your dinner," Thorny speculated.

"Again? I'm not hungry." It seemed to Ian that lately meals were being served every fifteen minutes.

"Ian, you need to eat something." Ian had grown shockingly thin and pale in the past few weeks, and Thorny was beginning to worry about him. The man just wasn't snapping out of this cold the way he should. Stepping to open the door, Thorny was surprised to discover Fern waiting.

"Yeah, Fern?"

Fern's large eyes darted around furtively. "There's a meeting going on I think you need to attend," she whispered.

"A meeting?" Thorny frowned. "What kinda meeting?"

"You'd better come with me, Thorny." Fern peered over his shoulder expectantly. "And you'd better bring Ian, too."

"Ian's sick, Fern. He can't go to a meeting." Suddenly Thorny found himself being propelled from Ian's room. "Hey, now hold on, Fern. What's going on?"

"Just be quiet and follow me. We've got big trouble."

Thorny couldn't imagine what Fern was babbling about this time, but he obediently fell into step behind her.

Working her way down the corridor, Fern stopped periodically to tap on doors, instructing the occupants of various rooms in her no-nonsense voice they'd better follow her.

By the time the hastily gathered entourage arrived in the recreation room, there was quite a large assemblage.

"All right, what's going on here!" Woody demanded, rapping the tip of his cane on the floor irritably. "They're gonna serve supper in a few minutes, and I don't want to have to scramble for my seat!"

"Just shush up, Woody. You've got bigger troubles than finding a seat at the dinner table," Fern warned as she closed the door and wedged a chairback beneath the knob.

"Oh, stop being so dramatic and just tell us what's going on, Fern!" Kenneth Laibrook added his voice to the ruckus.

"Chelsey Stevens was just fired," Fern said smugly, and Thorny could tell she was delighted by the stunned expressions that suddenly dominated the group.

For a moment, there was total silence in the room. Feet had stopped shuffling; chairs had stopped clanging. Her announcement had come as a complete surprise, and everyone was struck dumb.

Henry Rothman found his voice first. "Are you sure, Fern?"

"Of course I'm sure! It just happened a few minutes ago. Walter Bishop will take her place," Fern confided.

A smothered cry of protest escaped the crowd. "Walter Bishop?" Margaret Winslow repeated.

"It's true." Fern faced the disbelieving residents, stoking the coals of their rising indignation. "Ms. Stevens is in her office packing right now."

Thorny leaned against the pool table with his arms crossed, trying to digest the disturbing news. Chelsey Stevens fired. The thought pained him as deeply as it would have if she were his own child.

"Well, something has to be done about this." Making her way toward Thorny, Ida Munsington moved through the crowd quickly. "Do something, Thorny!"

Thorny looked at Ida solemnly. "What do you want me to do, Ida?"

"You have to get Ms. Stevens her job back. We can't just let her leave." Ida's eyes filled with quiet urgency. "She's . . . she's one of our own," she pleaded softly.

Thorny shook his head sadly. "I don't know what I can do, Ida. I don't have any authority around here."

Otto edged forward. "Do you know exactly how it happened, Fern?"

"No, I just heard that the regional director, along with Walter and Harriet Bishop, were in Chelsey's office earlier. It must have happened then." Fern began to ring her hands with growing frustration as the full ramifications of the situation began to sink in. "Oh, what are we going to do? Rosehaven will be horrible with Walter Bishop as chief administrator! He doesn't care about us the way Ms. Stevens does!"

Lars stepped forward to voice his opinion. "Thorny, maybe we'd better call your son. He'd know what to do."

"Greg?" Thorny wasn't optimistic that his son would be very willing to help. Though Greg respected Ms. Stevens, it was unlikely he'd want to involve himself with her problems. "I don't think Greg would know what to do, either, Lars."

"Well, someone has to do something," Louella decided. "We can't just let her walk away. I simply won't permit it."

The residents of Rosehaven all shook their heads in mute agreement.

Something had to be done; but not one single person could decide what.

While the impromptu meeting was taking place in the recreation room, Greg entered the front door of Rosehaven. As he started automatically in the direction of Thorny's room, his footsteps suddenly paused.

Why was he going to see Thorny alone? It suddenly dawned on Greg that Chelsey should be by his side when he broke the good news to his father. Then they could all share in the joy together.

Turning in the opposite direction, Greg strode down the corridor toward Chelsey's office. His eyes lit up as he saw her emerge, trying to manage an awkwardly large cardboard box.

Hurrying, Greg reached Chelsey's side and quickly reached to take the heavy load out of her arms. "Here, I'll get that for you."

Chelsey glanced up to see Greg smiling down at her. "It isn't that heavy," she protested mildly.

"I insist."

Chelsey relinquished her hold. As they started down the hall side by side, an uneasy silence stretched between them.

"I'm glad I caught you," Greg began.

"Oh?"

"Yeah." He looked into her eyes, and his gaze was apologetic. "I missed seeing you this weekend." As Greg stared at Chelsey, trying to gauge her reaction, he thought he saw her lower lip tremble.

"I...missed seeing you, too," Chelsey admitted as bright tears suddenly filled her eyes.

This, she thought, had undoubtedly been the worst day of her life, and now here was Greg to top it off. She was furious with him, not only for playing her for an absolute fool, but for giving her the absurd advice to stand up to her superiors. When she'd followed his suggestion, she'd lost her job. Now she was even more furious with herself because she was realizing that even after all he'd done, she still desperately wanted to fall into his arms and let him hold her.

Seeing her tears, Greg urged softly, "Look. Let's go back to your office for a few minutes." He needed to be alone with her. He wanted to hold her in his arms and tell her how very much he loved her. He wanted to share with her all the mind-boggling conclusions he'd reached over the weekend.

Chelsey looked at him oddly. "I don't have an office."

"What?"

"I said I no longer have an office." Big, fat drops began to roll down her cheeks as she turned and started walking again. At this instant she feared what was left of her wavering composure would desert her completely.

For a moment Greg was stunned by her declaration, then he fell into step behind her, trying to make sense of her words. She no longer had an office? What was that supposed to mean?

Chelsey moved through the lobby and out the front door without a backward glance. The residents watched her leave with sad eyes.

Juggling the cardboard box, Greg followed her brisk pace, feeling at a complete loss for words. He had no idea what was happening or why she was so upset.

They covered the ground to her cottage in record time. After stepping onto the porch, Chelsey unlocked the door, went inside the living room, and pitched her coat on the sofa. Without a word, she disappeared into the kitchen.

Greg set the box on the floor and stalked into the kitchen behind her. "You want to tell me what in the hell is going on?"

Ignoring his demand, Chelsey continued filling the teapot with water. She plopped it on the stove with a clatter and turned on the burner.

"Chelsey." Greg walked up behind her, placed his hands on her shoulders and turned her around to face him. "What's wrong?"

"Nothing."

"Nothing? Come on, I'm not stupid." His eyes challenged her to dispute the claim.

No, she was the only one guilty of stupidity, she thought. She had no intention of telling him she'd found out about his despicable philandering, but she did want him to know that his so-called sound advice had cost her her job. "You remember the discussion we had about what I should do if Walter Bishop ever seriously threatened my job?"

"Yes."

"You said I should stand up for myself; tell them that if they didn't like my job performance, then they could just fire me."

"Yes. Is that what this is all about? You've had trouble with your job?"

Her eyes met his disbelievingly. "You might say that."

"Well, what happened? Did you stand up for yourself?"

She smiled. "Oh, most certainly."

A slow grin broke across Greg's face. "That's my girl. I'm proud of you. You finally told Walter Bishop to get off your back?"

"I certainly did."

"And you told your regional director he could fire you if he didn't like it?"

"That's right."

Greg's grin widened. So that was what was bothering her, he thought. She had a hard day at work. He was relieved to know that she wasn't upset with him personally but upset over an unpleasant encounter with her boss. "So what did he say?"

Chelsey enunciated the words distinctly, "You're fired."

Greg's grin promptly faded. "Oh hell."

"My sentiments exactly." Chelsey turned back to the stove, trying to swallow the painful lump that continued to swell inside her throat.

"They can't do that to you," Greg stated flatly.

"They not only can, they have, Greg. I'm fired. Kaput. Gone."

"Why? Did Pop have something to do with this?"

As angry as she was, she didn't have the heart to lay the blame solely on Thorny. If Walter hadn't been watching her the way Pudmuffin watched Cecil B., then chances were she would still be employed. "The consensus is that I wasn't performing my job satisfactorily—for a variety of reasons."

"That's a bunch of bunk, and I plan to tell them so!"

Chelsey shrugged, suddenly very weary from the whole trying ordeal. "Don't bother. It wouldn't do any good, and I'm not at all sure I'd even want that job back."

The kettle began to whistle as Chelsey reached for a couple of tea bags.

"You don't mean that. You love the residents of Rosehaven."

"Of course I love those people; that isn't the issue. I don't love Walter Bishop, and I refuse to work with someone who's forever looking over my shoulder, hoping I'll make a mistake."

"Then what are you going to do?"

"I don't know. I haven't had time to think about it. I suppose I'll start looking for a job first thing tomorrow morning."

"Well, look." Greg crossed his arms and leaned against the counter, surveying her flushed features. She was angry, and she had every right to be. But she'd feel differently once she cooled off.

Rosehaven needed Chelsey Stevens, and Chelsey needed the love Rosehaven gave her. Greg felt bad about the situation because in a way it was his fault that she'd lost her job. Apparently his well-meaning advice had backfired, but, then again, maybe things had worked out for the best. He took a deep breath and let it out slowly. "Well, you could marry me. That would solve your problem."

Greg realized it wasn't the most romantic proposal a woman had ever received, but he wasn't good at this sort of thing. The point was he loved her, and as far as he was concerned, she never had to work another day in her life if she didn't want to.

Chelsey glanced up with her mouth open. She was so completely stunned by his unexpected proposal that she nearly dropped the kettle she was holding. "What?"

"Marry me Saturday and forget all about looking for another job," Greg invited again softly.

She didn't know whether to laugh in his face or throw him out on his cheating ear. Was he proposing because he felt guilty about helping her lose her job, or because he felt guilty about stringing her along all this time?

Either way, he'd made a fool out of her for the last time.

"Thanks," Chelsey said casually before returning her attention to pouring hot water into the cups, "but I clean house on Saturdays."

It took a moment for her curt refusal to sink in, but when it did, Greg straightened his stance defensively. "Damn, Chelsey. I know there's no moonlight and roses, but don't you think you could be a little more . . . tactful about telling me to go to hell?"

She longed to ask him how tactful he thought he'd been by leading her to believe that he honestly cared for her, but she bit back the stinging rebuke. Let him be doomed to wondering what had suddenly cooled her ardor. It wasn't the revenge he deserved, she thought, but it would have to do.

Taking a cautious sip of tea, Chelsey ignored the hurt that suddenly filled his eyes. "I've had a bad day, Greg. I'd appreciate it if you would leave now."

The cold indifference in her voice baffled him. Something deeper than the loss of her job was going on, but he had no idea what it could be.

"Chelsey—" he swallowed his pride and took a conciliatory step toward her "—honey, tell me what's wrong. If it's about that senseless disagreement we had Saturday—"

"I'm really very tired, Greg." Chelsey cut him off sharply before he could finish. He wasn't going to worm his way back into her good graces.

"All right." Greg stepped back, his eyes growing more determined. "I'll call you later. Maybe you'll feel more like talking then." For an instant, his resolve to leave her faltered, and his hand reached out to touch her arm, but she brushed it away.

"Don't bother," she said coolly before dropping her gaze. She took another sip of tea and nearly gagged on the taste. She felt as if she were about to explode with pain, but she wouldn't give him the satisfaction of knowing she cared.

This time Greg looked mortally wounded. "Don't bother?" he repeated. He couldn't believe this was his Chelsey. She'd never been cruel or flippant before.

"That's what I said."

"Never?" He had to be sure she actually meant to sever their relationship.

She nodded mutely, her courage beginning to fail her.

"Hey...look." Fear crept into his eyes. She was serious about not seeing him again. "Don't you think we've gone too far for you to just decide on a whim that you don't want to see me again?"

For a moment, she recalled the nights she'd spent in his arms, impassioned, tempestuous nights that neither of them would ever forget.

Dropping the cup on the counter, Chelsey covered her mouth with her hand. She shook her head hopelessly and ran out of the room, leaving Greg standing in the kitchen alone.

Seconds later, Greg slapped his hand on the counter in frustration and went out in search of some answers.

"AND YOU HAVE NO IDEA what's bothering her other than she's lost her job?"

For an hour Greg had impatiently paced the floor in Thorny's room, trying to figure out what had made Chelsey suddenly turn so hostile. Greg knew she had reason to be angry with him. He shouldn't have encouraged her to take a stand that would eventually cause her to lose her job, but he knew that couldn't be the only reason she'd brushed him off like a pesky fly.

There was something else bothering her, and Greg was determined to get to the bottom of it.

"No—" Thorny shook his head bewilderedly "—I don't know what else it could be."

Greg sighed and sank dejectedly onto Thorny's easy chair. Thorny thought he looked like the ten-year-old who was forever breaking the neighbor's windows with his stray baseballs. "I don't know what to do, Pop."

"About what?" Thorny had been surprised to see Greg tonight, and even more surprised to learn he already knew about Chelsey Stevens's dismissal.

"About Chelsey, of course."

Thorny looked at his son, mystified by his sudden concern for Rosehaven's attractive administrator, whom Greg had repeatedly professed to have no interest in. Now all of a sudden, she seemed to have his utmost interest. "What about her?"

Greg wasn't certain he should tell his father about his relationship with Chelsey now, especially since she'd just given him every indication that it was over. "I . . . I hate to see her get fired."

"Well, we all do." Thorny proceeded to tell Greg about the meeting that had taken place earlier that evening. "Her dismissal has a lot of people upset, and we're all going to go to the office first thing in the morning and protest, but I don't think it'll do any good."

Greg sat silently staring off into space. His mind was on Chelsey, and the curt, almost spiteful way she'd refused his marriage proposal. For the life of him he couldn't imagine why. A week ago their relationship couldn't have been rosier. And the argument Saturday was so inconsequential it was laughable.

Was Neil Matlock back in the picture? The thought made Greg feel queasy. No, Chelsey had said she hadn't talked to Neil in weeks and Greg believed her. Then what could it be? His temper began to simmer again.

Maybe he should just take Chelsey at her word and forget all about her, he thought angrily. That's what he should do, but he knew he couldn't. He was hopelessly in love with her, and he couldn't bear the thought of losing her. He had to do something.

Thorny stood up and walked over to turn off the television evening news. "I can't imagine what happened. She seemed all right this morning."

"Who?"

"Chelsey."

"Oh, did you see her?" Greg asked distractedly.

"Yeah." Thorny sat back down and cleared his throat. "And I guess since you're here, this is as good a time as any to have a talk with you."

"A talk?"

"Yeah. We need to talk."

Greg ran his hands through his hair wearily, wishing Thorny could have picked a better time. Greg couldn't concentrate on anything but Chelsey. "What about, Pop?"

"Well, I want you to know I've apologized to Ms. Stevens for trying to put you two together romantically."

Greg glanced up in surprise. "You did?"

"Yeah. I told her I was really sorry about all the trouble I'd caused, and that Ian, Otto, Lars and I wouldn't be causing her trouble anymore." Thorny sighed. "I tell you, son, I feel real bad about the way I've been acting. We did the things we did only to bring the two of you together, but it just didn't work out."

"Pop..." It was on the tip of Greg's tongue to confess his deception. It was obvious Thorny regretted his misguided adventures, and it was time he knew Greg was in love with Chelsey Stevens.

"We feel real bad about her getting fired. Ian, Otto and Lars are afraid we might be part of the reason," Thorny continued.

"That's possible. I thought something besides Walter Bishop's ambition for her job caused the regional director to fire her."

"Yeah, that's what I'm afraid of. You know, I've been thinking. Maybe you should offer her a job with Bradford Electronics, maybe even give her a fancy title—something real important-sounding that would pay her fifty thousand a year and give her her own office." Feeling terrible about Chelsey losing her job because of him, Thorny figured an office and fifty grand a year ought to help make up for it.

"Fifty thousand?" Greg whistled under his breath. Thorny *did* feel guilty. "I don't think she'd accept it, Pop."

"How do you know? She has to live, doesn't she? Why would she refuse a job that would pay her more than Rosehaven ever dreamed of paying her?"

"I don't know, Pop. . . ." Greg stood up and started to pace the floor again. He'd gladly offer Chelsey a job if she'd take it. "What did she say about your matchmaking?"

"Well, she took it real well. She said she understood and for me not to worry."

"Yeah, she would say that," Greg agreed softly as he paused by the window and looked out, his eyes searching for the small cottage. In the distance, he could see the tiny glow from the light in the window. A searing loneliness swept through him, and he wished he was in that cottage with Chelsey safely tucked within his embrace.

"But you don't have to worry anymore, son," Thorny assured him brightly. "I got you off the hook."

"Oh?" Greg was only half listening now. "How'd you do that, Pop?"

"It was simple, really. I just told her you were seeing someone else, so she could stop feeling uneasy around you."

Greg's thoughts were elsewhere, so his response was automatic. "Oh, that's good. I appreciate that. . . ."

But Greg's voice trailed off when the meaning in Thorny's words hit him with the explosive force of a baseball bat between the eyes. He turned slowly from the window, his face registering disbelief. "You told her *what*?"

Thorny stood up and stretched. "I told her you were seeing another woman, so she didn't have to worry about my playing matchmaker anymore."

Greg thought he was going to be sick. "You told Chelsey. . . I was seeing another woman?" he repeated lamely.

Thorny nodded, grinning smugly now. "So you can rest easy. I have you all fixed up."

"Damn! You didn't! Say that you didn't tell Chelsey I was seeing another woman, Pop!" Greg suddenly snapped out of his shock and rushed to stand before Thorny pleadingly. "You didn't really tell her that, did you?"

Thorny drew away uneasily. "Well... I know you don't want everyone to know about that woman you're seeing, but I figured you wouldn't mind if Ms. Stevens... knew." Thorny thought Greg looked downright peaked all of a sudden. "You feeling all right, boy?"

Greg sank down weakly onto the corner of the bed, his mind refusing to believe his ears. Thorny had told Chelsey he was seeing another woman—that's why she'd broken off with him.

"Greg, what's wrong?" Thorny demanded. He'd never seen Greg look like this, and it had him worried.

"Pop, you don't know what you've done!"

"What have I done?"

"You've probably just ruined my life," Greg predicted glumly.

"Ruined your life! How'd I do that?" The boy wasn't making a lick of sense.

"The woman I've been seeing *is* Chelsey Stevens!"

Thorny's face went from shock to outrage in a matter of seconds. "I hope for your sake you're kidding me."

"Pop, look..." Greg pressed his eyes against the heels of his hands wearily. This wasn't going to be easy. "Chelsey wanted to tell you about us sooner, but I've been holding back. We've been seeing each other for the past few weeks. It... I thought we had become serious."

"If you're trying to be funny, Greg, I'm not laughing." The misery of the past few weeks could easily have been avoided if Greg was telling the truth when he said that he and Chelsey had been seeing each other. Thorny almost hoped, for Greg's sake, he was teasing again.

Greg sighed. "I'm not laughing, either, Pop. Chelsey just told me to get lost an hour ago. I couldn't figure out why, but I guess what you've just told me explains it."

"You mean to tell me you two have been seeing each other all along!"

"Yes, and if it weren't for your useless meddling we would have told you. In fact, I was on my way over to tell you when I discovered Chelsey had lost her job."

"Greg, if you weren't thirty-five years old, I'd tan your hide." Thorny's voice suddenly held the authority that used to bring Greg to his knees when he was a youngster. "You lied to me about that other woman, and you've lied to me about your supposed lack of interest in Chelsey. If you suddenly find yourself with a fuzzy sucker, then you have no one to blame but yourself, boy. No one but yourself!"

"I didn't lie to you," Greg defended himself. "Maybe I withheld the truth a little, but I thought I had good reason. You said yourself you should never have tried to pick a wife for me, and as far as the story about the other women, I only told you that to make you stop pushing me toward Chelsey. Lord! I had no idea you'd go tell her!"

Thorny didn't feel the least bit sorry for his son. He'd taught the boy to be honest and forthright. Apparently Greg had suffered a severe lapse of memory. Thorny might admit that he shouldn't have been interfering in his son's life, but Greg had been just as wrong when he hadn't let on that the woman Thorny had selected for him had turned out to be a sound choice. "Well, looks to me like you've got your tail caught in a crack, and I can't say I have much sympathy for you."

"Oh no, you don't! You're the one who started this. You're going to go to Chelsey and straighten this thing out," Greg ordered. He was beginning to panic. Chelsey was under the mistaken impression that Greg was a two-timer.

Thorny could be as stubborn as his son any day of the week, and he was about to teach him a lesson in parental wisdom that was long overdue. "No, son, I won't. You're the one who said you were seeing another woman. How do I know you're not lying to me now when you say it was Chelsey you were seeing all along?"

"Come on, Pop! Have a heart. Chelsey will never believe me if I tell her I'm innocent! You've got to help me!"

Thorny calmly walked to his chair, sat down and shook out his evening paper. Adjusting his reading glasses on the end of his nose, he said, "I'd love to help you, son, but I'm supposed to stay out of your personal life." Thorny glanced up and smiled. "Remember?"

Chapter Fourteen

Walter Bishop's office was overflowing Tuesday morning as the residents of Rosehaven swarmed in, in angry protest. "Please! Please!" he implored them. "If you'll just take a seat and quiet down, I'll answer your questions one at a time!"

"We want Ms. Stevens back!" Kenneth Laibrook shouted.

"Yeah! Ms. Stevens, Ms. Stevens, Ms. Stevens!" chanted the restless crowd as they stomped their feet noisily.

"Ladies and gentlemen, please!" Walter looked helplessly to Grace Martin, who sat wide-eyed, cowering behind her desk.

The tip of a cane shot out and tapped Walter on the shoulder soundly. "We want Ms. Stevens, sonny!"

"Woody, put that cane down or I'm going to take it away from you!" Walter snapped irritably. All of a sudden, Rosehaven had turned into a madhouse.

Woody cupped his hand to his ear innocently. "Eh?"

"I demand to know the meaning of this!" Walter said to the angry mob. "You people can't just come in here and take over!"

"We're demonstrating," Violet Appleton yelled.

"Against what?" Walter snapped, having become thoroughly put out with the lot of them. These people had to learn that Walter Bishop wasn't going to be a pushover like their former administrator. There was going to be some authority shown around here for a change.

Elected unanimously to serve as spokesman for the group, Thorny stepped forward to confront the unpopular new administrator. "We're here to protest the firing of Chelsey Stevens. It's not that we don't like you, Walter, but we want Ms. Stevens back."

"Well, she can't come back," Walter responded sharply. "And you can't just barge into my office like this."

"Why not?" challenged Henry Rothman. "Some people might think we're old and useless, but we still have a right to say our piece!"

A raucous round of applause broke out as Walter struggled to retain control. "Listen! Listen . . ." Walter pleaded, his eyes roaming the crowd nervously until they fastened on Mildred, who'd just jostled a tray of potted flowers. "Mildred, please be careful," he cautioned. Everyone knew Harriet's prized violets were not to be touched. "I realize you're all upset about Ms. Stevens, but the matter is out of my hands. Ms. Stevens has been terminated—"

"Boo, hiss! We want Ms. Stevens . . . we want Ms. Stevens . . . we want Ms. Stevens!" chanted the crowd as their feet stomped and their canes banged the floor.

"Everyone, just go back to your rooms and settle down! You may have been able to push Ms. Stevens around, but I will not tolerate this sort of behavior!" Walter threatened. "From now on I'm running Rosehaven, and there will be strict adherence to the rules. Disobedience will be dealt with severely."

Mildred cocked her head defiantly. "Is that so?"

With calm deliberation, she reached over and pinched the head off a brightly blooming violet.

Walter's eyes widened incredulously. "Mildred!"

"We want Ms. Stevens...we want Ms. Stevens...we want Ms. Stevens!" the group chanted.

Walter glanced frantically at his secretary. "Grace, don't just sit there! Do something!"

Grace looked at Thorny, then squaring her shoulders, she joined in the chant. "We want Ms. Stevens . . . we want Ms. Stevens . . . we want Ms. Stevens!"

THE FIRST THING Chelsey saw as she stepped out of her cottage the next morning was Greg leaning against the hood of her car.

She turned and started back into the house, but quickly changed her mind. She might as well face him. There was no sense in being childish about the matter. She was adult enough to handle the situation rationally, she reminded herself, trying to ignore the fact that she still wanted to wring his neck.

Walking briskly to her car, Chelsey inserted the key into the lock. A masculine hand came down to keep the door firmly closed. "I believe we need to clear up a small misunderstanding between us, Ms. Stevens."

"Oh?" She kept her eyes firmly averted from his. Desperately, she tried to ignore the powerful effect of his nearness. His familiar scent washed over her, bringing with it a flood of memories too intimate to confront without weakening. Sarcasm, she decided, would serve as her best defense. "Well, perhaps we can discuss it sometime when you have a moment between women."

Greg swore as she slapped his hand away and jerked the car door open. Her eyes snapped back to meet his defiantly. "You will excuse me?"

"Now, look! I knew something was wrong," Greg said accusingly. He stepped back into her path, deliberately blocking her entrance to the car. "Why didn't you tell me Pop was in your office yesterday morning?"

Chelsey's eyes met his solidly. "*If* you'll excuse me, Mr. Bradford, I have a job interview to attend."

"I won't excuse you." Greg reached out and moved Chelsey firmly away from the car door. Slamming it shut, he said, "This whole thing has gotten completely out of hand."

"I have no idea what you're referring to."

Amid her sputtered protests, Greg grasped her arm and propelled Chelsey toward his car.

"Greg, I have an interview!"

"Fine. I'll drive you." Opening the car door, he motioned for her to get in.

"I'd prefer to take my own car. Besides, it may take all morning."

"I'm free for the rest of the day."

Their eyes clashed again in silent confrontation. "Come on, Chelsey, give me a break," Greg pleaded. "Let me at least explain my side of the story before you condemn me to a last cigarette and a blindfold!"

"I'm not sure I want to hear your side of the story."

"That's not fair, Chelsey."

"I don't think you were fair to see another woman and string me along at the same time."

"Will you just get into the car?"

Their gazes defied each other stubbornly until Chelsey, with an exasperated sigh, slid into the passenger seat of the BMW and Greg slammed the door. Moments later, they pulled out onto the highway.

"Where's your appointment?"

"Near Ocean Avenue."

They rode in silence as Greg maneuvered the small car in and out of traffic. It was the first time Chelsey had ridden in his sports car, and in spite of herself, she enjoyed the feeling of excitement it provided.

"What position are you applying for?" Greg asked, hoping to start on a civil note.

"Does it matter? I just need a job at this point."

"Are you trying to get back into administration?"

"No. The ads in the paper aren't exactly chock-full of vacancies in that field, and I have to live in the meantime."

"Why don't you let me give you a job?" Greg offered.

His quiet suggestion caught Chelsey by surprise for an instant, but she snapped back, "I don't want you to give me anything."

Although the conversation remained politely strained, Greg knew what was uppermost in both their minds. "Chelsey, you're the only woman I've been seeing. I love you—you know that. I'm disappointed and damn mad that you'd think for one minute that I didn't love you!"

"Strange. Your father is under the impression you've been seeing one of your secretaries."

Greg glanced over at her. "One of my secretaries?" Thorny's story was getting more contorted by the hour. "Is that what he told you?"

Chelsey kept her eyes straight ahead, fighting back the tears that suddenly threatened. "Yes."

Greg shook his head in disbelief. "I have no idea where he came up with that one, but it isn't true."

"He said you'd told him."

"I told him I was seeing a woman—I didn't say who—so he would let up on you and me," Greg confessed. "I certainly never said it was one of my secretaries."

"You deliberately lied to him?"

"Well . . . sort of, and I'm not proud of it." Since the day Thorny had entered Rosehaven, Greg felt as if he'd been forced to use tactics he'd never considered before. "Thorny was feeling down the night I told him, and I guess I felt guilty. I just wanted to make him feel better."

"Without letting him know you and I were dating," Chelsey added.

Greg's face was apologetic. "I know it was a stupid thing to do, and I'm sorry, Chelsey. I never dreamed it would backfire like this. I told Pop the truth last night."

Chelsey ventured a timid glance at him. "You told him about us?"

"Yes. I told him we'd been seeing each other."

She didn't know why, but his words made a shiver of hope ripple up her spine. "Was he upset?"

"Yes. Not because we're seeing each other, but because I'd kept it from him."

"Can you honestly blame him? You know we haven't been fair about this."

"I know. It's my fault, and I probably deserve every ounce of misery I'm going through, but I don't want to lose you, Chelsey." Greg glanced at her hopefully. "Do you believe me?"

Chelsey wanted to desperately. But did she dare? "Does the name Cindi Richards ring a bell with you?" she had to ask.

"She works in the office. . . . Why?"

"Thorny said you'd mentioned that you'd taken Cindi to lunch. That's why he thought she might be the woman you've been seeing."

"Cindi? Oh Lord, Chelsey! Cindi's twenty-two years old. What do you take me for?"

"Have you taken her to lunch recently?"

"Once during secretaries' week when I took all six of the secretaries out for lunch. Then Rand Harrison asked me to arrange a luncheon so he could meet Cindi, and I drove her to the club."

He sounded so sincere, so convincing, that Chelsey's wounded pride began to abate. "Will Thorny back up your story?"

Greg frowned. "Would it matter? I'm telling you the truth." He'd been dreading this inevitable question. Thorny was just stubborn enough to make Greg get out of this mess the best way he could without an ounce of help from him.

Chelsey thought carefully about what to reply. If Greg was telling the truth, Thorny shouldn't mind admitting that he'd been mistaken about the facts. "I think it would make me feel better to hear Thorny say it."

"He won't do it," Greg said finally.

"Oh?" Greg saw Chelsey's left brow lift suspiciously. "And why not?"

"He says he's teaching me a lesson. He's mad because I'd told him to stay out of my personal life, and now all of a sudden he's decided that's just what he'll do. In spades."

"How convenient for you."

"Chelsey!" Greg shot her a pleading look. "You know how stubborn Pop can be! I can't help it if he's let me dig a hole and fall into it."

"Greg, I really don't want to discuss it." She'd spent most of the night going over the unnerving events, and now she was more confused than ever. She motioned for Greg to pull over as they approached the building where she was to have her interview.

"We have to talk about this sometime," Greg predicted. "I'm not going to let it end this way."

Chelsey sighed. "Greg, I've lost my job and my living quarters. I have to be out of the cottage by the end of the month. I'm sorry, but I can only handle one crisis at a time. Let me get my life back into some semblance of order, then we can talk." Right now she was too distraught to discuss the weather, let alone decisions that would affect the rest of her life.

As she started to climb out of the car, Greg reached out and stopped her. Cupping her face in his hand, he leaned forward to kiss her. Her hand automatically lifted to block his effort, but Greg gently clasped her face. His voice was low but firm as he warned her, "There are people who love you, Chelsey. Let us help you through this. Pop and the other residents at Rosehaven are worried sick about you. *I'm* worried sick." His eyes locked with hers. "You don't have to run around looking for a job. I'll give you a job at Bradford Electronics, one you're qualified for. You don't even have to be qualified," he amended. "Just tell me what you want, and I'll take care of it."

"No, thanks. I got myself in this; I'll get myself out." She didn't mean to sound ungrateful, because she did appreciate his offer, but she'd always had to rely on herself. Somehow, with the unsettling events of the past twenty-four hours, she didn't think it would be prudent to change course at this point.

Maybe Greg was telling the truth; maybe he was in love with her. Then again, maybe he wasn't. It was something she'd have to think about.

"Then let me give you some money to tide you over until you can get established again," he offered.

Chelsey felt her spine stiffen with resentment. What now? Did he expect her to become a kept woman? "No, thank you. I'll manage."

"You're being stubborn."

"That's possible."

"I've never looked twice at Cindi Richards or any other woman since you and I . . ."

"Started sleeping together?"

"That's putting it crudely, don't you think?" His tone indicated that his patience was wearing thin.

"Well, isn't that the way you view it?" she said coldly.

"No, it is not," he corrected her. Chelsey tried to pull from his grasp, but Greg drew her face closer to his. "And it's not the way it is between us." He shook her face gently. "I love you, lady, and you can be as stubborn as you want, but eventually you're going to realize that it was Pop, innocently or not, who has caused your immediate problems. I'm going to be by your side until we can get them straightened out. Then if you still want to send me on my way, I'll have to deal with it. Until then, we're going to see this thing through together."

An impatient motorist blaring his horn reminded them that they were illegally parked.

Greg gave Chelsey a brief but loving kiss before he finally released her. "I'll be waiting when you're finished with your interview."

"You don't have to—"

"But I will."

And thus was set the pattern of Chelsey's life for the next four days. Greg was waiting each morning when she came out of the cottage.

He'd take her to a nearby waffle house and insist that she eat a hearty breakfast before she began the day. Once breakfast was dispensed with, they'd spend the day driving from one job interview to the next, returning at dark to the cottage, tired and empty-handed.

By the end of the third day, Chelsey had gained two pounds and discovered that, for the most part, she was overqualified or otherwise ineligible, not to speak of utterly discouraged.

Greg had been the perfect gentleman, leaving her alone to wallow in her self-pity. He never tried to kiss her, never hinted at spending the night with her, and obediently avoided the subject of their shaky relationship.

Chelsey knew he was neglecting his own work in order to spend the day driving her from one interview to the next, but she'd been unable to convince him she could take care of herself.

On top of everything else, she had exactly one week left to vacate the cottage. She'd been so busy looking for a job, she hadn't had time to think about moving, let alone find a new apartment.

"I still think the only sensible thing for you to do is to let me give you a job," Greg told her as he dropped her off at the cottage Thursday evening. The day's results had been as dismal as the preceding three. "Believe me, Chelsey, it would be simpler for both of us."

"I'm not beat yet." She was close to it, she had to admit, but she wasn't going to let Greg know it.

He shrugged. "You're just making things difficult for yourself."

"And you." Chelsey felt bad about interfering with his work, but if he refused to listen to reason, there seemed nothing she could do about it.

"I can hold out as long as you can." He winked. "Goodnight, Chelsey."

"Goodnight, Greg."

"See you in the morning."

"No doubt."

"YOU'RE GOING TO WEAR a hat, Ian and that's that. It's raining again."

Thorny helped Ian on with his coat, and ignoring Ian's protests, Thorny pulled the warm stocking cap down over Ian's ears.

It was damp and cold outside, and if they had to stand waiting for the bus very long, Ian would get a chill.

He'd probably get a chill anyway, Thorny fretted. But it was Christmas Eve, and Ian had made up his mind: even if he had to do it alone, he was going to visit Elda's grave today.

Thorny thought it would be nice to get out for a while. Rosehaven had been in turmoil since Chelsey's departure on Monday. The residents had become uncooperative and openly rebellious. The Christmas mood was far from festive, although the halls and lobbies twinkled merrily with brightly colored lights.

"What time did you say the bus comes?" Ian shuffled into his bathroom to get his medicine. His cold had gone into his chest, and his cough sounded deeper now.

"Every half hour. Ian, you sure you feel up to going today? Maybe we should put it off until the weather clears up."

"We've been through this a hundred times. I'm going today, Thorny."

"We can go next week," Thorny cajoled, thinking how much worse Ian's cough sounded. "Elda's not going anywhere, so what's your all-fired hurry?" He'd never known Ian to be so stubborn.

"I might not be here next week." Ian came out of the bathroom carrying two brown vials.

"I wish you'd quit talking that way." Such talk made Thorny uncomfortable, but he said, "Where do you think you're going?"

Ian didn't choose to reply. He picked up his gloves and shuffled back to the doorway. "Did you check where Walter is?"

"Fern says he'll be at the Christmas program. She said she'd keep him distracted until we can get to the bus."

"Good." Ian looked at his watch. "We'd better get started."

Thorny had decided it would be best to slip out the service entrance. The cooks would be busy stuffing turkeys and baking pies.

If anyone questioned where they were going, Thorny planned to say that Walter had asked them to carry in the fruit baskets that had been donated.

The temperature was a damp forty-three degrees as they set out across the soggy grounds.

Normally it was a thirty-minute walk to the bus, but today it took them over an hour to get there. Ian had to stop and rest twice as a racking cough took control of his spindly frame.

"Ian, this is foolish," Thorny scolded. He'd hoped once they were on their way, Ian would realize he didn't have the strength to make it and would agree to go back. "I'm going to take you home and put you to bed."

Ian straightened from his latest coughing jag, ignoring the deepening rattle in his chest. "No, Thorny...I'll be all right." His teeth started chattering as Thorny reached over to pull the collar of his coat closer around his neck. The rain, which had been just a fine mist when they'd started, was falling heavier now. A north wind tore at their clothing, making them even more miserable.

Ian's eyes suddenly filled with tears. "Please, I don't care what happens to me.... I just have to talk to Elda."

"Can't you talk to her some place where it's warm?"

"No, I have to go to her."

"You're a crazy old fool, you know that?" Thorny wrapped his arm around Ian's bony shoulders and used his own bulk to shield his sick friend from the worsening weather.

"I know it sounds crazy, Thorny, but it's real important to me," Ian confided as they started walking again. "I just need to sit and talk to her for a few minutes...."

Thorny tried to ignore the loneliness, and the fear of approaching death, he saw in Ian's faded eyes.

"I'm scared, Thorny. And if I could talk to Elda... well, I think it'll make it easier for me when my time comes...."

Thorny sighed and patted Ian's shoulder understandingly. "I told you not to talk like that, Ian. You're going to be all right."

"I have to do this, Thorny," Ian reiterated quietly. "I know it doesn't make any sense to you, so just trust me."

"Okay, my friend." Thorny patted his shoulder again. "I'll take your word for it."

THE COTTAGE FELT CHILLY as Chelsey opened the front door. The ashes in the fireplace were a mute reminder that she'd been in too much of a hurry to put wood on the fire before she'd headed out this morning.

The nine o'clock interview at Winterhaven had been promising, but after meeting with the director, Chelsey had decided that the position wasn't right for her.

Rosehaven had been so much warmer, so much more caring. She knew she couldn't be happy working in any other environment.

So, she was back to square one.

"Looks like the fire's gone out." Greg followed her into the room, and in a few minutes he had a small blaze going again.

Chelsey had slipped out of her coat and put the kettle on. A quick glance at the clock told her it was nearing lunch-time.

"Are you hungry?" she asked.

Greg stood and dusted off his hands. "What'd you have in mind?"

"I have a couple of cans of soup." She'd given up trying to convince him that she didn't need his help. She knew she didn't, yet she had to admit it was nice to have him around. He'd been a firm, comforting anchor for her during the past few unsettling days.

"Sounds good to me. Would you have a sandwich to throw in?"

"Just peanut butter." She made the observation distractedly, forgetting that it was a simple peanut butter sandwich that had first brought them together here in her cottage.

But Greg remembered. He shrugged out of his jacket, his eyes meeting hers teasingly. "I love peanut butter, remember?"

Her pulse quickened at his thinly veiled reference. Spinning around quickly, she started for the kitchen. "I'll see if I have any bread."

Greg wandered along behind her, smiling at her almost desperate attempt to ignore him. "You going to work on the new résumé after we eat?"

"I guess . . . though I don't know what good it will do."

"It'll work wonders if you'll do what I suggested."

"For heaven's sake, Greg, I'm not going to put down that I've worked on the White House Staff. They'd never believe it."

"They never check those things, Chelsey! If you want a word of advice—"

"Which I don't," she hurriedly pointed out. His last word of advice had gotten her the ax.

Recognizing his gaffe, Greg grinned. "I still say if you'd pep up your résumé a bit, they'll sit up and take notice."

"There's nothing wrong with my résumé. I could've had ten jobs by now if I could live on the pathetic sums they called a salary."

Greg shrugged. "Whatever you say. It's all going to turn out the same in the long run."

She wasn't sure what he meant, and she was afraid to ask.

Fifteen minutes later, the fire had taken on a rosy glow, and the smell of tomato soup bubbling on the stove filled the cottage.

"It's a terrible day out," Greg observed as he walked into the kitchen and lifted the window curtain. Frowning, he looked out on the unpleasant weather.

"I don't mind the rain." Experiencing a strange sense of contentment, Chelsey went about making the sandwiches. She had no idea why she should feel so serene. She didn't have a job. Today was Christmas Eve, and her shopping was only half-finished. She was going to have to move within a frighteningly short span of time, and she didn't have the slightest idea where she would go, and yet she felt happy. It didn't make sense.

Turning from the window, Greg's attention was drawn back to Chelsey. Her back was to him, and the dress she was wearing clung to her in all the right places. He felt a sudden hot surge of desire shoot through him, a desire that he'd kept under careful control lately.

But today the cottage was warm and cozy. It was dark and rainy, and she looked so unbelievably desirable....

Though she couldn't see Greg, Chelsey sensed his hesitant approach. She froze as his arms circled her waist and drew her flush against his body. Her legs felt weak as he nuzzled her neck and pressed tightly against her, making her thoroughly aware of the direction of his thoughts.

"Why don't we forget the soup?" he suggested in a deeply suggestive voice.

"Greg," she murmured helplessly. She'd been so careful to keep her distance, but suddenly, caution seemed as illusive as a moonbeam. She couldn't deny that she'd missed the warmth of his embrace, the touch of his hands, the feel of his skin next to hers—and now he wasn't making it easy for her.

His mouth feathered warm kisses along her cheek, and she closed her eyes and leaned against him for support, wishing she were a stronger person.

It wasn't fair! She didn't want to be dependent upon him for her happiness; but she was, hopelessly so. He had come to mean everything to her, and it was too late to do anything about it.

Turning her slowly in his arms, Greg lowered his mouth to taste hers. Soft, sipping kisses made her whimper softly with agonizing protest. "Please..."

"My thoughts exactly. Please, Chels...."

He couldn't do this to her, she thought, but he was, so effortlessly, so calculatingly, and she was standing here permitting it.

Her arms came up to curl around his neck. With a sinking feeling, she knew she was just about to lose the battle.

As they melted into each other's arms, he groaned and kissed her hungrily. Moments later, their lips parted, and he whispered, "See? Isn't this nicer than arguing?"

She had to agree. Much nicer. "We haven't been arguing actually."

"We haven't? For days you've held me at arm's length, and I'm dying." Greg buried his face in her hair and held her tightly. "I want to hold you, Chelsey, make love to you, tell you all the exciting new feelings I've discovered about you and me. . . ." He was kissing her again, ardent kisses that made her mind reel with indecision.

She no longer doubted what he'd said about Cindi Richards. Chelsey had realized days ago that if Greg didn't love her, he'd had the perfect opportunity to walk away. But he'd stayed, neglecting his own duties to care for her. And yet she still didn't want to depend upon him. . . .

"Oh, Greg, I'm so confused."

He continued to kiss her until she lost the ability to reason. Moving his lips along the curve of her cheekbone, he whispered, "Let me help you. Together we'll sort out your confusion, and I promise we'll work it out. You can't just keep locking me out of your life," he pleaded as everything inside her demanded she give in.

"Turn off the burner," he commanded in a voice thready with building desire.

"Greg, no. . . ."

Reaching behind her, he performed the task. Then his mouth captured hers again in searing, aching need. Lifting her in his arms, he smothered her protests and carried her to the bedroom.

"This isn't going to settle anything," Chelsey tried to warn him as they moved onto the bed as one, but even she heard the wanting in her hollow words.

"There's nothing to settle. I love you, you stubborn woman." His mouth continued its passionate assault, pushing aside all rational thought as their clothes melted away like ice cream on the fourth of July.

"No. . . . Oh, Greg. . . ." Her breath caught and her words died away as he began to make love to her.

The phone by the bedside rang, its sharp shrill shattering the charged silence.

Greg's hand clamped over hers as she automatically moved to answer it. "Let it ring," he commanded.

"It might be import—"

Her sentence was cut short as he levered himself over her and swept them both away to a state of blissful oblivion.

LATER, THE SOUP had to be reheated. The sandwiches had to be made again because the bread had dried out.

Greg and Chelsey moved around the small kitchen, intermittently exchanging long, languid kisses. Somehow, the world was a nicer place to live in than it had been an hour ago.

"Now that we have that out of our systems, do you think we can discuss this rationally?" Greg asked, as he finished making the sandwiches.

Chelsey was about to admit she thought they should when the phone rang again. "Want me to get it?"

"Thanks. I'll serve the soup."

Greg picked up the receiver. "Hello."

Chelsey finished ladling the soup and walked over to take the call.

"It's Walter Bishop," Greg informed her tightly.

"Walter Bishop?" Chelsey took the phone out of his hand. "Yes, Walter?"

She frowned as Walter began revealing the purpose of his call. "Yes, he is." Her frown deepened. "No, I have no idea where they might have gone," she said a few moments later. Glancing worriedly at Greg, she added softly, "Yes, Walter, we'll be over in a few minutes."

Greg watched as she absently replaced the receiver.

"What did that SOB want?"

"Thorny and Ian are missing."

Greg looked at her blankly. "Missing?"

"Yes. Walter wants both of us to come to Rosehaven immediately."

Chapter Fifteen

Seated in Walter's office thirty minutes later, Greg and Chelsey watched as Rosehaven's new administrator paced the floor restlessly.

"I'm terribly sorry about this inconvenience, Mr. Bradford. I know you must be frantic, but I don't think we have to worry too much," Walter said reassuringly. "We have people out searching for your father and Mr. Landers, and I'm sure we'll have good news any moment."

Walter sat down behind his desk and began to fidget with a paper clip. "Would you like a cup of coffee while we wait? I think Grace just made a fresh pot."

"None for me, thanks." Greg sat beside Chelsey, listening to Walter's feeble attempts to explain why Thorny had left Rosehaven again without permission. So far, he'd failed miserably.

"Chelsey?" Walter asked, belatedly including her in his polite overture. She noticed he avoided looking her straight in the eye.

"No, thank you, Walter."

"Well, as I was saying—" Walter stood and began pacing again "—I don't understand how this happened. Your father's and Mr. Landers's records are both clearly marked with red flags, but somehow they just disappeared after breakfast this morning."

"Has Ian's family been notified?"

"Yes, they're on their way over."

"Have you asked the other residents if they know where Ian and Thorny might be?" Chelsey prompted.

"Yes, I'm sure one or two of them know where they are, but they've apparently decided to remain uncooperative on the matter."

Walter had grilled Fern, Mildred, Woody, Lars and Otto for any small clue about Thorny's and Ian's whereabouts, but they had been tight-lipped.

Greg casually leaned back in his chair, more amused than alarmed by Thorny's latest caper. He was sure Thorny could take care of himself. "Sounds like complete incompetence on your part, Mr. Bishop."

Walter paused in his tracks, and his left brow rose a fraction. "Excuse me?"

"I said it sounds to me like you aren't doing your job. Tell me, where do I file a formal complaint?"

Chelsey flushed and lowered her eyes, realizing Greg was about to even the score on her behalf.

"Well, Mr. Bradford, I...uh...see no need for you to file a formal complaint," Walter said. "The actions of your father in no way reflect upon my ability to run Rosehaven. Why, you know yourself that your father has a long history of disobeying the rules!"

"I think that's beside the point. I put Pop in Rosehaven so he would have the best of care, Mr. Bishop. One administrator has already lost her job because someone implied the exact same sort of incompetence." Greg smiled coolly. "Now, Walter, since you're the new administrator of Rosehaven, I expected that you would personally see to it that

Thorny didn't step out of line and that his whereabouts were monitored every minute of the day."

"Why...why, that's impossible!" Walter objected. "I can only do so much. I can't watch these people every minute of the day!"

"Walter, do you have to refer to the residents as 'these people'?" Chelsey objected.

"Now, you just stay out of this!" Walter warned. "I knew this incident would be blown completely out of proportion!"

"Mr. Bishop," Greg said calmly, his voice holding an edge of strained tolerance, "I suggest you address Ms. Stevens in a nicer tone." His eyes locked with Walter's, sending a silent, unmistakable message.

Immediately Walter realized his mistake. "I am sorry, Mr. Bradford, I didn't mean to raise my voice, but there's bound to be feelings of sour grapes here." His eyes darted away from Greg's steely gaze uncomfortably. "It's unfortunate your father chose this time to act up again, but I can assure you I've done all that's humanly possible to prevent this from occurring. There certainly can be no hint of incompetence on my part."

"Meaning that there was on Chelsey's?" Greg finished dryly.

Walter was instantly on the defense again. "I believe the record speaks for itself."

Chelsey glanced at Greg apprehensively. Walter's insinuations were so commonplace that their effect on her was mild, but she wasn't sure how Greg would receive them.

"Mr. Bishop, you're a miserable bastard," Greg stated calmly. "You managed to get Chelsey fired for reasons beyond her control, and now you're faced with the same problems." Greg smiled. "It's your job on the line this time, buddy, and I want you to know I plan to do everything within my power to see that you're thrown out of here on your fat, pompous—"

"Greg, please!" Chelsey looked at him pleadingly.

"See here, Mr. Bradford." Walter sprang to his feet, his face blotched an angry red as he bellowed self-righteously, "You can't speak to me this way. Why, I'll . . . I'll—"

"Gentlemen! Please!" Chelsey reached out to prevent Greg from coming off his chair in automatic challenge. She had to intervene before fists started flying. "I think we've lost sight of the fact there are two elderly men wandering around out there in the cold and rain. Perhaps this discussion would be better saved for a more appropriate time." She glanced at Greg worriedly. It was the first time she'd ever heard him raise his voice in anger. "Don't you agree?"

Greg was somewhat ashamed of his uncharacteristic outburst, but he was a man who was fiercely protective of his own. And as far as he was concerned, Chelsey was definitely his own. "Sorry. I just lost it there for a minute."

She smiled. "I noticed."

Turning to Walter, Chelsey sought to calm him. "Would you mind if I spoke with a few of Thorny's and Ian's friends? They might be able to remember something that would help us locate them."

"Everyone has suddenly developed amnesia!" Walter snapped.

"Maybe not." Chelsey knew the residents would talk to her. "Do you mind if I speak to them?"

"Do as you please, but you won't learn a thing."

The three left Walter's office in uneasy silence. Chelsey smiled at Grace as they walked through the reception area. Walking stiffly into the hall, they started for the sitting rooms. It was late afternoon, and most of the residents were either napping or watching television.

They encountered Henry Rothman first.

"Hi, Henry."

Henry's eyes brightened at the sight of Rosehaven's former administrator. "Hi, Ms. Stevens!"

"Henry," Walter said, "Ms. Stevens thinks you might know where Thorny and Ian went. Do you?"

"Walter, I didn't say that," Chelsey remonstrated.

"Well, it's what you meant."

Henry's nose promptly tilted in the air. "I told you, Walter. I don't know where Thorny and Ian are." Henry smiled at Chelsey apologetically. "Or if I did, I must have forgotten."

"Henry, you are deliberately lying to me," Walter said accusingly.

Henry grinned. "Prove it."

"Thank you, Henry. We'll take your word for it." Chelsey patted his shoulder, and they moved on.

Fern was just coming out of the solarium as the three rounded the corner. When she saw Walter, she whirled and hightailed it in the other direction.

"Fern!" Walter called.

"I told you, I don't know where Thorny and Ian are, Mr. Bishop!" Her agile form darted around the corner before Walter could detain her.

"I'd bet a hundred dollars she does," Walter fumed.

They found Woody in the south lounge watching his favorite show—"The Newlywed Game."

Leaning over Woody's shoulder, Walter displayed all the manners of a sumo wrestler when he shouted, "Woody, are you sure you don't know where Thorny and Ian are?"

Woody glanced up sourly and said, "Eh?"

"Woody," Chelsey said, stepping forward as she recalled how she'd always suspected Woody could hear when he wanted to.

Woody turned, a smile breaking across his weathered features as he recognized the familiar voice. "Well, hi there, Ms. Stevens!"

"Hi, Woody." Chelsey smiled and ruffled the thin strands standing up on his bald head. "Do you have a minute? Can you and I go sit down and talk?"

"Sure, Ms. Stevens. Be glad to."

They moved to a couple of nearby chairs and sat, Greg and Walter following suit. Word spread quickly that Chelsey was in the lounge, and the room began to fill with residents eager to touch her hand or experience again the warmth of her perky smile.

Laughter filled the room, and a festive air took over. Walter left the room, muttering he'd be in his office. He was clearly annoyed by the reaction of the residents to their former administrator.

"Oh, I've missed you, Ms. Stevens." Ida clasped Chelsey's hand affectionately. "Are you all right?"

"I'm fine, and I've missed you too, Ida. How's Pudmuffin?" Though she'd only been gone a few days, Chelsey felt like it had been weeks.

Ida beamed. "Growing by leaps and bounds."

"And how's Cecil B.?" Chelsey asked Louella, who was hovering nearby.

"Divine, darling, simply divine."

"Mildred, how good to see you!" Chelsey found herself touching hands and smiling into familiar faces. "Kenneth, Margaret, you look lovely today. Violet, do you have a cold? I'm so sorry. . . ."

Greg watched the love poured out to Chelsey, and he smiled.

And she thought she had no family.

When the hellos and how-are-yous finally died down, Chelsey asked the residents to gather around her. "I have something I'd like to ask you."

The crowd immediately quieted down. A sea of eyes that had seen far more of life than Chelsey had stared back at her, eager and unified in their willingness to hear what she had to say.

"I'm aware that you've been asked if you know where Thorny and Ian have gone. Walter assures me you don't know anything, but I was wondering if perhaps someone might have remembered something ever so small that might help us to find them. Ian was running a fever this morning, and with the worsening weather, we're all very concerned about his health."

Chelsey pretended she didn't see the exchange of guilty looks. "Can anyone shed any new light on the subject?"

Heads were shaken, and Chelsey felt her heart sink. Like Walter, she strongly suspected they were covering for Thorny and Ian again.

"Ms. Stevens?"

Both Chelsey and Greg turned at the sound of her name. Ida was peering nervously around the corner. "I want to tell you something," the woman said.

Smiling, Chelsey got up and moved toward her. Ida beckoned her nearer.

Chelsey glanced quizzically back at Greg, then turned to Ida. "What is it, Ida?"

"Garden of the Saints Cemetery!" Ida spat the information in the same tone she might have used to give a hot horse-racing tip like Jeffrey's Baby in the third.

"Garden of the Saints Cemetery?"

"Yes, and you didn't hear it from me." Ida turned and scurried away before Chelsey could question her further.

"Why in the world would Pop and Ian be at a cemetery?" Greg asked when Chelsey relayed the information.

"If I'm not mistaken, that's the cemetery where Ian's wife is buried," Chelsey said thoughtfully.

"Well, I guess it's worth checking out. Come on." Greg began to propel Chelsey down the hallway.

"Shouldn't we tell Walter?"

"Not a chance. Let him get his own tipster."

A CEMETERY, AT BEST, is not a place where most people choose to spend a lot of time. And on this dismal, overcast and rainy day, Garden of the Saints was completely deserted except for two elderly men who made their way slowly among the tombstones.

It wasn't a pleasant place for Thorny or Ian to want to linger. The headstones rose up to taunt them, bleak reminders of the fragility of the precious thread of life.

"Are you warm enough, Ian?"

"Yes. Elda's over here, Thorny." The men moved to a grave site adorned with two brass vases filled with artificial red roses.

"Here she is, Thorny." Ian's voice was warm with love as his wrinkled hand reached out to tenderly trace the words carved in stone.

Thorny respectfully removed his hat as Ian fell to his knees on the wet ground. Ian reached to gently flick the raindrops from one of the plastic flowers. "Elda loved red, you know. The children always see to it that she has red roses."

"That's real nice, Ian."

"My name is going to go on the other side when I...well, later. I didn't much want it on there yet."

Thorny tapped his fingers against his hat uneasily. "Yeah, can't blame you."

"Would you mind if I had a few minutes alone with her, Thorny?"

"No. I'll be close by if you need me." Thorny wandered away, leaving Ian alone. He browsed through the rows of graves, reading the inscriptions on the tombstones. Mothers, fathers, brothers, sisters, children, infants. There weren't any favorites played here.

Thorny thought how pitifully short life was. Most folks spent half their allotted twenty-four hours a day worrying about the next one to come. A shame. It seemed to him there ought to be a more productive way to pass the time. If Thorny had learned anything in his lifetime, it was that tomorrow inevitably took care of itself.

Twenty minutes later, Ian found Thorny sitting on a bench, waiting for him. "I'm ready to go now, Thorny."

Thorny rose, ignoring the pain in his stiffened joints. The damp weather always made his arthritis act up. "Guess we'd better get started then. The bus will be along shortly."

They walked through the cemetery. Ian's coughing stopped them occasionally, but as soon as the attacks abated, they moved on.

"I suppose Walter will meet us at the door, mad as a hornet," Thorny predicted.

"We don't really care what Walter does, do we?"

"No, we don't."

"Strange Christmas, don't you think?" It was hard to believe that tomorrow was Christmas Day.

"Yeah, but you've made mine a lot nicer than it would have been," Ian said, before returning to his earlier subject. "It's a shame what Mr. Bishop has done to Ms. Stevens. He shouldn't be allowed to get away with it."

"I know. I told you about Greg's seeing Chelsey, didn't I?"

"Yeah, that's what you said. I'm glad to hear they finally noticed each other. Maybe you'll get to move back home yet."

"I'm not holding my breath, but I'm still hoping."

Thorny knew he would eventually tell Chelsey that Greg hadn't been two-timing her, but he was going to make the boy sweat for a while, even if it did mean he'd remain in Rosehaven longer.

"Do you think Greg might end up marrying her?"

"Don't know, Ian. I can't figure the boy out. We'll just have to wait and see. I don't think they're too happy with each other right at the moment."

"Well," said Ian, pausing to catch his breath, "I sure hope he doesn't let her get away. It's a darn shame people don't realize what they have until they lose it."

"Yeah, I hope he doesn't lose her."

"You know, Thorny, getting to visit with Elda was the best Christmas present I've ever had. Thank you. You've been a true friend."

"I'm real glad you got to visit her, Ian," Thorny replied.

Their gazes drifted back to the cemetery one final time. "Yeah, sure hope those two youngsters don't waste valuable time coming to grips with their feelings," Ian said softly. "Life's just too darn short."

"THERE...OVER THERE! I think I see them." Chelsey pointed to the two bedraggled men sitting on a bench at the bus stop as Greg slowed the car. The windshield wipers were slapping furiously, trying to keep up with the pelting rain.

"That's them all right." Making an illegal U-turn, Greg pulled the Cadillac alongside the two men and stopped. Chelsey rolled down the window. "Taxi?" she offered.

Thorny looked at Ian and shrugged. He knew it—caught again. Slowly they rose to their feet, and Thorny helped Ian to the car. The warmth of the heater felt exceptionally good to the two men as they settled meekly in the back seat. Thorny had been trying to flag a cab for twenty-five minutes, but not one could be found.

Greg pulled back into the line of traffic, waiting for Thorny to offer some sort of explanation. When it appeared that one wasn't forthcoming, Greg sighed. "Okay, Pop. Want to clue me in on what you're doing ten miles from Rosehaven in the pouring rain?"

"Visiting."

"Visiting?"

"That's right, visiting."

Ian began coughing, and Chelsey reached back and handed him a handful of tissues. "Ian, why would you venture out in this kind of weather? Your cold sounds as if it's getting worse."

"I'm all right, Ms. Stevens. It's just that I had something important I wanted to do." Ian blew his nose, trying to still the bone-rattling chills that suddenly came upon him.

Chelsey shrugged out of her coat and reached over the seat to hand it to Thorny. "Put this around Ian's shoulders," she instructed him. More satisfying explanations would have to wait. She turned back to Greg. "I don't know whether we should take Ian back to Rosehaven or straight to the hospital."

"Rosehaven is closer. We'll have the doctor check him immediately."

Thirty minutes later, Ian was safely back in his bed. Members of his family and various Rosehaven residents were gathered worriedly outside his door. The doctor had arrived, and they were awaiting word on his condition.

Thorny knew it wasn't good. When he'd taken Ian's hand and led him inside Rosehaven, he could feel the man's skin burning with fever.

But Ian had remained jubilant that he'd made the journey. He'd smiled and squeezed Thorny's hand reassuringly. "Thank you, Thorny. I appreciate what you've done for me today."

"You need to get to bed," Thorny had responded gruffly, trying to hide his growing fear. Ian would be lucky if his visit with Elda didn't prove to be fatal.

"It's okay, Thorny. There's nothing at all to be afraid of," Ian had assured him when he'd seen the worry in his friend's eyes. He had smiled then, and there had been a radiant look of contentment on his face. "It's okay, really," he'd said.

Greg interrupted Thorny's thoughts as he handed him a cup of hot coffee. "You okay, Pop?"

"I'm fine."

"I see you've changed your clothes."

"Yeah." Thorny eyes grew suspiciously misty. "I'm just a little worried about Ian."

"Pop, why would you allow Ian to go out in this sort of weather?" Though Greg knew Thorny was happy-go-lucky at times, he'd never known his father to be irresponsible. "Why would you take such a risk with his health?"

Thorny reached into his back pocket and retrieved a handkerchief. "Son, I believe they call it love."

"Love?"

"Yeah. Funny thing, love. You can't explain it; you can't dominate it; can't control it. Men die for it, over it, in the name of it, and yet everybody wants it." Thorny wiped his nose, then replaced the handkerchief in his pocket. "Ian wanted to visit his wife's grave, Greg. He asked me to take him."

Greg squeezed his father's shoulder affectionately. "Well, why didn't you say so? I would have taken you."

"Ian wanted to do this on his own."

"I understand."

"Do you, Greg?" Thorny turned his eyes to meet ones that bore a striking resemblance to his own. "Do you really understand what I'm saying, son?"

Greg shifted his stance uneasily. "About love?"

"Yes. True love doesn't come along that often, Greg. When it does, a man would be a fool to try and ignore it."

"Pop, sometimes it isn't that easy," Greg said softly. He knew Thorny was thinking about Chelsey and him.

Thorny sighed. "Anything worth having is seldom easy."

Greg wasn't sure when Thorny had gotten smarter than him, but it had happened.

Thorny eyed his son levelly. "You and Chelsey were together today. Does that mean you've worked out your differences?"

"We're trying, Pop."

"Would it help if I cleared up the misunderstanding about Cindi Richards?"

"No, Chelsey knows you made an honest mistake." Greg glanced around, suddenly realizing that Chelsey wasn't among the small group waiting in the hallway. "Where is Chelsey?"

"She said she wanted to pick up a few items she'd left in her office."

Greg glanced down the familiar corridor. "I'll be back in a few minutes, Pop." He walked away while Thorny remained with Ian's family.

Greg entered the administrator's office and noticed Grace was still working. "Hi, Grace. Is Chelsey here?"

Grace held her fingers to her lips and pointed to the closed door. "In there."

"Alone?"

"Yes, I don't know where *he* is."

"Can you see that we're not disturbed for a few minutes?"

"Of course."

Greg found Chelsey sitting in her old chair, sobbing.

He stepped behind the desk, pulled her up into his arms and hugged her. "Let it all out, honey. Let it all out."

This was the first time he'd seen her break down, and he was relieved she was finally allowing herself the privilege.

Burying her face in his shoulder, Chelsey took Greg at his word and cried until there were no more tears left. Sitting down on the chair, Greg held her on his lap and wiped her face the way he would a small child's.

"Do you feel better?"

"Oh, Greg, I feel so... so empty."

"Empty? Why?"

"I feel like I've let them all down."

"Let who down?"

"The people here. They're like my family."

"And how have you let them down?" he chided. "They love you, honey. You can see it in their faces."

"I've let them down by not being here for them. Poor Ian, if I had been here maybe he wouldn't have gone out in this rain."

"Come on, Chelsey—" Greg cocked his head wryly "—you know that's not true. Pop said Ian wanted to visit his wife's grave." Gently he wiped away a stray tear with the pad of his thumb. "And you should know that when a man wants to be with his woman, nothing's going to stop him."

"Maybe not. Walter Bishop might be a better administrator than I was, but I don't think he'll ever love the residents the way I do." She broke into sobs again.

When she regained control, Greg kissed the tip of her reddened nose. "And they love you, and I love you, very, very much."

Their mouths touched, and they savored the sweetness.

"You know, Chelsey, we don't know what life will deal any one of us," Greg said. His lips met hers again briefly. "It's a bad break that Walter set you up to lose your job, but it's not the end of the world. You can't blame yourself for what's happened. You've been good for Rosehaven, but now it's time to get on with your life."

She rested her head wearily against the width of his chest. She thought it was such a nice chest, warm, masculine. "But I have no idea what's going to happen to me, Greg."

He grinned and slowly eased farther down on the chair with her. He winked knowingly. "Now, let's just see if the two of us can put our heads together and come up with something."

SOMEWHERE AROUND FOUR O'CLOCK on Christmas morning, Thorny lost a good friend, but heaven gained one heck of an auto executive.

By Monday, the Garden of the Saints would have another of its own, and the opposite side of Elda Odelia Landers's headstone would finally be complete.

Epilogue

It was late Christmas evening, and throughout Rosehaven the smell of turkey and mince pie still lingered pleasantly in the air. Here and there stray bits of wrapping paper printed with mistletoe, holly and reindeer mingled with discarded red and green ribbons.

Most of the residents were in their rooms, resting from the day's hectic activities. The hall lights had been dimmed, and the calm that had replaced all the earlier hustle and bustle was welcomed.

Christmas was over for another year.

It had been a trying day for Thorny. He'd decided the quickest way to get it over with was to go to bed early. Just as he was climbing into bed, Greg tapped on his door.

"You asleep yet, Pop?"

"No, son. Come in." Thorny pulled his woolen robe back on and slid his feet into his slippers. "Something wrong?" Thorny couldn't imagine what Greg was doing at Rosehaven at this hour. They'd eaten breakfast together this morning, then exchanged presents. Thorny had received special permission to spend the afternoon with Ian's family, and Greg had gone home to phone Camille and Herb to wish them a Merry Christmas.

Greg sat down on the bed beside his father. Thorny looked older tonight, and it made Greg realize for the first time that his father wouldn't be around forever. A world without Thorny—Greg didn't want to even consider it. "There's nothing wrong, Pop. I just wanted to make sure you were okay."

"No different than I was when you left this morning," Thorny assured him, admiring Greg's attire. He was dressed in a tweed suit and carrying a black cashmere topcoat.

"Pop, I know you've lost a good friend today, and I wanted to say I'm sorry. Friends like Ian are hard to come by. I know you're going to miss him."

Thorny nodded. "Yeah, it's not going to be the same without him."

"Is his family doing all right?"

"It hasn't been easy, but they're holding up well."

"Actually there is another reason I stopped by," Greg admitted, deliberately switching to a happier subject.

"Oh? What's that?"

"I have one more Christmas present for you."

"Oh? Did one get misplaced behind the tree?"

Greg flashed a quick grin. "Not exactly."

"Well, let's have it." Greg always went all out at Christmas, buying far more presents than necessary. Thorny just hoped it wasn't another tie. He had enough ties to stretch from California to New York, with a few left over.

Greg rose and walked back to the door. "You'd better like this," he warned good-naturedly. "It's one of those no-return, one-of-a-kind, you-bought-it-it's-yours sort of gifts."

"I'll like anything you get me." Except another tie, Thorny thought.

Greg opened the door, and Chelsey stepped into the room, dressed in a beautiful white wool suit and carrying a small bouquet of orchids.

At first, Thorny thought she was carrying a present, but when he saw the flowers, he looked back to Greg expectantly. "Well?"

"Well, this is your present."

"What?"

"Your new daughter-in-law."

Thorny's eyes came back to Chelsey, who was smiling at him happily. "Hi, Pop," she said softly.

For a moment Thorny was speechless, then, "You two are married?"

Greg and Chelsey looked at each other and grinned.

"A wise old man once told me it would be foolish to ignore love," Greg confessed. "For once, I was smart enough to take his advice."

"Greg," Thorny warned, feeling his hopes begin to spiral in spite of himself. "Are you telling me a big windy again?"

"Naw, I decided to give that up, Pop. You've taught me crime doesn't pay. Chelsea and I flew to Reno and were married this afternoon."

"Well, I'll be darned." It was exactly what Thorny wanted, but least expected. For the first time in his life, he was floored.

Greg drew Chelsey possessively into the crook of his arm, stealing a brief, but thorough kiss before he turned back to an astounded Thorny. "That's all you can say? I'll be darned?"

"Well—" Thorny thought for a moment "—how about, it's about time, boy. I was beginning to get real worried."

Greg grinned. "I may be slow, but once I make a decision, you can count on me to follow through with it."

"Well, hallelujah! I did get the right kid at the hospital!"

They chuckled as Greg leaned over and hugged his father. "Well, what do you think, Pop? You think I can't pick 'em?"

"You think *I* can't?" Thorny countered boastfully. "After all, who found her first?"

Thorny broke the embrace and stood up to give the bride a big bear hug. "Welcome to the family, honey. I've been waiting for this moment for a long time."

Laughter suddenly filled the room as hugs and kisses were exchanged all around. It was hard for Thorny to believe a day that had started out so wrong could turn out so right.

The news was just too good to keep to themselves, so Thorny took the newlyweds by their hands and dragged them out into the hallway.

"Pop, have a heart. It's our honeymoon!" Greg protested.

"There'll be plenty of time for that," Thorny scoffed. "Let an old man have his fun."

For the next fifteen minutes, they went up and down the corridors, knocking on doors and spreading the news.

Even Pudmuffin seemed pleased, and gave her unqualified lick of approval.

"Well, we've done it, old boy!" Otto and Lars exclaimed. Thorny just stood there and beamed.

Never had Ian's absence been so acutely felt, but somehow Thorny thought he knew.

When the initial excitement finally began to subside, Greg and Chelsey went back to Thorny's room to share a piece of fruitcake. Fern had given it to Thorny that afternoon and made him promise to eat every bite.

As he sliced the rich, chewy concoction, Thorny realized he'd never seen Greg so happy. Not even with Mary Beth. "So, what are you two going to do now?" Thorny asked as he spread real butter on his piece of fruitcake. One stick of the forbidden treat had been provided by Greg in Thorny's Christmas stocking.

"Now?" Greg looked at Chelsey, his eyes not quite revealing his true intentions. "I'm going to take my wife home."

"I didn't mean right now. I meant, what do you plan to do now that you're Mrs. Greg Bradford, Chelsey?"

Thorny was clearly fishing. He'd accomplished his purpose of getting Greg married again, but he still had his main goal yet to achieve. He wanted to know how soon he could start packing.

Chelsey looked at her new husband and smiled. She planned to do many things, none of which were suitable topics of discussion with her new father-in-law. "Oh, I don't know, Thorny—"

"Pop. Call me, Pop, honey."

"Okay, Pop." She reached over and squeezed Thorny's hand. "Greg and I have been talking. He wants to invest in a small business for me to run."

Chelsey's eyes sparkled like emeralds as she warmed to her favorite subject. "I want a smaller version of Rosehaven, Pop. I want a place where I can bring Woody, Otto, Fern, Ida, Louella...all of my family and give them a home, a real home. I'll have nothing but the best. Nurses and staff who really care. It'll take time, but I'm going to do it."

Thorny listened to her excited recitation with growing despair. True, living in a place like Chelsey envisioned would be nice, but Thorny just didn't want to go there. There would still be rules, and Thorny was tired of everyone else's rules. He wanted to make his own.

He wanted to go home.

"Well, what do you think?" Chelsey asked, realizing Thorny's mind had wandered.

"Oh . . . it sounds real nice."

"Does it sound like somewhere you'd like to live, Pop?" Greg asked.

"Well . . . of course, if Chelsey's going to be there," Thorny said halfheartedly. He'd hate to start right off being a pill, but he supposed he'd have to. He wasn't about to give up on moving back in with Greg, though.

"Greg, I've been thinking. Maybe Thorny would be more comfortable living with us," Chelsey suggested, casting an impish glance in Thorny's direction. "Since I'll be around to see to his needs, Camille could be assured that he's being well taken care of. What do you think?"

Greg looked at Thorny and grinned. "Aw, Pop wouldn't want to do that."

"Hey, yes! Hold on there . . . I might." Thorny shot Greg a despairing look. The boy was about to ruin everything! "I hadn't really thought about it, but that might be nice. I'd try not to be a bother, and I can always come here, or your new place, and visit my friends. Yes, I think that might work out real nice," Thorny decided, as if he'd never considered the idea before.

"Really." Greg crossed his arms tolerantly. Thorny had missed his calling, he thought. He had become remarkably good at acting.

"Yes!" Thorny grinned innocently at Chelsey. "Moving back to Greg's sounds like a real fine idea."

"Then it's settled." Chelsey's eyes were aglow with love for her new family as she said tenderly, "First thing tomorrow morning, you can move back home, Thorny."

"Hold on." Greg stepped forward defensively. "Not first thing tomorrow morning, Mrs. Bradford. For the next two weeks, I want my wife all to myself."

Thorny shrugged and looked at Chelsey apologetically. "I always did have to make him share. Take your honeymoon, sonny. I can wait."

"Well, I can't," Greg confessed, drawing Chelsey to her feet. Their eyes met lovingly. "Come on, Mrs. Bradford, let's go home."

AFTER GREG AND HIS NEW WIFE had left, Gilda came in to give Thorny his medicine. She wasn't much to look at, but Thorny admitted she was a dear old soul, and he was probably going to miss her.

"Did you have a nice Christmas, Thorny?" Gilda asked as she handed him his medicine. She turned to fill a small paper cup with water from the pitcher beside his bed.

"Yeah, it was real nice, Gilda, real nice."

"Heard your son got married this afternoon. That must make you happy."

"Sure does...oops...Lordy! Was that a *mouse* I saw run under the bed?"

Gilda's eyes widened. She gave a frightened hop, then immediately stooped down to peer under the bed for the rodent. Thorny reached over and pinched her fanny.

Bolting upright, Gilda realized she'd been duped again. "Thorny Bradford," she said, wagging her finger at him, "I've warned you about that!"

Thorny chuckled and tipped his medicine into his mouth. Son of a gun, he hadn't lost his touch! "You're gonna miss me, Gilda."

Gilda snorted. "And where do you think you're going?"

"Why, haven't you heard?" Thorny flashed her one of those million-dollar, Bradford grins, guaranteed to melt the coldest woman's heart. "I'm going home, honey. I'm going home."

Take 4 books
& a surprise gift
FREE

Harlequin American Romance

COMING NEXT MONTH

#265 KATHERINE'S DREAM by Leigh Anne Williams

Taylor House had always meant home to Katherine, so when its future was threatened she returned home to Massachusetts to fight for her heritage. Pitted against brash local attorney Peter Bradford, she found that she could fight the lawyer but she couldn't fight the man, whose passion was her destiny. Don't miss the first book in the Taylor House trilogy.

#266 ALWAYS A BRIDESMAID by Julie Kistler

Everyone in the family counted on Maggie Wentworth to solve his problems. She could never leave home, not even for John Meredith, who tried using wit—even seduction—to worm his way into her heart. But how could she give him what he needed when it meant letting go?

#267 STRINGS by Muriel Jensen

Judy Cassidy took great care of her three summer charges, Mitch Kramer's devilish children. She couldn't help but fall in love with their seaside antics. That left only one other family member—but Judy wasn't about to let him take hold of her heart.

#268 THE MESSAGE by Stella Cameron

Page was committed to her bicycle courier service, even if it meant riding the streets alone at night. Ian Faber was intrigued when she delivered his pâté and champagne, and vowed to find out all about her. Page thought she was in trouble then—little did she know she'd soon be accused of a crime she didn't commit.